THE

ONE
BEFORE

BOOKS BY MIRANDA SMITH

Some Days Are Dark
What I Know

THE
ONE
BEFORE

MIRANDA SMITH

Bookouture

Published by Bookouture in 2020

An imprint of Storyfire Ltd.
Carmelite House
50 Victoria Embankment
London EC4Y 0DZ

www.bookouture.com

ISBN: 978-1-83888-938-8
eBook ISBN: 978-1-83888-937-1

To Whitney, Jennifer and Allison:
You are far better sisters than the characters I write.
I'm happy you're mine.

PROLOGUE

June 16, 2006

Celia stepped outside and met the sizzling heat, a stark contrast to the icy air pumping from her Honda Civic. As she left the parking lot, gravel and bronze sand slid between her flip-flops and feet. Once she reached grass, she hopped out of her shoes and wiped them clean. Now she was perfect again, from her braided blonde hair to her red-tipped toes.

"You're late," Ronnie said as he passed. He was wearing sunglasses and a visor, but she knew his eyes were on her. He liked to look at her. Everyone did.

She shifted the weight in her hips and smiled. "You gonna hold it against me?"

Ronnie started to say something but shuffled away instead. Celia loved the power she exerted over men. It was a God-given gift—one she planned on using until she took her last breath. She wiggled out of her tank top and Soffe shorts, folding the clothes neatly inside her duffel. She draped a whistle around her neck and started rubbing sunscreen into her already tanned skin, careful to reach the spots that would peek beneath her red one-piece.

Once ready, she pulled down her sunglasses and climbed the white wooden lifeguard stand, adjusting the attached umbrella to an angle that was just right. She sat there, looking out at the liveliest place in her sleepy hometown. Families had come in swarms to Whisper Lake that year, one of the busiest seasons she could remember. She'd been coming here most of her life, but this was only her second year as a lifeguard. Everyone in Whisper Falls frequented the lake during summer; not much else was offered, except for the County Fair at the end of August.

Celia settled into a comfortable position, peering over her rims at all the people she recognized. She spotted her youth minister, a former math teacher and the man who changed the oil in her car. Several classmates were in the sand preparing a volleyball game. Throughout her shift, each person she knew would catch sight of her and wave. Even people she didn't know eventually ogled her. All of them admiring her beauty, her athleticism, her strength.

This was Celia's favorite place in the world. A hot summer day at the lake, sitting on her throne, looking down on those around her. *It's going to be a good day*, she thought, leaning back and closing her eyes.

She could never have predicted this day would be her last.

CHAPTER 1

Madison

It's my fault we're moving.

I always knew we'd end up in Whisper Falls; agreeing to marry Cooper Douglas cemented that future. Still, I thought I had some time. At least five years, maybe ten. I'll miss the city, the pulsating excitement just outside my door. I feel that life source dimming with each mile marker I pass. The traffic thins, and the landscape flattens. I think we've reached the other side of nothingness, but the GPS insists we keep going, until we're off the highway completely, traveling narrow, two-lane streets.

The route leading to our house is bare of civilization but filled with natural beauty. The only mark of human intervention is the narrow road with its faded white median. Tall trees—don't even ask me what kind—stand along the edges, their fallen leaves resting politely on the grass as if by design.

Finally, I see the house. Our house, I suppose. Before we left Atlanta, Coop and I decided to play a game where I told him what I expected the house to look like, without seeing any pictures. I'm about right. Two stories. Wraparound porch. There's no shed in the back like I imagined, and the house is white brick, not red.

I park in front of the detached garage. I step outside, staring at the house, and take in a deep breath. It's true what they say. The air is cleaner here. Soothing. It can almost rid me of my anxiety with a few deep inhales. Almost.

Behind me, Coop turns into the driveway. He's hauling a rented trailer, which contains all the belongings from our apartment. My things filled less than a dozen boxes. Coop had more stuff, and he'd only been in Atlanta for two years. He exits his vehicle, stands behind me and wraps his arms around my waist.

"So, what do you think?"

"Pretty close to what I imagined," I say. I lean my head to the left, my hair blowing in the breeze. "I think I like the white brick better."

He squeezes me, then walks to the porch. I follow him. "Of course, this house is temporary, if you want it to be. We can always buy our own, or even build."

"Give me a tour. I can't decide if I like the place until I see the inside."

After a brief walkthrough, I decide I definitely like the place. The wooden floors are original and clean. There's a fireplace in the massive living room. Upstairs, there are four bedrooms. The master is the biggest and has a small balcony overlooking the front lawn. I stand there, my fingers wrapped tightly around the iron railing. I look ahead at the Great Smoky Mountains in the distance. I try to picture every morning like this. Can I do it? Can I be happy here?

I think back to when we made the decision to move, after I told Coop what I'd done. It no longer made sense to stay in the city when he had the Douglas publishing empire to take over. He would have stayed in Atlanta for me, but I ruined that.

Coop never made me feel that way, though. Like I'd done something wrong. Instead, he kicked the Whisper Falls sales pitch into high gear, pulled up photos and highlighted our substantial cost-of-living cuts. I agreed moving was the best decision, even though it was the last thing I wanted to do. My life in the city was unsalvageable; the least I could do was follow Plan B quasi-enthusiastically.

Coop joins me on the balcony, kneading the tension from my shoulders.

"You said this used to be your aunt's house," I say. "How long has it been vacant?"

"Five years or so. Mom kept the lawns maintained and renovated the interior. It feels brand new."

"Your aunt. Did she, you know—"

"Die in the house?" He grins, despite the morbid topic.

"Yeah?" Although beautiful, the house is over a century old. It screams of hauntings.

"You and your active imagination." He kisses the top of my head and walks back inside.

Coop's aunt isn't the only ghost on my mind. He's told me several stories about his hometown in the two years we've been together. The most memorable was about his high school girlfriend, Celia Gray. She drowned in the waters of Whisper Lake the summer before he started college. The event was a defining moment in his life; it haunts him, and now it haunts me. We both knew moving here would disrupt his past, but I'm hoping, at the same time, it will erase mine.

CHAPTER 2

Helena

I miss my daughter.

For a few years, I felt her presence with me wherever I went. Now I only feel her absence. Grief has carved me up inside, leaving me hollow in some places, tattered in others.

You can't overcome the loss of a child. It's the most unnatural of occurrences, the heaviest of losses. If you lose a parent, you're an orphan. If you lose a spouse, you're a widow. What are you when you lose a child? You're me. Bitter and cold and angry.

Plenty of other people are in my position. I see them each week at the meetings. At some point, the others pull their lives back together. Find a new purpose. Those parents always say the hardest part is not knowing why. Never understanding what happened. Not seeing what their child could have one day become. I'll tell you what's worse than that. It *is* knowing. Because I *know* what happened to my daughter. I tried—time and time again I tried—to get someone, anyone, to listen. No one would. They wanted proof. They wanted evidence. All things I couldn't provide.

I could only give them a name. Cooper Douglas. I know he killed my daughter, and one day I'm going to make him pay.

CHAPTER 3

Madison

We're off to join Coop's family for Sunday brunch. I know little about my in-laws. Coop's father died a few years back, and I've never met his siblings. His mother, Josephine, visited Atlanta once; she insisted on buying dinner to celebrate our engagement. Seeing her again feels different now that I'm one of them. On their turf. The water thinning their bloodline.

Coop describes his family as close-knit, yet he made the conscious choice to separate them from our relationship. When we lived together in the city, he never suggested I accompany him on his visits to Whisper Falls. He's kept me at a distance; moving here bridges that gap. As we make the short drive to Josephine's house, I sense Coop's nervousness rising. He's quiet, with a tight grip on the wheel.

"Are you okay?" I ask, after several minutes of silence.

Coop exhales and forces a smile. "I don't know what I'm so worried about. I know they're going to love you." He squeezes my knee. "I suppose I'm adjusting to the idea of living here again."

I'm also adjusting, still reeling from the move and the life we've left behind. "What do they know about me?"

"All good things. They know you're a journalist. Born and raised in the city." He laughs. "They know you make me happy."

I smile, fiddling with the ring around my finger. Suddenly, I feel a pang of sadness, like I'm some ragamuffin the Douglas family is rescuing. I wish I had someone other than Coop with whom I could share this new life, although, truthfully, I've been on my own longer than I'd like to admit. I don't have a relationship with my parents or anyone from my childhood. Beth and Matt, my closest friends, are back in the city.

"Here we are," Coop says, stopping the car outside a black gate. He rolls down the window and punches a code into the security system. The gates open, leading us down a twisty drive lined with more trees.

"Wow." I knew his family had money, but I wasn't quite expecting this.

"A dramatic entrance, eh?" There's a hint of embarrassment in his voice. Not many people can relate to his family's level of wealth. I wonder what that does to a person, coming from so much? It must make one guarded with everyone. Friends. Schoolmates. Lovers.

"It's beautiful," I say, trying to hide the shock in my voice. In the distance, the sun hovers over a large body of water. It seems to have appeared out of nowhere, hidden behind the greenery of the massive landscape. "Is that a lake?"

"The back end of the house overlooks Whisper Lake. You'll see more as we get closer."

Suddenly, I remember Celia, and it's like this ghost from his past is sitting in the car with us. Whisper Lake is beautiful, but I know the murky currents hold secrets. They hold danger.

We take a sharp turn, and now the Douglas manor is in full view. As we pull closer, it becomes larger. It's two-stories, but wide, easily spanning six thousand square feet. Dark wooden beams hoist a large balcony on the second floor. Coop parks our car beside a circular fountain at the front. We both sit in silence, staring at the massive house.

"Are you ready?" he asks.

I nod, too intimidated to speak. I can't shake the feeling I've entered into a world meant for someone else.

We don't knock. Coop uses a key to unlock the front door. Somehow, that simple action makes this place feel real. Like it's part ours. I can't believe Coop, the same person who shared my one-bedroom apartment, calls this his childhood home.

"We're here," Coop calls out. His voice echoes. *Echoes* throughout the large space. There's a grand staircase ascending from where we stand. Coop walks forward, and I follow him, trying to appear at ease. Like I belong. I'm hoping his family won't realize within minutes that I don't.

Coop leads me through several rooms until we reach two French doors. He pushes them open, and we walk onto the back deck. There's a dining table there, already covered with a white linen cloth and multi-colored chrysanthemums. Josephine is standing there tampering with the centerpiece. She turns.

"Finally, you're home," she says, holding out her arms to hug Coop. He bends down and embraces her.

"It's good to be back." Coop releases his mother and straightens his posture, placing his hand on my lower back. "You remember Madison."

"Of course." She gives me a hug. "Lovely to see you again."

"I love your outfit," I say to Josephine, sensing my jersey dress is informal brunch attire. She's wearing a bright red skirt and blazer, a pearl broach fastened to her left lapel. Unlike Coop's golden mane, she has dark curls that stop at her chin. There are soft lines around the corners of her mouth and eyes.

"I always dress up on Sundays," she says, sitting at the head of the table. "You and Cooper should consider joining us at church."

"Don't start," Coop says, taking a seat.

"Have I said something wrong?" Josephine leans back with both hands in the air. She looks at me. "Are you religious, Madison?"

"Yes." I skid my chair closer to the table as I sit. "I've not been a member at a specific church in a while, though."

"Sounds like that should change," she says, unfurling a napkin. "First Presbyterian has a wonderful congregation. I'm sure you'll fit right in."

"We can find our own church," Coop says, failing to mask his annoyance.

"Sure you can. I just think it would be nice to have someone join me besides Roman. It's not like Regina will go."

The back door opens, and a slender young woman walks out carrying a tray. She's wearing a cream turtleneck, and her straight hair almost reaches her waist. Her mane is darker than her mother's, though. It's intentionally dyed black, which only heightens the alabaster hue of her skin.

"My little heathen joins us at last," Josephine says, pouring lemonade into her glass.

"I brought food at least." Regina places the tray in the middle of the table. "This one is a chicken pot pie, and I've got a vegetable pie in the kitchen."

"A heathen and a tree-hugger." Josephine wears a sardonic smile.

Regina pretends to curtsy, then faces me. She looks me up and down, and I can't help wondering if she's comparing me to previous girlfriends she's met before. "You must be Madison."

I smile, swallowing down my nervousness. Something about the look on Regina's face makes me feel like a consolation prize. "It's great to finally meet you. Coop's told me all about his family."

"I'm sure." Regina rolls her eyes, then shoots a look in Coop's direction. "Where's Roman? Won't he be joining?"

"He had some errands to run," Josephine says, inspecting the pie in front of her. "Regina is our personal chef of sorts. She owns Nectar, the best restaurant in town."

Coop stands and cuts three slices. He serves Josephine, me, then himself. Regina walks into the kitchen, returning with a plate of vegetable pie. For several minutes, there's silence as everyone eats.

"This is the best part about moving back," Coop says, covering his mouth. "You're the greatest cook in the south, Regina."

"It's really impressive," I say, flattening the napkin in my lap. "I can't wait to visit Nectar."

Josephine finishes chewing and looks at Coop. "You think that's the best part about returning to Whisper Falls?"

"One of the best," he says, his tone dulled.

Regina's eyes narrow, bouncing between Coop and Josephine. "Say, this is brunch, right? I could whip up some Bloody Marys and mimosas."

"That's distasteful this early on a Sunday," Josephine replies, shooing at her with a fork.

Regina tilts her head to the side and guzzles her lemonade. "Maybe if Roman were here."

Beside me, Coop's face reddens. I know he wants me to be comfortable around his family, an impossible feat when they can't be at ease around each other. Regina's suggestion has merit; I sense Douglas family functions run smoother when alcohol is involved.

"What are your plans at the *Gazette*, Cooper?" Josephine asks.

"It'll be a busy week. My calendar is already filled with a slew of community events and meetings."

"Your father would be so proud," she says, reaching out to squeeze his hand. "He always knew you'd be the best person to run the business."

I hear a sigh coming from Regina's direction, but I don't look. Coop told me his maternal great-grandfather started the *Whisper Falls Gazette*, and the publication has remained in the family ever since. When Coop's father died, his second-in-command took over until Coop could.

"I feel guilty for the time I'll be stealing from Madison," he says. "I'd like to establish a routine before the wedding rolls around."

"I'm happy you mentioned the wedding," Josephine says, holding up her glass. "We have loads of planning to discuss."

"Here we go." Regina rolls her eyes, but I sense she enjoys watching the family tension unfold.

"There's not much left to do," Coop says.

Josephine turns to me. "Cooper booked First Presbyterian for the ceremony. I assume you have a dress."

"I do," I say. "We finalized most of the decisions before the move."

She looks at Coop. "You still need flowers and decorations and entertainment."

"Madison is capable of planning her own wedding," he says.

"Yeah, Mom. Give the girl a break," Regina says. "She's not working right now. She'll have loads of time on her hands."

We all stare at Regina. I feel slighted by her unnecessary comment, but I don't think she can help herself. In the half hour I've known her, I've picked up on her innate ability to aggravate people.

"It's not about that," Coop says, jerking his head away from his sister. "This is Madison's big day. She should be free to do as much or as little as she wants."

"I'll give you the names of some event planners I've used in the past," Josephine says, turning to me. "Most are based out of Knoxville. You wouldn't want to use anyone in Whisper."

"That would be great. Thank you," I say, hoping this will end the conversation. Josephine is straddling the line between helpful and intrusive. I squeeze Coop's knee under the table, signaling him to stand down.

The back door opens, and Roman, the oldest of the Douglas children, walks onto the porch. It must be him because he looks just like Coop, minus the blond locks. He's tall with thick hair that hovers over his eyes in curly brown tufts. "Sorry I'm late," he says, rolling up his sleeves. "Did I miss anything?"

"We've covered religion, the wedding and Coop's job," Regina says, crossing her legs. "What's next, Mom? Politics?"

"Relax, Reggie." Roman rustles her hair a bit too harshly. "It's Sunday."

"I'm Madison," I say, standing to greet him.

"So, you're the woman who stole ol' Cooper's heart?" He gives me a hearty hug, lifting my feet into the air.

"Easy," Coop says, helping me back into my seat.

"It's great to finally meet you," Roman says, before he starts stuffing his face.

"Are you still managing Mom's rental properties?" Coop asks him.

Roman nods. "Yep. And I'm in charge of the landscaping around the house."

"This property is beautiful," I say, turning to take in the complete view. "Josephine, you have a gorgeous home."

"Thank you," she says, scanning the faces of each person at the table. "I'm just happy to have everyone back. The place feels complete now."

After our meal, we enter the library—a symbol of privilege in itself. I've never been to a home that had an entire room dedicated to books and trophies. Roman walks to the bar cart by the fireplace and pours a drink. Given his ruddy complexion, I don't think it's his first.

"Before you get settled, I have a small surprise," Josephine says, walking up behind us and placing one hand on Coop's shoulder, the other on mine. "I've asked Roger to snap a picture of the happy couple."

"A picture?" I ask.

"Do we have to do this now?" Coop asks, his irritation from earlier rekindled.

"Hush it up. You've been engaged for months," she says, tapping his shoulder. "We need to put your announcement in the social's section."

"They've just moved back," Roman says. "Madison doesn't even know anyone."

"It's only a declaration of your engagement," she says. "We like to feature those sorts of things in the *Gazette*. And this is a particularly important announcement. You're the first Douglas to get married."

Both Roman and Regina flinch, as though the comment was intentionally meant to hurt them. Clearly Coop is Josephine's golden boy, in more ways than one. She exits the library.

"Roman's right. Madison doesn't know anyone," Coop says, sitting in a velvet armchair. "I was thinking maybe you could show her around, Regina?"

Regina looks at Coop, then me. "Sure. It would give us a chance to get to know each other. How's Friday?"

"Great," I say. "Hopefully I can unpack between now and then."

"It's a date." Regina returns to whatever she was doing on her phone. Moments later, Josephine escorts Roger into the room, a slender man in his sixties with a camera in his hands. She introduces him as her house manager and most loyal confidante.

"Where do you want us to stand?" I ask, wanting to appear a good sport.

"By the fireplace," says Roger. "We'll get a nice sliver of the bookcase in the back."

"Sounds perfect," Josephine says, stepping behind Roger so she can see the frame.

Coop stands behind me, placing his hands on my waist. I put my left hand atop his, making sure the ring has all the attention it deserves.

"You both look wonderful," Josephine says before Roger starts clicking.

"Mighty fine couple," says Roman, taking another sip of his drink.

We stand motionless, smiling. When Roger puts the camera down, Coop leans forward and whispers in my ear. "See? They already love you."

I smile wider and squeeze his hand. Maybe I'm built for this life after all.

CHAPTER 4

Madison

Downtown Whisper Falls is exactly what I pictured it would be. Quiet. Traditional. Boring. Market Avenue is the center of the community. The street is littered with brick rectangular buildings, each no more than three-stories tall. Much like the autumn leaves, their colors range from red to orange. Between each building are narrow, shadowed alleys lined with weeds, nature's attempt to retrieve what has been taken.

It's a short walk to the *Gazette* headquarters. A small bell jingles overhead when I enter. The lobby is cramped, but I can see the space stretches beyond the receptionist's desk. The secretary, whose placard reads Misty Walsh, is peeling stickers and placing them on folders. Her hair is curly, and her bangs are straight. She's wearing a denim dress with buttons down the front.

"How can I help you?" she asks, smiling.

"I'm here to see Coop— eh, Mr. Douglas."

"Do you have an appointment?" I'm sure Misty would know if Coop was expecting a visitor.

"No, just popping in."

Misty picks up the phone. "What's your name, sweetie? I'll see if he's busy."

"Madison," I say. "I'm his fiancée."

Misty puts down the phone without pressing a button. "Goodness, girl. Why didn't you say anything?" She pulls on a latch and swings the counter upward.

Misty pulls me into an embrace. My arms are scrunched against my sides as she continues to squeeze. When she pulls back, she scans my face, then torso. "You're a looker. Guess you'd have to be to lock Cooper down."

"Thank you." I think. I'm not really sure how to take that comment, or such a lively hug from a complete stranger. Gosh, this place is nothing like the city.

"I've been working the front desk since Cooper was a kid." Her palms touch and she smiles. "His father would be so proud with how he's turned out."

"Care to show me his office?" I ask, making my voice airy and light. I don't want to appear rude, but I'm not used to encountering strangers who know so much about Coop's life.

Misty leads me to the back corner and knocks on a door. There's a glass window overseeing the workspace. The blinds bounce upward, revealing my handsome fiancé. He's holding a cell phone to his ear. When he sees me, he motions for me to enter.

"I'll be up front," Misty says, closing the door as she leaves.

Coop's still on the phone. I look around the room, which reminds me of my own editor's office back at the *Chronicle*. Three bookcases behind his desk are filled with style guides probably not touched in years. Two chairs are positioned in front of his desk. I sit in one. After a few minutes, he puts the phone down and releases a big breath. He walks over to me and kisses my lips.

"This is a nice surprise," he says. He sits in his chair and spins in my direction. "Bored at the house, huh?"

"A little." More than a little. I've never lacked obligations and responsibilities and meetings of my own to attend. I'm not used to living life on the sidelines. "I have other motives for being here, though."

"Oh?"

"Lunch," I say, holding up a Tupperware container of sandwiches. "It should be about that time, right? I thought I could steal you for an hour."

Coop walks from behind the desk. He places one hand on my shoulder, using the other to twirl a strand of hair. I don't flinch, like I did when Misty was pawing at me. I welcome his touch. "I wish I could, but I have a Kiwanis luncheon I have to attend. It starts in a half hour and I can't get out of it."

"Oh." I rack my brain, trying to remember what a Kiwanis is. "Well, maybe after?"

"My calendar is filled up. I'm still struggling to find my footing here. Maybe sometime next week?"

It's not like Whisper Falls has a lot of breaking news. In Atlanta, Cooper and I covered all types of stories. Crime and coercion and politics. The *Gazette* mainly focuses on community, unless something extraordinary happens. He's the face of the paper, the face of Whisper Falls.

"Okay. It's not like I'll have plans."

"Don't be like that," Coop says, pulling me into a hug. "Give this place a chance. It's never going to be as exciting as Atlanta, I'll admit that, but you'll find your place."

"I know." The words sound like a lie, even to me.

"Thanks for the sandwich. Maybe we can plan lunch sometime next week. You still need to try out Nectar."

"Yeah, that would be nice," I say, backing toward the door.

"Don't take off right away," Coop says. "Let me tour you around the office."

"Maybe next time." I don't feel like being introduced as Coop's fiancée to a dozen different people. I pat my stomach. "Hunger calls."

As I make my way to the front door, I soak up the room around me. The controlled chaos of people talking on phones, typing to meet deadlines and skimming Facebook feeds. Everyone working in their own productive bubble on either side of a cubicle. It's like a miniature version of the newsroom at the *Atlanta Chronicle*. Looking back, it was a humdrum I never knew I would one day miss.

I wasn't expecting to get fired. In fact, I was eyeing a promotion. One of our key staff writers had snagged a position on the west coast, and his vacant desk was like a glowing neon sign making the entire newsroom salivate. Everyone wanted his job, but very few were in the running. I was one of those few. That's why when I sniffed out a promising story, I chased it.

Bernard Wright had already been in the Atlanta news for weeks. He was a fancy restaurateur in the area known for making millions by turning abandoned shacks into 5-star dining establishments. His restaurants attracted national reviews, and one was even featured as the set for some reality cooking show. In recent weeks, however, Wright wasn't in the news for being a businessman. His face was plastered across every publication because a handful of female employees had alleged sexual misconduct against him.

One of his former employees reached out to me. 'Chrissy'. That wasn't her real name, but it was the alias I used in my article. She told me how she'd started working for Bernard Wright during the summer between her sophomore and junior years of college. It started as a part-time gig, until she realized she raked in more money serving steamed lobster and chilled shrimp than she ever would in elementary education, her chosen study track.

By the time 'Chrissy' was meant to resume her fall classes, she had dropped out, and Wright hand-selected her to work in one of his new restaurants downtown. Her income increased even more. She wasn't just a server; Wright gave her managerial tasks, which meant she often worked late nights checking inventory. She said Wright was flirtatious with her at first, but friendly. Like the father of a friend, always respecting the boundaries between them.

As the months passed, his behavior became more aggressive. He'd put his hands on her hips and whisper in her ear, his lips touching her skin and making her freeze. She told me Wright eventually made a pass at her, then another. Until one night, she was too scared and intimidated to protest his advances. She thought their arrangement was exclusive, until she heard about the lawsuit being brought against him by other employees. The other women's stories inspired her, reminded her she wasn't alone and gave her the strength to speak. That's why she reached out to me.

We had several interviews; each time she revealed more details about her relationship with Wright, a man already labeled as a monster in the regional media. Understandably, she wasn't ready to open up right away. As she divulged more details during our conversations, I felt sick. When I was alone, I cried. I hated hearing the first-hand details of what another woman had endured under the heavy fist of male authority. But more than anything, I was proud of 'Chrissy' for coming forward with her story, and I felt honored she'd entrusted me with telling it.

Her vivid account of working alongside Bernard Wright was meant to be the feature that landed me the new title I desperately wanted. It was like my entire future was unfurling before me: the wedding with Coop and the prestigious promotion with the higher paycheck.

I had never been more wrong.

CHAPTER 5

Madison

It's finally Friday. Regina knocks on the door fifteen minutes late, which means I've been sitting alone, fully dressed, in the living room for the past half hour. She's wearing black pants and a leather bomber jacket. Her hair is curled, pinned up on one side with a barrette she likely pulled from the Douglas heirloom collection.

"You look cute," she says, scanning my black skinny jeans and off the shoulder top.

"Thanks," I say, closing the door and locking it. I'd invite Regina inside, but I'm afraid she'd see the house's state of disarray. "Where are we going?"

"The most popping place in town," she says, sliding into her car. All the Douglases have nice cars; I figured that out when I visited Josephine's home. Her driveway looked like the miniature lot of a luxury dealer.

"Are there many bars here?"

"More than you'd think," she says, starting the ignition. "There's one bar for every two churches. People have to have a place to sin so they can have a reason to repent."

"I see." I take out a tinted balm and slick it over my lips. "Coop called in between leaving the office and heading to some fundraiser. He told me to text him where we end up and he might join us."

"*Coop.* That's cute." She shrugs. "Do you always call him that?"

"Most of the time, I guess."

"Fun, fun, fun," she sings. I can't help but feel Regina is pulling a prank, and I'm not in on the joke. I start to put two and two together as we get closer to town. We drive past the *Gazette* and all the places I thought we might end up and pull into the crowded high school parking lot.

"What's this?"

"It's Friday night in Whisper Falls," she says. "That means football."

I watch as people of all ages exit their cars and migrate toward the stadium. *This* is her joke. She's tricked me into thinking we're having a proper night out. She must sense how much I'm craving excitement, and clearly this isn't it.

"I thought you were showing me around town."

Regina unbuckles her seat belt. "Trust me. Everything you need to know about Whisper Falls you can find out here." She exits the car, poking her head back inside. "You coming?"

The announcer's voice booms louder as we make our way to the gate, the cool breeze tangling my hair. When we reach the ticket booth, Regina flashes a laminate card and the man working the gate waves her in.

"What's that?" I ask, looking at the card.

"We buy a family pass every season. We should get free admission considering the cash Mom donates to this place each year." She slides the card back into her YSL wristlet and marches toward the concession stand. "Popcorn?"

"Not hungry," I say, as an older man in a flannel jacket bumps against my shoulder. Regina purchases her concessions and finger waves to at least five people I've never seen before. Everyone knows her, which means they're all looking at me, wondering who I am and already deciding I don't belong.

As she walks away, Regina rams into a woman about our age wearing a handmade T-shirt and leggings. Her blonde curls are stiff and scrunched, a hairstyle I've seen at least three times since entering the gate. When she recognizes Regina as the person who knocked her shoulder, she scowls.

"Sorry, Bridgette," Regina says, avoiding eye contact.

"Didn't know you cared about football," she says, one hand on her hip.

Regina nods at me. "I'm taking my sister-in-law around town. This is Cooper's fiancée, Madison."

"Nice to meet you," I say, holding out a hand. Perhaps initiating a handshake will keep people from smothering me with unwanted physical affection. Bridgette doesn't take it.

"Cooper's fiancée?" She looks me up and down, her assessment noticeably more critical than Misty's was earlier in the week. "I hope she can swim."

It takes a second for her comment to register. She's making a sick reference to Celia, the beautiful teenager who lost her life to the Whisper Lake tides. Within seconds, I transition from confusion to outrage. I'm about to speak, but Regina butts in.

"Oh, bite me, Bridgette," she says, her dark hair jiggling with the shake of her head.

Bridgette winks. "I bet you'd love it if I did."

Regina pushes past her, and I follow. "Who the hell was that?" I ask, after we're a few steps away.

"Bridgette McCallister, née Rollins. Total skank. She slept with like half the basketball team my freshman year. She's one of Celia's old cheer buddies."

Hearing Celia's name is like a punch to the gut. For so long, she's been this nonexistent being Coop and I avoid discussing. I forgot I'm in her world now, where people know more about her than I ever will. They likely know more about Coop, too.

We approach the field, which is surrounded by a black fence. The scoreboard reveals the second quarter is almost over and the

Whisper Falls Wildcats are down seven points. I start walking to the bleachers, but Regina stops me.

"Where are you going?" she asks.

"Aren't we here to watch the game?" If she hadn't noticed my dissatisfaction yet, she does now.

"We're here to watch people," she says, leaning against the fence and facing the crowd. I dodge a family with small children climbing the concrete steps and stand beside her. "You've had the pleasure of meeting Bridgette. Expect to see her at every local event. She's full of hometown pride. Gah, the only thing worse than peaking in high school is peaking in eighth grade."

"Isn't that a little harsh?"

"You heard what she just said, right? She hasn't gotten any kinder with age." She returns her attention to the crowd, unbothered. "You see the woman in the purple sweater with the black bob and glasses?"

My eyes follow her outstretched finger. The woman she's brought to my attention is standing, holding a poster that reads *Go Cats*. I nod.

"That's Kim Fuller. She's the elementary school principal. She's always posting inflammatory statements on social media. All this alt-right stuff to get people riled up. Her husband is sleeping with the school librarian, and everyone in town knows it but her."

She turns and nods toward a man standing near a huddle of cheerleaders. "That's Gary. He owns a car dealership and has a rap sheet a mile long. People say he's a little too friendly with the teenagers, if you catch my drift. That's why his second wife left him."

I shake my head, struggling to connect faces to this influx of information. "Why are you telling me this?"

"You need to know things about people when you live in Whisper, otherwise you won't know who to trust." She sips through her straw and nods somewhere else. "The skinny guy with the faded letterman jacket? He's a known CI for the cops."

I only half-listen as Regina talks. I absorb my surroundings, trying to determine where I fit in amongst all these people. I wonder where Coop fits, too, or at least, how he once did. In his youth, was he an athletic idol storming the field? Did Celia cheer him on from the purple and black platform to my right? By the time Regina has pointed out a former stripper, a pill dealer and a disgraced policeman, I've had enough.

"Look, I didn't come here for this," I say, crossing my arms.

"Why did you come here?" And I can tell she's not asking about the game. She's talking about *here*. Whisper.

"Because I love Coop. We're building a life together. I have no interest in these strangers' secrets."

She crinkles her nose. "Aren't you, like, a writer or something? You dig up people's dirt for a living."

"I am a real journalist. I was a..." My frustrations prevent me from finishing. My skin burns hot, and not just from the large field lamp hovering overhead. "You know what? I'm leaving."

Regina leans further into the fence. "Where are you going? It's not like we have Uber."

"I'll figure it out."

I march past the band as they rip a tune. The stadium chatter lessens as I re-enter the parking lot. It dawns on me I really am out of options. I hear footsteps behind me picking up pace and then see Regina, popcorn bag still in hand.

"Come on, city girl. You can't call it a night yet." She jingles her keys. "Let's go. I've got another place to show you."

We barely speak as she drives away from town and the paved streets turn to dust. Before long, the headlights stretch over Whisper Lake. She parks the car in a grassy spot by the water.

"If it were summer, I'd have all sorts of spots to show you," she says. "The lake is the only part of Whisper that doesn't irk me."

"What are we doing now?" I feel like her game isn't yet finished.

She pulls out a bottle of bourbon and clear cups that look like they've been lifted from a motel nightstand. "The only thing there is to do in Whisper. Drink and stare at nothing and talk shit."

She pours a gulp's worth into my cup and hands it over. I pause before downing the shot.

"Atta girl," she says, stepping out of the car. I join her. A gust of wind blows past us, cooling the heat underneath my skin. We're surrounded by darkness, the chirping of crickets in the trees and the sound of soft ripples in the nearby water.

"If you're so miserable living in Whisper Falls, why don't you just leave?" I ask. Clearly, she isn't happy here, and after a week of isolation interspersed with clumsy introductions, I can see why.

"Some people have no choice but to stay."

"I don't buy that. You, your brothers… you have options. Education. Money. You act like you're being forced to stay. You're not."

"All that stuff comes attached to the purse strings. You think I'd be able to afford culinary school on my own? Or that Cooper would be able to run his own newspaper? It comes with being a Douglas. Even if it sucks sometimes, it'd be pointless to give all that up."

I look across the lake, watching as the moon reflects on the water, a single cylinder of light. I've never felt more distant from Regina, or Coop. I can't imagine what it's like to be given what the rest of the world struggles to obtain, and still bottle such bitterness. It's difficult to tell whether Regina likes me. More than anything, I think she's been lonely for a long time, making it difficult for her to connect with anyone. The only reason she's survived in this town is because she's a Douglas, a fact we both know, and she resents.

"I really want to be happy here," I admit. "I'm trying."

"You're different from the others." For once, she looks sincere, pushing back the long black strands around her face. "I can tell you love Cooper, not just the dollar signs."

"Were others after dollar signs?" I ask, wondering what she's getting at. I'm well versed when it comes to Coop's dating history, but I don't know how many exes he's introduced to his family.

"One or two." She takes a big gulp. We both stare at the water, as if it's pulling our gaze, forcing us to think. Asking us its questions.

"What was she like?" I ask.

"Who?"

"Celia."

She smirks. "Hasn't he told you?"

"He told me about what happened, not much else." I wonder where on this lake her body was found. If it floated near the bank where we currently stand. "Do people bring her up a lot? Like Bridgette did tonight?"

"They usually aren't so forward. Some people, like Bridgette, would rather relish in the drama."

We're silent for several seconds. There are questions I want to ask her, things I want to know. Things that, for whatever reason, Coop has never felt comfortable telling me.

"Like I said, he doesn't talk about what happened."

"Even if he did, he wouldn't tell the truth." She finishes her cup and clears her throat. "Celia was a wicked bitch."

"Regina! She was a teenager who died."

"So? Good people die every day."

I roll my eyes at Regina's boorish outlook. "How bad can someone be at seventeen?"

"Have you been seventeen?" She laughs, folding her arms across her chest. "Celia was cruel to everyone she ever met. Probably had her eyes set on Cooper since she was in elementary school. I don't think he ever appreciated the bullet he dodged when she died."

"Coop told me she was popular. That her death changed people."

She laughs. "Told you he wouldn't tell the truth. Celia was nothing like the saintly image this town has resurrected. You can't believe everything you hear."

It's interesting how quickly Regina has dropped her earlier role as a gossipmonger. Only an hour ago, she delighted in telling me all her neighbors' secrets. "Should I believe the things you said tonight? About Bridgette sleeping with half the basketball team?"

"Maybe." She chuckles and takes another sip of her drink. "Thing is, I've never liked her. I couldn't give two shits about her tarnished reputation. That's what we do in Whisper. We choose our side and defend it to the death."

I roll my eyes again. Regina will take some getting used to, but there's truth in what she says. I think of Misty's reaction to meeting me, praising my arrival, compared to Bridgette's callous dismissal. This town certainly takes sides. I close my eyes and focus on the gentle sound of water lapping against the shore, trying not to let the ugliness of this place tarnish what beauty exists.

CHAPTER 6

June 16, 2006

Celia's shift ended at six, when the lake closed to the public. People could still congregate there, and did, but they were no longer under the watchful eye of the Whisper Falls Guard. She put the whistle to her lips and blew, signaling to the remaining swimmers it was time to exit and find a spot further down the bank.

When the water was clear, she strung the flimsy chain blocking off her section of beach and folded the flaps of her lifeguard stand. She filled out her hours by hand and left the clipboard hanging from the back of the chair for Ronnie, her boss, to find in the morning. When she arrived at the gravel lot, there were only two cars remaining: her purple Civic, and Cooper's shiny black truck. He leaned against his vehicle, thumbing his iPod.

The mere sight of him took her breath away. He was shirtless, wearing trunks in the same shade of red as her suit. The whistle hanging from his neck dangled over his taut, tan midsection. His hair was blond, but a few strands at his crown were white from long hours sitting in the sun. Anyone looking at Cooper Douglas could see his good looks, but Celia saw more than that. She saw potential, something she considered a massively underrated relationship incentive.

He crossed his arms as she approached, so Celia added a little more swing to her hips. They'd been fighting for weeks, and she wanted to win him over. She pushed her sunglasses into her hair, so he could see the bright blue in her eyes.

"Your section packed up?" she asked, in her sweet, southern drawl.

"Yep." His stance didn't budge, neither did his face. Cooper was upset, and Celia had an idea what about.

"Bridgette said they're having a bonfire by the south bank tonight. Think Roman could score us a couple beers?"

"I don't feel much like partying tonight, Celia," he said. "We need to talk."

"What about?" She cocked her head to the side, letting her braid fall over her shoulder.

Before Cooper could answer, a white Jeep pulled into the lot. The music was blaring, and a collection of limbs sprawled out of the open windows. When the brakes hit, a smattering of dust spread around the tires. The driver popped up, looking at them over the windshield.

"Y'all heard about the party tonight?" asked Jim, a scrawny, acne-prone seventeen-year-old with a shell necklace around his neck.

"I was just telling Cooper about it," Celia said, happy the cavalry had arrived in time. Cooper might be mad at her, but it was hard for him to resist peer pressure. Cooper always folded under pressure.

"We all know you won't turn down a good time," Jim said to Celia, but there was an edge in his voice. She looked at Cooper, but he refused to look at either one of them.

"What's that supposed to mean?" she asked.

"Stop pestering her," Bridgette yelled at Jim, scrunching to make room in the back seat. "Get in, Celia. I want you to braid my hair."

She started walking to the car but stopped when Cooper spoke.

"Can't come right now, guys. Mom needs me to run by the house."

"Aww," Bridgette whined.

Beside her, a girl with strawberry curls popped the cap off a beer bottle and took a swig. "Y'all are missing out," she shouted.

"Go on without us," Celia said, taking a step closer to Cooper. "We'll meet up later. We're hoping Roman will buy some more alcohol."

Jim slid back into the driver's seat and cranked the car. "See y'all after a while."

The car squealed out of the lot and onto the main road, leaving another cloud of dirt in its wake. The voices and blaring music faded, until there was nothing left but the sound of chirping insects and Cooper's heavy breathing.

"You think that's cute?" he asked, taking a step closer. "I told you I'm not in the mood to party."

"That's why I said we'd meet them later. We can go talk first, or whatever." She looked him up and down, letting him know she was willing to do more than talk, but he didn't seem interested. He was still angry. "You should thank me. It makes you sound cool when people remember Roman can get beer."

"In case you haven't noticed, I don't need Roman or beer to be cool."

"What's up with Jim? He was acting like an asshole, and you didn't even say anything."

Cooper shrugged. "Maybe everyone isn't as crazy about you as you think they are."

Celia flipped her duffel over her shoulder and gave Cooper a look she knew he despised. It was like she was laughing at him, but there was no smile. "If you wanna talk, let's talk," she said defiantly.

"Let's go to the dock by my house."

This was a good sign. It was their sentimental place. The location where she finally let him move past second base and where, months later, he told her he loved her. Maybe this relationship was salvageable, depending on how much he knew.

"Should I drive, or you?" she asked.

"I'll drive."

Cooper jumped into the driver's seat. Celia checked the locks on her car, climbed into Cooper's truck and fastened her seat belt.

CHAPTER 7

Helena

I'm reading the paper when I see it.

That bastard is engaged. *Engaged*. The word crawls all over me, tugging on my patience and biting at my wounds. This is what people don't understand about moving on. Even if I accept what has happened, there's always something in the present I can't tolerate. Something new I can't control.

I've always been an avid reader. I don't have just one subscription, either. I have my national newspaper I read because it makes me feel worldly, a few local publications and the *Whisper Falls Gazette*. I know what people think… if you don't want the past to bother you, leave it alone. I've tried to cancel the damned thing, what, three times? But I never go through with it because, in many ways, it's my only link to him, and he's my only link to her.

Even though I continue to read his family's shitty newspaper, I wasn't expecting this. On the front page of the social's section (of course it's the front), there's a recent picture of Cooper Douglas. He's probably standing in one of the fancy rooms of his family's pretentious house. He's smiling at the camera, his dimples pinned. His arm is around *her*. The new woman in his life. Madison Sharpe. She looks nice enough. Wholesome. Clean. Nothing on my girl, of course, but that's to be expected. What this picture doesn't show is the wool Cooper has pulled over her eyes; this Madison probably has no idea her fiancé is a murderer.

An hour later, I'm still wallowing in it. This defeated feeling. My daughter is gone. Her quirky laugh and her adorable sneeze. Her inquisitive nature. I've not experienced her warmth in years, a realization that leaves me hollow. And yet, Cooper Douglas continues not only living, but thriving. Taking over the family business (oh yeah, I noticed the recent inclusion of his name to the masthead). Getting married. I slam my drink against the table, as if the disruptive clack of glass on glass will make me feel better. It doesn't. Nothing does.

Madison Sharpe. Thanks to the oversharing of her generation, it doesn't take me long to uncover more about her. She has all the standard social platforms. With her white-blonde hair and edgy dark eyebrows, she looks every bit the city girl. Her petite frame is usually swathed in crop tops and rompers, a noticeable change from the cardigan and dress she wore in the engagement photo. She must already be conforming, molding herself to better fit the monster standing at her back.

Scrolling through her feed, I see she used to post pictures at brunch with friends, department store shopping and late nights in the back seats of taxis. That's stopped; she hasn't uploaded a photo in more than two months. Cooper must have a hold on her, already tightening his grip and forcing her to leave her life—her real life—behind. Now he's further isolated her, moving her to that backwoods Tennessee town. Looks like she worked as a journalist for the *Atlanta Chronicle*, then abruptly stopped. Did she leave her job for him? Forfeit her life?

I inhale through my nose, exhale through my mouth, all the while repeating the positive mantras my grief counselor suggested I chant when on the verge of overwhelm. I imagine I'm in this protective bubble and no one can pierce it. Try as I might, all I see when I close my eyes is him. Cooper Douglas, with his wealth and privilege, never forced to be punished for all he's done. Now all the ideas are returning, all the fantasies I've concocted over the years of ways I can punish him. They're irrational, yes. But no one describes revenge as rational. They say revenge is sweet. Oh, so sweet.

I swore I wouldn't return to Whisper Falls. My last visit accomplished little. If anything, it hurt my campaign to turn others against him. Gave the whole Douglas clan a reason to be on their guard about what I'd do next. That's why I won't target them this time, I decide; I'll go after her. I pick up the paper and look at the picture again. Madison Sharpe. *Does* she know her fiancé is a murderer? Does she? If not, she needs to.

If only I could have given my daughter the same warning. Of course, I had no way of knowing what danger she was in. How could I when she seemed so happy? I think back to the last time I saw my sweet girl. Of course, I didn't know it would be the last time. Maybe that's why it was so perfect.

She jabbered on and on about the end of the school year, a healthy mix of annoyance and interest about her classes. Kids that age love to complain about their routine, but they're a little afraid to try anything new. This time, she was different. She was in love.

"What's his name?" I asked. We walked along the uncrowded streets during one of our day visits.

"Cooper Douglas." She smiled wide and cracked her knuckles. "I don't know, Mom. I think this guy is the real thing."

The real thing. No words to describe it, really. Nothing adequate. The real thing makes you glow from within, ache with feeling. Man, did she glow that day.

"Tell me about him," I said, panning my hand from her shoulder to her elbow. "How did you meet?"

"At school." She tilted her head to the side and rolled her eyes, a tic that reminded me of my younger self.

"See, school can't be that bad."

"No, it's not bad." She grinned. "Nothing really seems bad anymore."

The real thing makes you think that at first.

"How long has it been?" I asked.

"Several months." She braced, like she was afraid I'd shoot her down. "I know we're young, but he's so understanding and supportive. He really listens. And he makes me laugh." Then she was laughing, some recent memory appearing in her mind. "At the same time, he's serious. He's guarded. I think it's because his family is loaded."

"Wealthy doesn't hurt," I said, poking her ribs.

That's what you do when talking about boys. Make fun and kid. But I could tell by the way she spoke this wasn't just any boy. This boy might become a man she'd one day marry. *The real thing.* The intensity of it all made my head whirl.

"Don't move too fast," I said, afraid of a lot of things, but more than anything that my giddy, bright girl would end up hurt.

"We're not. I mean, the feelings are there. We're taking things slow, but I am spending more time with his family."

"When do *I* get to meet him?" I hooked my arm into hers, leaning into her weight.

"Soon."

We didn't linger on the topic long. Thank goodness. It'd be that much harder to live with myself if our entire conversation that day revolved around Cooper Douglas. We kept talking about school and the latest season of *The Bachelor* and had a random debate over which was superior, cookies or brownies? That led to us getting ice cream, and we sat in the park until sunset.

Then, I hugged my vibrant, glowing girl goodbye. Never once did I think it would be the last time I'd see her. I've almost memorized every detail of that last embrace. Her vanilla smell and plush shirt and wet cheeks. Just because we didn't see each other often didn't mean we didn't want to. She missed me when I was gone, and I missed her. I still do.

Even the happy memories hurt now. It's unfair. All of this is so unfair. But I need to stop rehashing the past and focus on the present. On retribution. It's time Cooper suffers for everything he has taken away.

CHAPTER 8

Madison

Coop's workload carries over into the weekend. His responsibilities as editor-in-chief are more taxing than his role at the *Chronicle*. Most people would take it easy, not let the pressure of running a newspaper get to them because their family calls the shots. Coop's not like that. He wants to prove himself, probably *because* he's a Douglas. He wants people to respect his first name as much as they do his last.

I'd wanted to go furniture shopping. The limited furniture we brought from Atlanta barely covers a quarter of our new space. I'm running out of storage, which puts the rest of the unpacking process on hold. Coop suggested I go shopping with Josephine instead. *She's got a better eye for decorating*, he said. This first week, I've seen my in-laws more often than I've seen Coop. It's a different dynamic here, though. Family plays a larger role because there's little else to soak up the time.

I'm waiting on the front porch when a black SUV pulls into the driveway. The windows are tinted, but transparent enough for me to see Josephine in the passenger seat and Roman behind the wheel. It's hard for me to put my finger on what Roman's like exactly. He exudes Coop's charm but lacks his responsibilities.

"Nice day," he says as I slide into the back seat.

"It really is," I say, my gaze turning to the lush woods surrounding our house. Each day, the view alters slightly, the leaves an ever-changing presence. "I'm surprised by how beautiful it is here."

"Tennessee is breathtaking in the fall," Josephine says, as Roman backs out of the driveway. "That's when tourism spikes."

"I can see why," I say. I'd never thought of this pocket of the country as being a vacation destination, but according to Coop, I'm wrong. Perhaps it's because I grew up in the city, and time away usually meant booking a week at the beach. "Does Whisper get many visitors?"

"More the surrounding areas," Josephine says. "Gatlinburg and Knoxville and Chattanooga."

All places I've heard mentioned but have never been.

"Whisper could have been a tourist trap, but Mom put an end to that," Roman says.

"How so?" I ask, intrigued.

"Back in the early aughts, outside investors took an interest in this place. They thought Whisper Lake would be an ideal destination for a luxury resort," she says, as though retelling a fond memory. "They wanted to buy a hundred acres of land."

"Could have been our ticket out of here," Roman says. His reflection in the rectangular rearview mirror is smiling, but I sense an edge in his voice. "Could have made millions."

By all appearances, the Douglases are wealthy as is. I can't believe they were in the position to be worth even more. "What happened?" I ask.

"Mom refused to sell."

"They were offering *you* this money?" I ask Josephine.

"I owned most of the property. All landowners were required to be in agreement, and I was majority stakeholder." Somehow, she speaks about her finances and sounds self-assured, not greedy. "Roman's right. I held up the deal."

"It was like winning the lottery and refusing to cash in," Roman says, turning into the downtown area.

"Why didn't you?" I ask.

"Not everything in life is about money," Josephine says.

"Says the rich woman," Roman goads.

"Whisper Falls is charming and quaint. There aren't many places like it anymore," she says, speaking as though describing an old friend. "I couldn't imagine these same streets being littered with Burger Kings and mini-golf establishments and bait shops. Change isn't always good."

"You still seem a little bitter about the decision?" I say to Roman, wavering my voice to make it clear I'm only kidding.

"Yeah, yeah. I was a kid at the time. It wasn't my decision to make. It's something I like to think about now and then, though. How this place could have been different." He stretches his arm and squeezes Josephine's shoulder. "Really, I just like to give Mom a hard time."

It certainly would have changed the area. Aside from the profits for the Douglases, a deal like that could have brought more money to the area. Job opportunities and tourism. Do the people here even know about the opportunities Josephine has taken from them? Looking out the window, I imagine a different type of Whisper Falls. Try to decide if I'd be happier in that place. The car stops, and I see we're outside a large warehouse called Turner's.

"You'll see once we get inside," Josephine says, turning to look at me in the back seat. "This place has a little bit of everything."

Inside, Josephine introduces me to the owner, a man named Fred. He's short and round and all too eager to have us in his store. I'd only planned on picking up some pieces for the living room, but Josephine assures him we've got an empty house to fill. Watching the way Fred's eyes pop at the remark makes me blush.

We walk from one setting to the next: a living area, a patio set, a bedroom display. Josephine can't keep away from Fred, the two of them conversing back and forth. Roman walks to the back of the store and chats with the workers. There's a couple beside me talking to a salesperson. The worker looks familiar, but that can't be possible; I've not been here long enough to really know anyone. As

I walk closer, watching her, I remember she's the blonde from last night. The name tag on her royal blue vest confirms it: Bridgette, Rising Star.

The couple shopping for a new washer and dryer step away. Her attention turns to me, and I enjoy the quick flicker of recognition in her eyes. I move closer, unable to resist watching her squirm. Like I'm Julia Roberts in *Pretty Woman* giving it to the snotty salespeople on Rodeo Drive. She looks different now, her confidence from last night gone.

I've got her cornered between a display of dishwashers. She can't just ignore me, not with Fred and Josephine standing so close. Finally, she looks up and offers a strained smile.

"Need help finding anything?" she asks.

"You look familiar," I say, relishing this moment. I replay her comment from last night in my mind. *Hope she can swim.* Now I'm the one with the upper hand, and I like it.

"Bridgette Rollins? Is that you?" Josephine, standing behind me, steps forward and embraces Bridgette. I'm caught off guard considering how rude this woman was to Regina.

"Nice seeing you, Mrs. Douglas," Bridgette says. Her head over Josephine's shoulder, we lock eyes. I'm unsure if she's thankful for an interruption or if she's genuinely happy to see her.

Josephine pulls away, motioning to me. "Bridgette, I'd like you to meet my future daughter-in-law, Madison. She's just moved here from Atlanta."

"We met at the football game last night," I say, dryly. I can't help dangling the possibility I might bring up last night's comment, although I won't. I'm not yet comfortable enough with Josephine.

"That's right," Josephine says. "Your son is the quarterback, right?"

"Stepson," Bridgette says. "He's the second-string linebacker. Still only a sophomore."

"You must be so proud." Josephine turns to me. "Bridgette was one of my girls back when I sponsored the cheerleading team. Feels like ages ago, doesn't it?"

"Is that how you know Regina?" I ask Bridgette.

Bridgette and Josephine chuckle in unison. "Regina wasn't on the squad, not for lack of trying," Josephine says. "The school was short a sponsor, and I stepped up. Only did it for a year or two. Sometimes I miss being so involved."

"We had some good times," Bridgette says, her eyes bouncing from Josephine to me. Judging by her job and bitter attitude, I'd say it was the best of times for Bridgette.

"Lovely running into you," Josephine says, lightly touching Bridgette's hand.

"Let me know if you need help finding anything," she says, scurrying off.

She'd probably get a hefty commission if she stayed around, but she seems intimidated.

The remaining hour we're in the store, I barely see Bridgette. I'm too busy committing to furniture I don't have the funds to buy: a new sofa, some bookcases and a bedroom suite. The sign at the front of the store offers financing, so I can at least pay on my purchases between now and the wedding. At the sales counter, I'm stunned when Josephine announces she will buy everything.

"You can't," I say, beginning to sweat. "It's too much."

"Please," she says. "It's my duty as part of the renovation. I'm not going to throw the responsibility of furnishing the place on you."

"But it's our house," I say, my eyes darting to Roman. "I don't want you to think you owe us anything. You've already done plenty."

"Word of advice," Roman says, his voice low. "Mom's going to get her way. She never passes up the opportunity to spoil someone."

"I really do insist," she says, handing her card to Fred. "Go on outside. On the way home, we'll talk about what else the place needs."

I'm not used to such graciousness. The entire time we'd been shopping, I'd mentally calculated how much everything would cost, what the monthly installments might be and the potential down payment. I'm used to working for what I want. Sometimes, even with work, I end up disappointed. But, as Roman says, Josephine delights in indulging those she loves. I'm now one of those people.

As I walk to the car, I spot Bridgette outside. She's leaning against the brick wall of the building, smoking a cigarette.

"Hey, Bridgette," I say, marching toward her. I'm too close for her to walk away or duck back inside. "Can I talk to you for a second?"

"My break is almost over," she says, eyes flitting for an escape route.

"You seemed chummy with my mother-in-law," I say. "I wonder how she'd feel about that dig you made last night?"

"Look, lady. I don't know you—"

"You don't have to know me. What you said was rude. Making a joke about a girl drowning?"

She titters, taking another drag of the cigarette. "We don't need to get into this."

"Why? Because you know who I am?" *Who I am.* What do I mean by that? A Douglas? In a few short days, it's like the privilege has gone to my head. I take a deep breath and redirect. "I thought Celia was your friend."

"She was my friend." Bridgette tosses the cigarette on the ground, stomping it with her foot. "And Cooper killed her."

The scent of smoke rising from the ground turns my stomach. I step back, processing the magnitude of what Bridgette just said. Coop? *Killed her?* Then the anger returns. "What did you say?"

Bridgette smiles, having reclaimed control of the conversation. "You know that's what everyone in Whisper thinks, right? People don't say it anymore, out of respect for Mrs. Douglas, but we all know Celia's death wasn't an accident."

I'm confused. Of course Celia's death was an accident. That's all Coop ever said. How could anyone think he's capable of hurting—let alone killing—someone?

"Celia drowned," I say, my words sounding more like a question or guess than a statement.

"Yeah, the water in her lungs killed her. That doesn't explain why her skull was cracked. I'm guessing Cooper didn't tell you that part of the story." Bridgette looks over my shoulder. I turn to see Josephine and Roman exiting the store.

"Coop would never hurt anyone," I hiss, low enough so they can't hear.

"If you say so," Bridgette says, slinking around the side of the building. "Welcome to Whisper."

For a few moments, I stand there. I can barely think. I'm trying to process what Bridgette said and what it means, then I hear Roman calling my name from the parking lot.

"Are you coming?" he hollers.

"I'm going to run by the *Gazette*," I say, standing still. I don't want them to see the rosy flush in my cheeks. "I need to visit Coop."

"We can give you a ride," Josephine says, opening the passenger side door.

"No thanks," I say. "I'll walk."

CHAPTER 9

Madison

The distance between the warehouse and the *Gazette* is longer than I expected, but I need these moments alone. I need to process what Bridgette, with her wicked smile and chipped fingernail polish, said. Coop killed Celia. Could people actually think that?

In the two years we've been together, he talked about Celia periodically. There's been times I've wanted to dig deeper, ask more questions about her death, but I think to do so would be cruel. It'd be like demanding someone relive the worst day of their life over and over again, and for what cause? To ease my own insecurity? After all, Coop has graciously overlooked my own shortcomings.

I playback everything I know about the tragedy. Coop never mentioned foul play, let alone that people suspected him. And why would they—how could they—think Coop was to blame? He's the most mannerly and respectful man I've ever met.

As I get closer to Market Avenue, I see groups of people enjoying the Saturday sunshine. They're sitting on park benches and strolling along the sidewalks. On the surface, this place is beautiful, welcoming and warm. I can't help wondering if this is all some kind of façade. A shield this town wears to hide its nastier underbelly.

By the time I reach the *Gazette*, Whisper Falls feels like a ghost town again. Most businesses on this side of the street are closed for the weekend. Coop's the only one pulling extra hours, which is why the front door is locked.

I bang against the glass, simultaneously reaching for my phone to call Coop. I've almost finished tapping his name when the front door opens. Coop stands there, looking a bit startled.

"Madison?" His worried look drops slightly, and he smiles. He must be wondering why I'm here.

"Can we talk?" My voice is low and unenthusiastic. I step inside the building to find Coop isn't alone. There's another man here. He's shorter with thinning hair and pockmarked cheeks. He removes one hand from his pocket and initiates a handshake.

"Jim Nelson," he says, his firm grasp displaying the confidence his outward appearance lacks. "I don't think we've met."

"I'm Madison," I say, looking to Coop for an explanation. His name sparks recognition. Jimmy, one of his old high school friends. Coop has mentioned him before.

"This is my fiancée," Coop says. He places a hand on my hip.

"Pleasure to finally meet you," Jim says. "Cooper and I go way back."

"Jimmy is the Whisper Falls Police Chief now," Coop says.

The last thing I wanted was to be introduced to yet another family acquaintance. A friend, actually. Not after what Bridgette just told me. "I hope I'm not interrupting anything."

"No," Jim says, clapping his hand on Coop's shoulder. "I'm not here on business. Just noticed the car parked across the street and thought I'd check in on my old friend."

"You'll have to come by the house for dinner soon," Coop says. "Madison's spent the day furniture shopping."

"I'd like that," Jim says, nodding to me. "You should check out Turner's. They've got some great stuff down there."

I nod. It's been difficult trying to contain my upset at this impromptu introduction, and I'd rather Jim leave so I can talk to Coop.

"You still have my number?" Jim asks as he walks out. They stand on the front step, laughing and high fiving. Beneath their suits and titles, they seem little more than young boys reliving their youth. Coop is smiling when he walks back inside, shutting the door and locking it.

"Everything okay?" he asks.

"Not really," I say, looking away and taking a seat in the armchair beside the window, the cracked leather poking at my skin. "I just heard something really awful."

"What is it?" Coop leans against the front desk, crossing his arms. "Did something happen with my family?"

"Nothing like that," I say, thinking back to how I reacted in the parking lot with Roman and Josephine. They must have deemed my sudden departure rude, especially after Josephine had paid for our new furniture.

"Tell me what's going on," he says. "You're worrying me."

I take a deep breath, considering where to start. "Last night, Regina and I went to the football game."

"I know." He'd been asleep when we returned from the lake, and I barely had time to speak with him this morning before he was off to the office again. He laughs. "I bet you stuck out like a sore thumb."

"There was this woman there. Bridgette. She made a rude comment to Regina about Celia." I struggle to say her name. "Bridgette works at Turner's. When I saw her, I tried confronting her. That's when she told me people think you killed Celia."

Coop stares at me, waiting to see if there's more, then he looks down. "Bridgette doesn't know what she's talking about."

"I gather she's not the most reliable source," I say, scooting closer to the edge of the chair. "But is what she said true? Do people really think you had something to do with Celia's death?"

He exhales, and I can see his body stiffening. "Some people."

I stand, dropping my bag on the chair. "That's crazy. Why would people think that?"

"It's a nasty rumor that got started years ago. I didn't tell you about it because I don't want you to feel uncomfortable."

"What makes me uncomfortable is hearing about this from strangers. I don't want to be blindsided by catty comments."

"Did Regina say something—"

"That's not the point," I say, defiantly. "Whatever story there is about you and Celia, I need to hear all of it. Now."

He holds eye contact, then nods. "We were both lifeguards at Whisper Lake. The day she went missing, we spent an hour or so at my family's dock. I left to go to a party. People thought I might be involved because I was the last person seen with her. And that's it. There's nothing connecting me to her death."

He's told me about that day before, but the scenario materializes more clearly now. I have a frame of reference, locations and faces I can picture in my mind. And a sickening twinge in my gut about the accusations being made. "Bridgette said her head—"

"Her skull was cracked." For the first time, he looks angry. I'm entitled to these details, but they're understandably hard for him to give. I'm dredging up memories he's long buried. "She drowned. Probably knocked her head against something while she was in the water. There's a lot of dangerous spots on the lake."

"Why wouldn't you tell me you were accused of killing her?"

"I've defended my honor enough to the people around here. I shouldn't have to do it in my own home."

"I'm not accusing you, Coop," I say, hurt that he'd even suggest it. I know Coop isn't capable of something as horrendous as murder. Of course, from his perspective, I can see how this might feel like an ambush. I take a deep breath, lowering my voice. "You have to understand, I was shocked when Bridgette said that. I only wanted to know why it was said."

"You called her a source," he says, his voice hurt. "You're treating this like it's some type of lead. We're talking about my past. My life."

It's my nature to investigate. That's what made me a great journalist, but I've learned to curtail that impulse when it comes to my personal life. I only snooped through Coop's belongings once, when he first moved into my apartment. He had a stack of old *Gazette* papers. I went through them and found a picture of another woman. It wasn't a scandalous photo, but my insides boiled with envy, which simmered into shame. Had I been younger, the discovery would have initiated a weekend-long squabble. With maturity came the realization I couldn't go through other people's belongings and be upset over what I uncovered. Coop was entitled to his privacy, and I let it go.

But this is different. I've been confronted with something I knew nothing about, and I won't be able to move past it until I have all the answers. Coop must have known I'd hear the rumors eventually. Why wouldn't he give me a fair warning before moving here? I'm about to ask more questions when the phone rings. It's not one of our cells. The ringing is coming from the landline behind the receptionist's desk. Coop flips the counter, picking up the receiver.

"*Whisper Falls Gazette*... yeah, it's me... no, I haven't found it yet." He starts rummaging through a folder, then slaps his hand against the desk. "I will... give me a minute." He covers the phone with his hand and looks at me. "I've got to sort something out, but I want to finish this conversation. Can we talk at home?"

"Yeah, sure." I stand hurriedly, then remember I have no way of getting home. "I don't have my car."

"I shouldn't be much longer." The look in his eyes tells me he feels guilty, torn between his work and trying to provide the comfort I need right now. "Wait across the street at Nectar, if you want. I'll be an hour. Tops."

I don't say anything, just release a deep breath and stomp out of the office.

CHAPTER 10

Madison

Unlike its neighbors, Nectar looks like it was built this century. Black framing outlines horizontal panes of glass, making the entire dining space visible from the sidewalk. Given the warm weather, the windows are lowered, allowing a nice breeze to follow me inside.

Round, wooden tables are scattered around with metal chairs tucked underneath. The walls are decorated with abstract paintings, nothing remarkable, but nothing ordinary either. In the center of the room, there's a large workspace covered with various breads and baked goods. Regina stands there, sprinkling flour onto a gigantic mound of dough. I'm impressed; I'd been expecting a diner, and instead got a friendly reminder of Atlanta farm-to-table bistros.

"What can I get you?" asks a girl with an olive apron covering her bottom half and a floral tattoo cascading down her arm. Her name tag reads Maple.

I'm still looking around, taking the place in. "Is there a menu?"

Maple points above, and I see a hanging chalkboard with each item written out by hand. "Daily specials are by the front." Maple walks away, grabs a coffee pot and refills the cup of a nearby customer.

Regina is still smacking and kneading the dough when she sees me. She wipes a fallen hair away from her face, leaving a smear of flour on her forehead.

"Didn't think I'd catch you here," she says, wiping her hands clean and walking toward the counter. "I thought Mom and Roman took you shopping."

"They did. I'm waiting on Coop to finish up at the office." I'd rather Regina not pick up on the fact I'm upset. "I love the design of this place. It's so modern and—"

"Not Whisper Falls?" Regina finishes my thought.

"It's not what I was expecting."

"Cooper's not the only member of the Douglas family to leave Whisper. I attended culinary school up north and spent the summer after graduation working at all these enviable little restaurants. When it came time to open my own place, I decided Whisper Falls needed some culture."

"Well, it looks great." My eyes float to the menu dangling above our heads. "Of course I haven't tried the food."

Regina laughs. "Prepare to really be impressed."

I'm not hungry, but I order something anyway. I settle on a salmon BLT paired with garlic potato wedges. Regina said it was a favorite dish, and Maple seconded the opinion. I find a table in the corner, next to a small stage with a barstool and microphone. This seems like the type of place to offer live music on the weekends. To my left, I see a corkboard littered with business cards and flyers. Advertisements for the local florist and dry cleaner and tax preparer. A bright orange poster advertises a website called *The Falls Report*.

It's getting close to dinner time and people are starting to pile in, their arrival made known by the ding of a bell. The turnout is decent. There's a cluster of young adults plugged into their laptops at the table next to mine. A woman in a navy coat sits by the window drinking coffee and reading the newspaper, probably the *Gazette*. Occasionally she looks at me, offering a stare that says *you're not from around here*.

My phone buzzes with a text message. It's Beth.

Checking in, stranger. I miss you!

I feel guilty. The stress of the move and this past week has prevented me from reaching out as much as I should.

Miss you. How's the baby?

Beth and Matt are expecting a baby girl. I'm happy for her, even though the timing of the delivery means she won't be able to attend the wedding. She doesn't need to make the drive from Atlanta so late in her pregnancy, and I wouldn't want her to take any risks on my behalf.

Twenty-six weeks and healthy, she replies.

Much love. Promise to call soon.

What I want to say is I'm lonely. That I'm insecure about my role in this family and bothered by what my new neighbors still say about my fiancé. That everywhere I turn in this town, I'm faced with another reminder of the mysterious Celia Gray. But I won't tell her any of this. Unlike me, everything is going right in Beth's world. Her career and husband and baby. I don't want to be a buzzkill.

By the time I've finished texting, Regina moseys over, ignoring the lines of people standing by the register. She's holding two trays of food in her hand. "Thought I'd join you," she says, pulling out a chair.

"Aren't you working?" I ask, nodding toward the front.

"I still have to eat. We have another hour before the place really gets busy," she says, squirting a mound of ketchup on her plate. I notice the bottle says organic, homemade. "Besides, I want to know what's bothering you."

"Nothing," I say, picking up and dropping a potato wedge.

"Bullshit. Something's got you all sour. Mom getting on your nerves yet?"

"She's been great," I say, making a mental note to call Josephine later tonight. I regret how I took off earlier. I debate whether to open up about what happened at Turner's. Something about Regina reminds me of home, like we're both not cut out for Whisper Falls. We could be friends, if only she'd let her guard down. I think she's so used to being different she doesn't know how to react to someone genuinely trying to earn her approval. "Remember that girl from last night? Bridgette?"

Still chewing, Regina drops her shoulders and rolls her eyes. "What I'd give to forget."

"I saw her again today. She works at Turner's furniture store."

Regina nods. "I forgot about that. I don't think she's been there long. She usually can't hold a job for more than a few months." She wipes her mouth. "Did you talk to her?"

"Briefly. I wanted to confront her about that comment she made. She told me the people here think Coop killed Celia."

Regina leans forward. "You didn't know?"

"Did I *know* that people think my fiancé is a murderer? Your brother? No, I didn't know that."

Regina shakes her head. "Don't let Bridgette get to you. She's a nobody."

"It's the fact *other people* think Coop was involved. How am I supposed to build a life here knowing people think that? My gosh, I just met the police chief."

"Jimmy is a family friend. He knows Cooper had nothing to do with Celia's death. Lots of people do. It's just people like Bridgette who won't let the past go."

"Why do they think Coop was involved?" In some ways, it feels like a betrayal to have this conversation with his sister, but she's being more forthcoming, and these are things I need to know.

"Rumor was Cooper got angry and hit her with something before she went into the water. People look for someone to blame after a tragedy, and they've waited generations for the great Douglas family to fall."

"Could someone have really done that? Hit her over the head?"

My mind returns to last night's conversation at the lake. I didn't expect Regina to have so much anger toward Celia, a girl who died thirteen years ago. Her words were filled with hate, a stark contrast to what Coop has said. Of course, he doesn't talk much about Celia. When he does, he portrays a girl taken before her time. Regina portrayed something else.

"He had nothing to do with it, if that's what you're asking." It's the first time her voice lacks that sing-song element. She's tense and defensive.

"I know. Celia drowned." She needs to know I'm on her side. When it comes to Coop, I'll always be on her side. "But doesn't it bother you? Knowing people still say these things about him?"

"It does, but we've been defending him for a long time. Some people are determined to believe what they want to believe. Around here, people will take rumor over fact any day." She leans back. "We know the truth. That's all that matters. I think Celia climbed to the top of Miner's Peak to jump off the rope swing and hit her head on the way down."

"Regina?" Maple shouts from the register. "Someone has a question about the gluten-free menu."

"Be right there." Regina sighs. "Just talk to Cooper. It's a hard topic for him. For all of us, really."

"Thanks," I say, noting my meal has barely been touched. Nothing to do with Regina's cooking, rather my own nerves. I stand and push past the people crowding around the entrance. Coop still hasn't texted, and I don't feel like returning to the *Gazette* headquarters. Instead, I stroll until I reach a small courtyard in the center of downtown. The plaque on the sidewalk reads: *Whisper Falls Memorial Gardens: Always Remember, Never Forget.* There's a small gazebo covered in flowers and a series of benches circled around it. I choose one and sit, waiting for Coop to finish at the office.

Whenever Coop mentioned Celia's death, he never said people thought he was to blame. Maybe he didn't want to breathe fresh life into an old rumor. Maybe part of him was afraid I'd run for the hills. I exhale in frustration, shooing away my mental images of Celia and Bridgette. The scent of pollen and dirt drift upward, tickling my nose. There's a potted collection of wildflowers resting next to my bench. Looking across the way, I see each bench has its own arrangement beside a memorial plaque. I stand, looking to see what my bench represents, to whom it pays tribute.

Underneath my seat is a picture of a blonde girl with striking blue eyes, hypnotic really. The inscription reads: *In loving memory of Celia Gray. May your light shine on us all.* My eyes dart back to the girl's face—Celia's face—which, in some ways, appears harsher now. Like she's taunting me. As I scamper away, the sign at the entrance reminds me to *never forget.*

All I want to do is forget. About Celia. About the past. I'd like to make a home of this place without constantly feeling followed by ghosts.

CHAPTER 11

Helena

I got a glimpse of Madison today, but I didn't have the nerve to talk to her. Not yet. One of my first stops after arriving in Whisper Falls was Nectar, the uppity eatery owned by none other than Regina Douglas. I snagged a spot by the window, attempting to familiarize myself with this town again and the people in it. When I saw Regina behind the counter, I felt a rush of nervousness. Thankfully, she was preoccupied with kneading and chopping; she didn't notice me.

Imagine my surprise when halfway through my sandwich and waffle fries (which I reluctantly enjoyed), Madison approached the counter. I did a double take, finding it hard to believe my luck. It's only my first day back in Whisper Falls, and here comes my target. Some would say it's the lack of options in this backwards town, but I think it's something else. Kismet. Fate.

That ashy hair is hard to confuse with anyone else. It had to be her. I watched as she had a brief conversation with Regina. The two don't yet seem comfortable with one another, and I wonder how else Madison is struggling to adjust. She didn't seem particularly happy as she sat alone, waiting on her order. But maybe that's just her. Resting Bitch Face, is that what they call it? Madison definitely has that. In fact, the only time she smiled was just before her food arrived, when she was staring in her lap, presumably texting someone. Probably Cooper.

She looked up at me once, but then lazily drifted her gaze to the other diners without giving me a second thought. I'm used to going unnoticed these days. As a young woman, I turned heads. Now, I'm easily overlooked in crowds because my looks have faded and I'm always alone. Practically invisible. It's been that way for years, which is why I'm not intimidated to come back here and do what must be done.

Watching Madison saunter out of the restaurant, I could see she didn't possess any of the loneliness and bitterness that plagues my existence. Perhaps she has some insecurity. Beyond that, she has her whole life in front of her. She bears all the promise any girl her age should, the promise my own daughter exuded when she was still on this earth.

The last time I saw her was nothing like the last time we spoke. By then, the brightness I'd seen in her that day was gone. I'd felt it dimming for weeks. I could sense her holding back, cutting our conversations short. Not only did Cooper Douglas take her away forever, he took little bits of her leading up to that day.

"Tell me what's wrong, sweetie," I said to her over the phone.

"Nothing," she said. But I knew something was off. Something personal was pulling her spirits downward. I needed to know what it was.

"Is it your boyfriend?"

"Gah, Mom." She sounded like an annoyed teenager full of resentment. If only she'd seen I had once been a young woman, capable of understanding. "I don't know. I love him, I know that. But there are things we need to work out."

"Like what?"

"Just some stupid rumors," she said, her voice starting to crack. "We need to talk, but I'm hoping things will blow over."

Rumors. A parade of faces flashed through my mind. Other young, vibrant girls. Had he chosen one of them over my daughter? None of them could compare, surely. Her father used to fool around on me, and I could remember that throbbing feeling. The resentment building, becoming too heavy to carry. That rejection, ripping the glow away, leaving nothing but gloom.

"I'm sorry, honey."

"Nothing's happened yet," she said, failing to sound positive.

"Everything will be okay. You know I'm here for you."

"I know."

"Maybe it's time for another visit?" I needed to see her. Hiding her feelings was too easy over the phone.

"Soon, Mom." Then there was a sound in the background. "Cooper is waiting. I need to go."

"I love you, honey," I said, but she had already hung up.

The waitress with the arm tattoo returns to my table, interrupting my memories. Perhaps it's a good thing, as I was right at the point where things turned bad. "Can I get you anything else?" she asks.

"All good here. Thanks."

I exit the restaurant, looking over my shoulder one last time at the sister. She was a teenager last time I saw her, and it looks like she hasn't gained five pounds since then. Thankfully, she doesn't recognize me. I don't think the brother would remember me, either.

From where I stand, I can see the *Gazette* headquarters. I wonder if I should confront Cooper myself. Maybe I should just get a glimpse of him. Or cause a real scare by throwing a rock through the window. The idea makes me laugh, but I realize that's the old me. Dealing with Cooper directly didn't work last time, nor did causing a scene. That's why I must go through Madison. I'm a stranger to her, and she's an outsider here, which makes her easier to isolate.

I walk in the opposite direction. I reach a small courtyard with a gazebo. If I recall correctly, this place was under construction last time I was here. I had thought the bulldozer and lumber were eyesores in the middle of this quaint town square. The sign reads: *Whisper Falls Memorial Gardens: Always Remember, Never Forget.* I remember reading, in the *Gazette* actually, about this place. I'd wanted to return to Whisper Falls for the dedication, but that was in the thick of my drinking days. Even I couldn't handle my crazy then, though I'd like to think I'm better at controlling myself now.

There are six memorial benches, each one paying tribute to a fallen Whisperanian. When I arrive at the third bench, I see her picture and plaque:

In loving memory of Celia Gray. May your light shine on us all.

My breathing gets wobbly and I fall to my knees. I stare at her beautiful face. I think of what Cooper must have done to her. The only thought worse, is that he got away with it. I begin crying. At first my sobs are shallow, then they fall heavy and deep. I'm wailing in the middle of the courtyard as I might if I were alone in my motel room.

On the sidewalk, strangers stop and watch, but they don't dare approach. Their stares are confused, then sympathetic. We humans are drawn to tragedy in the same way we're mesmerized by fire: its power, its unpredictability, its warmth. Being near heartache reflects how cold we never realized we were. We watch on thinking, *Those poor people.* We never dare to think, *Poor us.* The only time we are untouchable is when faced with another person's misfortune.

I'm on the other side of things now. Let them look; I don't care what they think. They're catching a small glimpse of the grief I live with every day. None of them know the connection I feel to this beautiful girl. None of them could understand the determination I have to bring her justice.

And just like that, my passion for vengeance is renewed. Cooper Douglas will know what it's like to be on the other side of grief. I'll make sure of it.

CHAPTER 12

June 16, 2006

Cooper sat on the dock, his bare feet cooling in the water. Celia was still sitting in his truck. Just as they arrived, Celia's mother called. Even though they were in the midst of their own argument, he knew she would answer. She always did. Celia and her mother had a complicated relationship. He was happy he didn't have to meet the woman. He thought it was shitty she gave up on Celia as a child. His family dynamic was so different. His parents were strict at times, but they always made him feel safe, secure and wanted.

He knew Celia never had any of that. It's what most people at school couldn't understand about her. When her catty side came out, they didn't see all the feelings of inadequacy she suppressed. That same vulnerability made him love her, and he thought a quick conversation with her mother might put Celia in a slightly more sentimental state. He needed a softer Celia right now. Because even though he loved her, he wouldn't stick around if she was cheating on him.

His car door slammed, and Celia thundered down the bank leading to the dock. She'd unraveled her braid and changed into a white bikini. He expected she'd claim it was for the party later, but he knew better. She was trying to distract him through sex appeal, a trick that might have worked on any other day. But not now.

She sat beside him, crossing her legs and propping herself up on her elbows. She smiled, and he could smell the citrus body spray seeping from her pores.

"What did your mom say?"

"Just a bunch of this and that." Celia looked away, at the trees plunging into the lake. "She's already planning another visit to Whisper."

"If she wants a relationship with you, why doesn't she just move here?"

She sighed. "I don't know. Right now, we can talk and visit without her feeling like a total screw-up. Things might sour if we're around each other twenty-four seven."

"But she's your mom."

"My aunt does what she can." She looked at him, her eyes distant. "Right now, Mom is more like a friend. That's what I need more than anything."

"I don't get it." He knew better than to push the subject. Celia didn't like talking about emotional things. When things got heavy, she usually just took her top off to lighten the mood. But he resented this woman he'd never met for taking advantage of Celia. She'd robbed her of her innocence and didn't even know it. She'd made her cruel.

"I know we're not here to talk about my mom." Celia hooked her arm around Cooper's and leaned her head on his shoulder. "Will you tell me what's been bothering you all week?"

"You don't have any idea?" He gently unlaced his arm from hers and scooted away. "What's going on with you and Steven Burns?"

"Oh my gosh." Celia tossed her head back, letting her locks dangle. "That's what you're upset about?"

"I've heard from three different people who saw you with him at last week's bonfire—"

"There were lots of people at last week's bonfire. Is that why Jimmy was acting all weird earlier?"

"Jim is my best friend. He's not okay with you cheating on me," Cooper said. "What's going on with you and Steven?"

"Maybe if you came out more, you'd know. But no, you're always busy running around doing Mama Douglas' bidding."

"My family has nothing to do with this."

Celia smirked. She dipped her shins in the water and leaned back. "You can either believe me or listen to town gossip. I have no desire to be with the likes of Steven Burns."

"It's not just that. I found that T-shirt in your car last week. And you've been so shifty lately every time you get a call or text."

"I told you, the shirt belonged to my cousin. And I don't know what you're talking about. *Being shifty.* What's making you so paranoid?"

"It's just the way you act with people, Celia. Like we're all little puppets. You play people, and I don't like the idea of being played."

"We're on the same team, Cooper." She cupped his chin and wiggled his face. "I adore you. I'm practically counting down the days until I graduate, and we can get married."

Cooper pulled away. He tugged a nearby dandelion out of the grass, flicked off the bud and threw it in the water. He watched it float, then sink. That's how he felt. Like he was sinking. When he was around Celia, he didn't know what he wanted. Couldn't tell what was true and what was a lie. He was sick of feeling like he wasn't in control.

"I'm not settling down with someone the whole town calls a cheater."

"Who gives a shit what this town thinks?"

"I do. I like it here. My family is important. You need to change the way you treat people. It sends the wrong message."

"Oh, Cooper." Celia leaned forward, resting her elbows on her knees. "I'm not some ball of clay you can mold into your liking. I know your family has brainwashed you into thinking you're important because you're a Douglas, but don't you forget, I'm special too. I'm Celia Gray."

Cooper rolled his eyes. "Stop deflecting, Celia." Usually he thought her attitude was cute, but right now he was annoyed.

Whatever she was trying to pull, it wasn't going to work this time. "I'm getting tired of your games."

He wanted to say more but stopped when he heard footsteps. They both turned to see who had joined them on the dock.

CHAPTER 13

Madison

We remain silent until we arrive home. The confines of Coop's car aren't the right place to revisit such a claustrophobic topic. My attempts to ask earlier came off as another accusation. Coop doesn't like talking about Celia, and I oblige him by not bringing it up, not picking at his life's greatest tragedy. But there's another layer to this situation now, it seems, and I'm not prepared to live in Whisper Falls without knowing all the details.

Coop returns from the bedroom having changed into a T-shirt and sweatpants. I'm sitting by the fire, my jacket still on and my arms crossed.

"I'm sorry what Bridgette said upset you this much," he says, sitting beside me.

"Of course it upset me," I say. "Accidents happen. Tragic deaths happen. But for people to accuse you of a crime—"

"Bridgette was one of Celia's friends. Used to be one of my friends, too. After her death everything became so divided." He looks away, as though the sight of me hurts him. "It was the darkest time in my life. I couldn't even mourn Celia without being labeled a murderer. I don't like to talk about it."

"That's understandable," I say, reaching my hand out to touch his. "But I'm here now. I can't stand walking into a room and thinking people know something about you I don't."

"Fair enough." He nods, pulling away his hand so he can prop both elbows on his knees. "You know, I think if Celia's body had been found the same day she drowned, the rumor would have never been started. It was the days while she was still missing that created all this nonsense. It gave people time to make their own theories. Too much time."

"How long did it take to find her?"

"Ten days, or something like that." He shakes his head, as though trying to remember the facts whilst dispelling the heartache. "By the time her body was found, people had already made up their minds about what happened."

"Why do they—"

"Why do they think I killed her?" He looks at me with pain in his eyes. I can see all of this is hurting him, that I'm hurting him, but I have to know. "We were supposed to go to a party that night, but I showed up without her. Our friends knew we'd been fighting, so they thought—" Try as he might, he can't continue. He covers his mouth with his palm.

"What were you fighting about?"

"Dumb high school stuff." Now he stands, pacing in front of me. "I can barely remember. Celia had this way of irritating people, and honestly, I'd had my fill of it, but I'd never—"

"I know you wouldn't have hurt her, Coop." I stare into his eyes, hoping he'll see that I believe him. Not for a second did I think Coop could be capable of harming another person, and I regret the way I confronted him earlier suggested otherwise. I only want to know why others think he did.

He nods, and, for the first time all day, I feel like we're on the same page. "So, you can see why they'd blame me. I was the boyfriend. Last person seen with her. It made for a good story, and people liked to tell it. This town had resented my family for years, and Celia's death finally gave people permission to take it out on one of us. I felt the full brunt of everyone's hate. My whole life I walked around Whisper like I was a god. Overnight, I became public enemy number one. I was only a kid."

It's visible now, his upset over the way he was treated. I've never heard him express his displeasure with Whisper so openly. He's made hints in the past, but now I understand he has a plethora of unresolved issues with this place and the people in it.

"I'm sure there were some people who defended you," I say, hoping.

"There were. My family always had my back. Certain friends, like Jimmy. More than a few people have changed their stance over the years, especially when they need a loan from Mom or a little extra publicity in the *Gazette*."

"Anyone who knows you understands you could never be involved in something so sinister," I say, placing a hand on his chest. "That must count for something."

"People shout accusations and whisper apologies." He releases a dry laugh, which fails in masking his pain. "People may not treat me like a murderer anymore, but at one point they did. The sting of that never goes away."

I think of what that must have been like. Coop would have only been eighteen at the time, the moment when most people discover life, explore new possibilities. It must have stunted him in some ways, wrestling with both grief and resentment towards those around him. It explains why he's so cautious now, why he keeps everyone, including me, at a distance.

"I can't imagine how hard it must have been for you," I say, touching his cheek. "But I'm here now. I believe you, and I won't let anyone spread lies about you."

My phone rings, displaying a number I don't recognize. I answer.

"Madison?" There's a pause. "It's Josephine. Cooper gave me your number. I hope you don't mind."

"Not at all. Everything all right?"

"Just fine. I'm calling because I wanted to pass along the names of the event planners I told you about. Cooper has given me strict orders not to intrude, so I'll entrust you to make arrangements."

There's a pause, as though she expects me to say something. I don't. She reads off the names and I write them down. "However, I would mention my name. It might help with their sense of urgency. And, of course, my feelings won't be hurt if you decide to look elsewhere. Although I can assure you the names on this list will help you plan a beautiful wedding."

"Thank you, Josephine," I say, turning in an ineffective attempt to gain privacy from Coop. "I'd also like to apologize for the way I took off earlier. I had such a lovely time shopping with you, and you've been so kind—"

"It's all right, dear," she says, interrupting my ramblings. "After speaking with Regina, it's quite understandable why you were so upset." So, Regina told her mother about our conversation, or maybe just that one part? I'm not sure if it helps or hurts that she knows what Bridgette said.

"Again, I had a great time today." Josephine and I are still in that awkward phase where we have yet to build a bond of our own. I want her to like me, and I already sense that, at least in her mind, I'm a fitting daughter-in-law, unlike Regina who seems to reject her mother's influence.

"Living in Whisper Falls requires some adjustments," she says. "I only wanted to make sure you're okay."

"I'm fine," I say. "Thank you."

Turning back, I see Coop is standing by the fireplace. His anxiety from earlier seems to have eased. I hope we've moved past this hurdle. That our conversation today was a necessary step in better finding our place here. Today has tested us, put salt on his old sores. People forget that salt on a wound, however painful, can promote healing. Nothing is ever truly resolved when left untreated. Nothing is ever truly overcome when left ignored.

CHAPTER 14

Madison

For the rest of the weekend, it feels like we're getting back to normal, getting back to us. In many ways, Bridgette's comment gave me more insight into Coop. It made me understand why Regina is so vindictive toward those around her. The relationship between the Douglases and this town is a complicated one. At least now I have a better understanding why. They've given so much to this place. They've supported its people and their businesses, only to be rewarded with rumors and accusations.

I'm determined to move forward. I don't want to inherit Regina's bitterness or Coop's shame. I'll find my footing in Whisper Falls, despite how foreign it feels. The first step in all that is the wedding. Major details, like the location and dress and date, have already been decided upon and booked. We agreed it would be easier to finalize the finishing touches (the flowers and decorations and caterer) once we'd moved. On Monday, I call the event planners Josephine suggested and arrange a series of one-hour consultations, in hopes of finding someone to help me juggle the remaining tasks.

I spend the rest of the week unpacking and making room for our new furniture. By Thursday, I drive to Whisper Falls Park for a mid-morning run. Maybe I'll be one of those housewives who picks up jogging. I'd prefer yoga or Pilates, but they don't offer any classes here. I already checked.

I can see the whole park in its entirety. It's almost empty, save a mother and her children on the swings and a woman sitting alone on a bench. There's a white and blue playground in the center of the running track. I start jogging, knowing the sooner I elevate my heart rate, the less I'll feel the early morning chill lingering in the air. Like everything else in Whisper, this workout is different. I'm used to weaving through crowds on narrow sidewalks, music blaring from my earbuds. I'm not even listening to music, instead taking in the unique melody of the crunching leaves, a little girl's laughter in the distance and my own breathing.

As I start my third round, my body begins to sweat. I'm getting faster, puffing out all the frustrations I've attempted to ignore since the move. All the anger I have toward myself for having to leave. All the lingering questions I have about Celia Gray and her death. A strong gust of wind unsettles a bundle of leaves, blowing them into my path. Along with them come a few pieces of notebook paper. I look to my left and see the woman by the bench scrambling.

I grab the papers swirling nearby. "Are these yours?" I shout.

The woman turns, holding papers in one hand and brushing back her brown, shoulder-length hair with the other. She's about my age and wears a puffy olive coat. "I guess that's what I get for trying to do work outside."

I approach the bench, offering the documents I recovered. "Hopefully you aren't missing anything important."

"Thanks. I'll sort it out later. Writers fare better when they stick to a desk." She smiles. There's a small stud piercing her left nostril.

"Do you work for the *Gazette*?"

She laughs. "No, but I can't blame you for asking. It's the only paper we have around here. My stuff is a little more offbeat. It's a blog, really, but I like to think I start reporting where the *Gazette* leaves off."

"I'll check it out. What's the name?"

"*The Falls Report*," she says, sorting her papers. The name triggers a memory.

"I remember seeing a flyer about that at Nectar."

Another laugh. "I guess I'll take advertisements where I can get them." She holds out her hand and shakes mine firmly. "Bailey Bloom."

"Madison Sharpe," I say, matching her grip. "I'm new to Whisper."

There's a brief look of recognition, then she smiles. "You're Cooper Douglas' fiancée, right?"

I don't think I'll ever get used to being labeled as that. Like my only purpose exists through Coop. "That's right."

She sits on the bench. "You should know all about the *Gazette* then."

I sit beside her messy stack of papers. "I'm actually a former journalist myself."

"Oh yeah? Which paper?"

I tell her and see her eyes light up. That's what I'm used to being known for, the gritty writer at the famous paper. I miss being that girl. "Of course, I'm not doing that now," I say. "Coop started running the *Gazette*, so we moved here."

She nods, not saying anything. She's scanning something on her laptop, then slams it shut. "Well, I wish I could say you've made a wise decision in moving, but I'm sure you've figured out there's not much to do here."

"It's very different from the city."

"Call it like it is. There's no opportunity in this town. Barely any culture, which is part of the reason I started *The Falls Report*. I wanted to offer something that wasn't funneled through the great Douglas machine." She stops, clearly wondering if she's offended me.

"I think that's great," I say. I'm certainly not going to fault the woman for trying to usher reluctant Whisper residents into the new century. And she's right about the Douglas reach. They own the town's best restaurant, produce its news source, sponsor its sports—all of it coming from the same family with the fancy house by the lake. I'm joining that clan, and yet a part of me will always feel like I don't belong.

"When did you stop writing?" Bailey asks. "I'd love to look up some of your old articles."

"It's been a few months, but it feels longer." I look down and pull the sleeves of my shirt. "I miss writing sometimes. Nothing like chasing a story."

"Ain't that the truth. Why don't you have that fancy husband of yours get you a job at the *Gazette*?"

"Nepotism." I shake my head and roll my eyes. Coop and I have had this conversation a dozen times. His staff is limited. He can't bump someone out for the sake of creating me a position, not that I'd expect him to. The *Gazette* doesn't have a high turnover rate, so it's hard to say when I'll return to the newsroom. Hopefully my former scandal will have subsided by then.

"I'm sure things will turn around." She hoists her bag over her shoulder, misplaced papers peeping from the top. "Life's not hard when you're a Douglas. You'll see."

By now, my pulse has stabilized, and I no longer feel like running. Bailey walks away, leaving me alone on the park bench. She's the first person I've met with whom I could see sparking a friendship. She's a writer, wanting to track down stories and make people listen. I used to be like that, until I messed it all up.

My job at the *Chronicle* was the type of position undergrads dream about snatching after graduation. It didn't come easy, either. I put in time making coffees and running errands. I proofread copy until my eyes stung, but I never complained. I never came in late and never argued about working a little later. Slowly, I started getting more and more assignments. I became one of the youngest staff writers at the *Chronicle*. Soon after, Coop and I started dating. Eighteen months later, we were engaged. I had my city, my man and my paycheck. I was living the dream.

The 'Chrissy' feature had been live three days when my editor, Bill, called me into his office. He said questions had been raised about the authenticity of 'Chrissy's' claims. Nothing unexpected given the controversial subject matter. I provided him the same information she gave me: old check stubs, photographs and the names of former co-workers.

Another two days passed before I was called into the office again; Bill explained our fact-checker had found further discrepancies. They couldn't confirm 'Chrissy' had ever worked for Bernard Wright or any of his businesses. They couldn't even confirm she'd attended college. It wasn't just parts of her story that weren't lining up—nothing she'd told me checked out. Her only connection to the Bernard Wright enterprise was that she once applied to work as a hostess in one of his restaurants and was denied. Everything she'd told me was a lie, and she'd taken extra measures to fabricate documents.

Bill called me into his office for a third time. "You've put us in a tough position, Madison," he said, scratching his gray mustache.

"We'll run a retraction," I said, still convinced we'd be able to fix the situation. "The information she gave me checked out at the time. I believed her story."

"We're not the only ones fact-checking what you wrote," he said, flapping the paper on his desk. "Bernard Wright's defense team is using this to prove these women have a vendetta against their client."

I closed my eyes to try and shake the nausea. That's when I understood. Wright's defense team planted this trap, a last-ditch effort to improve their client's image, and I fell for it. "Just because 'Chrissy' fed me a fake story doesn't mean these other women are lying."

"I know," he said, defeated. "But it raises doubt. It hurts their case."

My intent had been to help them. Selfishly, I wanted to benefit myself, too. I wanted that promotion, which is why I was less vigilant about triple-checking everything 'Chrissy' provided. I believed her. I trusted her.

"I can do something to help. I can write a series on how rare it is for women to false report. Or talk to some of Wright's other accusers. I can do *something*."

"Madison," he said, his voice stern and deep. "A retraction won't be enough. We're going to have to let you go."

"This is the only mistake I've ever made—"

"It was a big one." He looked away, clearly bothered by his decision, though convinced it was necessary. "You're a good reporter. Give it some time, and you'll still have a career. You can even use me as a reference."

"I don't want a reference! I want my job here. I want a second chance."

"I can't give you that right now." His face softened, as he tried to make the situation appear better than it was. "Go live your life. Plan your wedding. Learn from this, and you'll be better next time."

I think about that conversation all the time. I think about 'Chrissy' and the other women I damaged by writing that story in the first place. Mistakes cast ripples; they penetrate your surface, the life you thought you had, and expand onward from there. I didn't just ruin my own future. I jeopardized the women who spoke out against Bernard Wright and endangered the women he might encounter moving forward. My restless desire to lock down a story potentially unleashed a dangerous person into the world.

I messed up. Admitting to what I'd done was difficult. Coop was beyond supportive. I'd already accepted his proposal, but if I hadn't, his reaction solidified my desire to spend the rest of our lives together. He didn't blame me or point fingers; he kept me from doing those things to myself. Sometimes I wonder if he'd be as quick to forgive a member of his own staff for the same mistake. Regardless, he saw past my worst moment and loved me anyway. That's what we all need in life. People who choose to see the best in us, even when confronted by our worst.

Outsiders aren't as understanding, which is why I avoid telling the truth about my termination. Sympathy is granted sparingly; it's typically reserved for forms of tragedy. An unpreventable illness.

An unprovoked crime. We forget most people are the source of their own unhappiness. When you're the cause of your hardships, people are less willing to forgive. I'd rather be seen as the doe-eyed wife-to-be. Even she's less foolish than I feel.

CHAPTER 15

Madison

Last night, I struggled to sleep. After I returned from my run, I made sure the house was in order for the potential wedding planners I'm meeting today. Coop and I drank wine after dinner, and I drifted to sleep with images of bouquets and dresses and hors d'oeuvres dancing in my head.

Halfway through the night, I awoke from a horrible dream. It was summer. Coop and I were in a boat—I can only assume on Whisper Lake—sprawled across the deck. We stripped off our suits, and took turns dipping into the icy waters. I was smiling and happy and free. On my last plunge, I stayed under the water, a cluster of air bubbles percolating near my ears. When I swam to the surface, something grabbed my feet, pulling me. It all felt so real. Within seconds, my emotions sprang from delight to confusion, then terror. I don't know what it was—who it was—pulling me downward, but I couldn't break free. It was dark when I woke up, sweating and panting. Coop slept peacefully beside me, but I was unable to fall back asleep.

After sunrise, I tiptoe downstairs and start the coffee machine. I'm determined to make this day a good one; the wedding consultants will be stopping by this afternoon. I want to spend the day organizing our ceremony and reception, but that's difficult to do when the chill from my nightmare lingers.

It's more than the bad dream. If anything, I'm angry these lies have been orbiting around Coop for the past thirteen years. There's something about this Celia story that doesn't fit, a piece that's missing. I get the urge to do something I haven't done in ages. I flip open my laptop and type in the name: Celia Gray. Of course, I've done this before. It's my nature to investigate, but I've tried to be different with Coop. That's why I've not pushed as much as I should. I love him. More important than that, I trust him. But I feel different now that I'm here, so far away from my usual comforts.

In the past when I searched Celia's name, little comes up. Since her death, most media outlets have transitioned to online forums, even the *Gazette*. Many articles were lost in the transfer, including the ones written about Celia. There were a couple articles about her body being found, but little else. Today when I type in the name Celia Gray, a recent link appears. It's an article that was written only two days ago on *The Falls Report*. I rack my brain, trying to figure out why it sounds familiar. I realize this is Bailey's website, the woman I met in the park.

Scrolling through the archives, I see Bailey likes to write about the town's history. She has a series devoted to the old railway system that used to be based here. She also has reviews of different Whisper Falls restaurants. I return to the article that first brought me to the site. It's titled, *"Guess Who's Back in Whisper…"*

Howdy, Whisperers. Those of you who still subscribe to the local brainwash paper might have recognized a noticeable change to the masthead. That's right. Following his predecessor's retirement, Cooper Douglas has finally taken over as editor-in-chief of the Whisper Falls Gazette.

As many of you know, the Douglas family has owned the newspaper for generations. After graduating with his master's degree in communication (I'll let you sift through the irony on that one), Douglas spent several years interning at some of the most notable publications across the southeast. He's brought this expertise back to Whisper Falls and, when asked for comment, said, "I hope to carry on the great legacy of community and history the Whisper Falls Gazette *has been entrusted to uphold."*

Cooper is the second son of community benefactor Josephine Douglas and the late Ryan Douglas. Josephine's great-grandfather started the Gazette *back in the 1920s. The success of the* Gazette *led to several other regional newspapers and amassed a great fortune for the family.*

For those of you who don't remember, our local royals played a unique role in one of Whisper Fall's greatest mysteries: the death of Celia Gray.

I sit back, my fingers hovering over the keyboard. My stomach turns as I read her name over and over again.

At the time of Celia's disappearance, a multitude of rumors swirled, cementing her status as a cautionary tale for generations to come. As I'm sure you know, Celia's body was found in the lake ten days after she was reported missing. The discovery answered the question Where?, but the condition of her body raised more. Particularly How? and Why?

Celia lived with her aunt and three cousins in a two-bedroom house by the railroad tracks. She was a B-average student, who excelled at cheerleading and volleyball. Friends describe her as "bubbly," "happy-go-lucky," and "always looking for a good time." Like most Whisper Falls teens, seventeen-year-old Celia spent the summer working as a lifeguard at the lake.

As many of us can remember, a summer in Whisper Falls is best spent splashing around in the cloudy waters, toes stuck in the mucky bank. On Friday, June 16, Celia ended her shift patrolling the shores. Like most lifeguards, she made plans to meet up with friends. What she did that day remains a mystery. Did she go fishing under Watts Bridge? Spark a bonfire by the south bank? Climb Miner's Peak and swing from the rope swing?

All these suggestions floated around, but no one knows exactly what Celia did. She was last seen with Cooper Douglas, her high school sweetheart.

Cooper later met up with friends at a party, but Celia wasn't with him. No one was concerned at first. She wasn't reported missing until three days later. This enacted a days-long, multi-state search. Most people thought—even hoped—Celia had crossed state lines to be with one of her estranged parents or embarked on a road trip with friends.

All hopes were extinguished when her body was found floating in the waters of Whisper Lake. Wherever Celia ended up that day, it appears she didn't go very far. Decomposition suggested she'd died around the time she was reported missing. What led to her death was equally difficult to pinpoint. Water in the lungs made the official cause of death drowning, but a fractured skull proved she was hit with a heavy object shortly before entering the water.

The coroner ruled her death accidental, a decision that caused an uproar. Many people in Whisper Falls demanded more information be collected. Several unanswered questions remained. Where was Celia in the hours between when she was last seen and her death? Why did it take ten days for her body to be found? What caused her head injury?

People spun their own theories for years. Celia's mother made several trips to Whisper Falls, vowing to find justice for her daughter. Rumors about Cooper Douglas' involvement ran rampant, prompting the Douglas family to hire their own private investigator to re-open Celia's case. Two years after her death, the hired PI concluded Celia had fallen from a great distance and hit her head on an unseen rock in the water. This conclusion satisfied most, but for some, questions still linger...

"Good morning," Coop says. He walks into the kitchen dressed and ready for work. He stops when he sees the shock and fear on my face.

CHAPTER 16

Madison

"What's wrong?" Coop asks. He moves to the refrigerator and pulls out a bottle of water. He twists off the top, never taking his eyes off me.

"Nothing," I stammer, looking away. My first reaction is to deflect my emotions, but it's pointless; I'm obviously shaken. I scoot the laptop in his direction. "There's an article online. About you and Celia."

"What?" He pulls out the chair beside me and scans my laptop. "*The Falls Report?*"

I nod. "Read it."

He pulls my computer closer, scrolling his thumb against the trackpad. When he finishes, he shakes his head. "This website is only a gossip forum. If you knew the writer—"

"I do know the writer," I say, defensively. I cross my arms. "She didn't tell me she had written anything about you."

"Of course she didn't." He returns to the fridge and retrieves a carton of orange juice. "Bumping into you was probably planned."

"My name wasn't mentioned. But you… the way she wrote about you, she was all but accusing you of Celia's murder."

"Like I said. It's one step above a Facebook rant. You can't let this sort of thing get to you."

"It's not just the article," I say, kicking back my chair with my feet and looking out the window. "We've barely been here two weeks, and it seems like all I can think about is Celia Gray. People are making comments and writing articles. There's a memorial bench beside your sister's restaurant. It's like I can't shake her."

"What happened to Celia scarred this community. Bad things don't happen here. It's different than the city. It's harder for people to let go." He returns to his seat, leaning over the table. "We already went through all this last week."

"I know, but I can't just shake off what people say about you. That article was thick with innuendo." I slam the laptop shut. "Doesn't it make you angry?"

"At the time it would have. The only thing that makes me angry now is seeing the toll it takes on you." He covers my hand with his. "We know the truth. All that matters is that we're on the same page. Everyone else can eff off."

I smile reluctantly, wishing I could adopt his self-assured mindset. Perhaps he's more bothered than he'd like to admit, only putting on a brave face for my sake. One detail in the article still nags at me.

"What about your parents? The article said they hired an outside investigator to look into her death."

"They did." He leans back. "They were fed up with people saying I killed Celia. The easiest way to refute those claims was to prove there wasn't any foul play. The investigator confirmed her death was accidental."

"If the facts prove there was no murder, why wasn't that enough for people to stop blaming you?"

"You're a journalist. What's the better headline: 'Girl Drowns After Falling from Cliff' or 'Teenager Murdered by Wealthy Boyfriend'?"

Coop isn't just brushing things off. He's conditioned. He's used to being placed under this speculative microscope, determined to walk past the accusations with his head held high. Innocent people shouldn't have to live like that, making the choice between their reputation and their dignity. He wouldn't be subjected to such treatment if we lived anywhere else.

"Coop, why did we come back here?"

"I always wanted to build a life here. I'm not going to let a few people and their opinions take that away from me." He stands, pushing his chair under the table. "Besides, someone had to run the *Gazette*. It's not like Roman can do it. Regina would dry the place up just to spite my mother. I need to move past this so I can restore my family's honor. It's my fault it was taken away."

Something inside me drops at the thought Coop still blames himself. That he believes this tragic incident tarnished his family name. I hate that I've resurrected those feelings now. We could have had a peaceful morning if it weren't for my snooping. "I shouldn't have even mentioned the article."

"It's natural for you to have questions. Just don't let what people say get the best of you." He gives me a hug. When he pulls away, he smiles. "We should grab lunch today. Forget about this morning and enjoy ourselves."

"I wish I could," I say, regretting I started the day with an interrogation. "But I'm meeting with the wedding planners."

"Say no more," he says, walking to the front door. "I hope you find the right person."

I already have, I think, smiling as he walks away.

CHAPTER 17

Helena

I've started drinking again. Not because I enjoy the taste, but because I'm trying to work up the nerve to follow through with my plan. I've let my grief lie dormant for years. I surrendered to the idea I'd exhausted all my options. That was until I saw that engagement announcement. It made me realize I still have some fight left, and I'm going to funnel it all into ensuring Cooper Douglas doesn't get the happily ever after he's stolen from me.

In many ways, Madison is my only hope now. Everyone else is tired of listening to my story, but Cooper's role in all of this affects Madison as much as it does me. Taking her from him will give him a taste of what it's like to lose the person you love. If I could only make Madison understand why I'm convinced Cooper is dangerous! His behavior in those early days spoke volumes.

After two days of unanswered phone calls, I knew something was wrong. No one had heard from my daughter. Not my ex. Not our extended family. I hoped there was a simple explanation for her absence. I found myself pulling apart every detail of her life, trying to find someone who might know her whereabouts.

I was ashamed I didn't know more about her friends. The closest thing I had to a contacts book was her social media posts. I went through each one, messaging every person tagged in the past six months. All of them responded, but none of them had spoken to her in recent days.

I contacted the police department with limited information to give, but the most important piece was that my daughter was gone. "You don't understand," I pleaded with them. "She wouldn't just take off. She's not like that."

"Young girls are unpredictable sometimes," the officer told me, rambling on about some stunt his own daughter had pulled. He didn't mention that his daughter, despite whatever wild, outrageous thing she'd done, would be home for dinner that night. She'd be sitting across from him, safe and sound. My daughter was gone and no one—her friends, parents, police—knew where she was.

"Look into the boyfriend," I told them. "It's Cooper... something."

"It would help if you could provide a last name."

"I can't remember his last name!" I shouted, weak from the lack of sleep and beginning to shake. "He was with her the last time we spoke. It's a small place. You have a first name. He can't be that hard to find."

I could feel their judgment. They didn't appreciate an outsider coming into their community and giving them orders. "We're doing all we can," they said.

That was the first in a series of lies. They weren't doing enough because they still hadn't found her. Our family made flyers and posted them around town. Some of her friends contacted me; they didn't have useful information, but they offered to help in any way they could. In the blur that was those first, frightening days, I never heard from a friend named Cooper.

She'd been missing a week when her classmates organized a vigil. I didn't much like calling it that because a body hadn't been found. I still had hope, but at least they were trying to raise awareness. More people arrived than I could have dreamed. Of course, drama attracts an audience. Always has. There were so many faces, most of them young, some tear-stained, all curious. Did any of them really know her? Did they know where she'd gone?

After a while, it became too overwhelming. I slipped away from the crowd and rushed to the outdoor bathrooms. I'd meant to splash my face with water but ended up throwing up. Fear really sank in that day. She'd been gone a week. Seven days. My girl would never put me through this heartache intentionally. What if she never came back?

I exited the stall, defeated and alone. Outside, I stood by the water fountain, watching my daughter's mourners in the distance. All this grief and hoping and prayer. The weather was sunny and perfect, much like in the park on the last day I saw her. Surely that wouldn't be our last moment together. It couldn't be.

"Sad, isn't it?"

I turned to see who was speaking and saw a tall young man with a pale complexion, his blond hair swiped just above his brows.

"Excuse me?" I asked, caught off guard.

"Sorry," he said. Like me, he appeared to be avoiding the crowd. "I thought you were with the vigil."

"Oh, that. Yes, I am."

"Did you know her well?"

"All her life," I said. I resented the extra attention I'd received in recent days. I didn't want sympathy, I only wanted to find my daughter.

"She was really special," he said, looking over the crowd, then down at his feet.

"Were you friends?" I did enjoy the stories people shared about her. I thought maybe he had one, a happy memory that could bring her back, if only for a moment.

"For a while." He reached out his hand for a handshake. "I'm Cooper Douglas."

My jaw dropped as I realized this mystery boyfriend wasn't only at the vigil but standing right in front of me. "Helena," I said, refusing his hand.

My name connected immediately. We'd never met, but surely she'd told him about me. He took a step back. "I'm sorry for your loss." He darted away. I could almost see the tail between his legs!

"Cooper, wait." I chased after him. "I've been trying to contact you. I'm hoping you might be able to tell the police—"

"I've already talked to the police." He turned his back to me. *Turned his back.* At my own daughter's vigil. He tried to ignore me.

"She told me the most wonderful things about you, you know." I wanted him to view me as friendly, not some sniveling mourner. Maybe he wouldn't be quite so on edge. "I know you were with her the day she disappeared. You could know something helpful and not even realize it."

"I don't have anything to say to the police," he said. "And I don't have anything to say to you."

He turned and I saw his face. I saw the fear. He was too young to hide it. That's the moment I knew he was involved. Why else wouldn't he try to help me? Why wouldn't he search high and low, as I was? Unless he knew there was no one to find.

"What did she talk to you about that day?" I asked, chasing him through patches of grass until we reached the gravel parking lot. "Can you tell me? Please."

"I'm sorry. I have to go." He hopped into a truck and drove away.

I've never forgotten his reaction that day. His cruelty for not answering my simple questions. He was younger then, afraid and intimidated, but that didn't stop all her other friends from coming to her defense. I hoped our chance meeting had only spooked him and he would reach out later with more information. Instead, his parents hired a lawyer to conduct communication with the police. Cooper never contacted me again.

The entire situation could have been handled differently. He made his choice then, as we all do. As far as I'm concerned, Cooper Douglas deserves every ounce of heartbreak I'm about to throw his way.

CHAPTER 18

Madison

I lead Mrs. Phillips to my front door and bid her goodbye.

"Josephine has my contact information, if you need me," she says, holding her handbag in front of her.

"I appreciate you making the trip here," I say, propping the door open.

She leaves. I return to the living room and collapse onto the sofa. It's been a bizarre day. I went from confronting Coop to parading wedding planners around the house.

I've met three potential candidates so far: Mrs. Roberts, Mrs. Teague and Mrs. Phillips. All women differed in both appearance and personality, and yet they managed to present the same ideas. They'd suggested we have the ceremony at First Presbyterian, as planned, but instead of a reception by the lake, they thought we should renovate an old barn on the property. Slap walls with white paint and string fairy lights. *Barn weddings were all the rage*, they claimed. Even their color suggestions had been the same: burgundy, navy or orange. I'd spent the entire morning listening to the same event described by three different people. I'm undecided if this is a lack of originality, or Josephine's indirect way of inserting her opinion.

The doorbell rings, announcing the arrival of my last consult. The woman standing on our porch looks much like the others, wearing black slacks and a coral sweater.

"Are you Madison Sharpe?" asks the woman when I open the door.

"I am."

"Then I must be at the right place." She gives the front porch another look, then holds out her hand to shake mine. She smiles weakly. "Anne Richards."

"Come inside," I say.

Anne, like the others, absorbs her surroundings like a sponge. She's inspecting the place for potential and wealth. Even if her preliminary assessments disappoint, she knows I'm marrying a Douglas, and that alone is enough to impress.

"Let's go into the dining room," I say.

I can see Anne has a thick binder tucked inside her handbag. She takes a seat and pulls out the notebook, placing it on the table. There's a slight tremble in her hands. She's nervous, unlike the previous candidates who oozed confidence and flair. "It's been years since I've been in Whisper Falls."

"You're from Knoxville?"

"That's right." Her mouth twitches as she begins to speak, then pauses. "To be honest, I've not done a lot of events lately. Some of my examples might seem outdated."

"That's fine," I say. "My expectations aren't very high."

Anne laughs, as though she understands the hidden meaning that Josephine's are. She clears her throat. "Can you remind me what you've established so far?"

"I have my dress. The ceremony is at First Presbyterian, and we'd like to host an outdoor reception somewhere on the Douglas property. That's what I mainly need help organizing."

"Beautiful." Anne nods along and takes notes as I speak.

"Have you been there?"

"Ages ago. The Douglas family is very philanthropic. No telling how many parties they've hosted over the years."

"I started planning this back when we lived in Atlanta, so most decisions are set. But we don't have a caterer. Or entertainment. Or flowers. I'm hoping that's where you come in."

"I can certainly help." She stops writing, puts down her pen and stares at me. "Tell me, Madison. What do you want for your big day?"

I cross my legs and think. I'm certain the other planners didn't ask this question. Instead, they rambled about what was on trend or what they'd done before. "I've always been a fan of white weddings," I say. "You know, when the attendants wear white, too."

"It's nontraditional, but that can be very beautiful."

"And I'd like some flowers sprinkled around the reception, but I think a mix of different candles could be very romantic."

"I love that idea. Anything else?" Her nerves are diminishing. I think she prefers hearing my ideas over suggesting her own.

I look toward the ceiling, trying to think. "I guess that's another reason I'm looking for a planner last-minute. I don't really know what I want. I was never the girl who sat around and thought about her wedding day. I only wanted to find the right man."

"And have you?" she asks, holding eye contact. "Have you found the right man?"

"Coop is wonderful." I smile, feeling my own nervousness subsiding. "When I get overwhelmed about all this other stuff, I try to focus on that."

Anne clears her throat and looks at her notes, as though she's searching for the right words. "You're right. Finding a good man is the most important part. Everything else is secondary."

Anne pushes forward the folder she's brought. As I flip through the pictures, she answers more questions. The more we talk, the more it feels like a conversation, not an interview. Anne isn't trying to impress me; she wants to please. She's managed to remind me that our wedding is about Coop and me, not Josephine or the latest trends in *Brides* magazine.

"I realize it's a struggle to travel here each time we make plans," I say, seeing our hour together is nearly over. "I don't mind traveling to Knoxville, if that would make things easier on your behalf."

"It seems there aren't many decisions left to be made. I don't foresee us needing many sessions. Besides, it's nice to leave the city, even if it's only for the afternoon." She smiles. Anne has kind, almond-shaped eyes and a narrow nose. Her charm is more apparent now than it was at the beginning of our meeting.

"When is the next time you can come to Whisper Falls?"

"Would next Thursday work? That will give me time to contact florists. Maybe we could choose centerpieces?"

"Sounds great." My chest fills with joy at the idea we're finally moving forward and making decisions. This wedding, which for several weeks has seemed stalled midair, is happening.

Anne puts the notebook back into her purse. "Does this mean you'd like my help in coordinating your big day?"

"I think we have a similar understanding of what I'd like. I'd love for you to be a part of it."

"Thank you." Anne smiles from ear to ear. I think this yes means more to her than it would have to the other women. They would have flaunted their Douglas family win. Anne seems happy she is enough. "I'm delighted to get to know you."

I follow Anne to the door and watch her leave. This time when I return to the living room, I feel satisfied. This might be the first decision I've made since moving to Whisper Falls that I know is right.

CHAPTER 19

Helena

Finally, something is working out. I got the job. There were a lot of ways this could have blown up in my face. My mission could have easily ended before it began, but, for once, I think fortune is on my side. Fate wants me to get involved. The universe wants to finally right all the wrongs.

Whisper Falls is a gossipy town. After a few days of frequenting Nectar and other high-traffic establishments, I caught wind Josephine Douglas was searching for event planners. *Her golden boy was getting married*, people said. Whisper natives weren't surprised one bit she was passing over local options in favor of a wedding consultant in Knoxville. That's what sparked my idea, as far-fetched as it might have seemed.

I baited at least a dozen wedding planners before one took a bite. Anne Richards not only confirmed she was meeting with the future Mrs. Douglas; she provided all the information I needed.

"You'll be in Whisper Falls this weekend?" I asked Anne over the phone, posing as one of Josephine Douglas' house managers.

"This weekend?" Anne sounded flustered and annoyed. "I thought our consultation was this Friday at two."

"There must have been a mix-up," I said. "Ms. Sharpe booked all of her appointments for this Saturday."

"I won't be able to make it then. I'm available Monday if Ms. Sharpe—"

"I'm incredibly sorry, but decisions will need to be made quickly. The wedding is only three months away, as is. I'm sure you understand."

Anne didn't sound very understanding when she hung up the phone. She, like the other planners Josephine contacted, must know this is a high-dollar affair. My aim wasn't to inconvenience Anne; she was simply the first planner on my list to admit she had an appointment in Whisper Falls. She gave me all the details I needed to pose as her from that point forward.

From the cramped corners of a place called Computers and Coffee, I researched Anne's website. I printed off a few pictures from recent events and added them to a folder. My cover would be blown immediately if I didn't create some kind of backstory. Thankfully, an event planner wasn't much of a stretch. Believe it or not, I was once known for orchestrating fabulous parties, back when I was younger and less bitter. After my daughter's death, I could no longer muster the enthusiasm. And yet here I am, polishing up the best parts of the old me, for Madison.

I arrived during Anne's appointed time slot. For a moment, I didn't know if I could go through with it. I feared Madison might figure me out, know I was some fraud with an ulterior agenda. Then I reminded myself Madison had no reason to suspect anything. As long as there weren't any other members of the Douglas family present, I'd be fine. Josephine would remember my face; Madison couldn't pick me or Anne out of a crowd.

My confidence plummeted when I walked inside the house. Standing in Cooper Douglas' foyer was almost too much to bear. My eyes scanned the new furniture that filled their living room. According to the gossipers in Whisper, Josephine Douglas had dropped a ghastly amount of money at some place called Turner's to furnish this place. For a brief moment, I wanted to stampede into the living room and break every vase, use the shards to carve into the fabric of their new sectional. Why should he get all this normalcy? Why does he deserve a beautiful home and a darling bride-to-be?

I reeled my thoughts from that dark tunnel, focusing instead on her. On Madison Sharpe. She's blonde and beautiful and pretty much all the things you'd expect a guy like Cooper Douglas to tie down. Boy, has he tied her down! She's all about her new little life in Whisper Falls, using her induction to the Douglas clan to her advantage. I'm guessing that's why she didn't even try to find employment. Why is it women these days are so ready to throw away their own value for a man? My girl wasn't like that.

At the same time, I don't think she's oblivious to the monster with whom she shares her bed. Her eyes are too bright and her smile too wide. Beneath her cheery façade, I sense a layer of insecurity. Loneliness, perhaps. It takes a truly lonely person to spot another. I guess that's what happens when you trade in your entire life for a shiny ring! It won't take long to build a rapport with her, I can tell.

Of course, I'd sound like an absolute crazy person if I revealed my true intentions during our first visit. I need to build a bond first. Make her know she can trust me. Trust is vital if I want her to believe a word I say, and she needs to believe me. That's the only way I can turn her against Cooper.

So I listened as she talked about flowers and colors and candles. I'd assumed she'd desire a reception in some barn followed by a photography session in an itchy cornfield. That's the aesthetic these days, according to my research. Madison is different from the girls around here though; it's hard to say for the moment whether that works in my favor.

I'll humor her during our next visit by bringing flowers. I'll print off more pictures, and maybe we can even sample a menu or two. I'll help her plan the wedding of her dreams because that's what she needs from me right now. In the end, none of it will matter. Because there's no way in hell this wedding will happen. I'll make sure of that.

CHAPTER 20

Madison

I haven't felt this giddy about the wedding since I bought my dress. My meeting with Anne serves as a reminder that my future with Coop is happening, regardless of any unsightly roadblocks I might encounter along the way. I pull up Anne's website and click through images. Most of the photographs aren't weddings; it seems in recent years she's focused more on community fundraisers. She probably thought that would hurt her chances of getting the job.

On the contrary, I find Anne's detachment from bridal trends refreshing. She didn't enter our appointment with preconceived notions of what my wedding should be, unlike the previous planners I met with. Instead, Anne was willing to hear my suggestions, my vision. I'm at ease with her, and I haven't felt that way often since moving to Whisper Falls.

For years, I've defined myself through my job and personal achievements. With that gone, my confidence has plummeted. I think that's why I've felt more insecure about Celia, and the idea people think Coop is to blame amplifies those emotions. From the time he told me about his teenage girlfriend who drowned in the lake, it's bothered me. I resent the hold she seems to have over both our lives, although Coop has always provided reassurance about his feelings for me.

One memory remains fresh in my mind. It was the night we got together to celebrate Beth and Matt's engagement. We used to be inseparable: Beth and Matt, Coop and me. Before Coop, we were more of a trio, seeing as Beth and Matt had been together since college. Coop and I had only been together six months at that point, but we'd already cemented our status as a foursome. To celebrate, we got hammered in my apartment after a fancy dinner. Two bottles in, Matt suggested we play drinking games.

"It'd be like college all over again," he said, his bald head gleaming underneath the overhead light.

"Come on," Beth said, swatting his arm. "Aren't we too old for that sort of thing? We're supposed to be sophisticated." She did a wobbly shoulder shrug soaked in sarcasm.

"It'll be fun," Coop said, squeezing my waist.

We tried to recall popular games from our schooldays but couldn't remember any of the rules and felt ancient when we pulled out our phones to google them. Instead, we sat on the floor answering questions; after each round, everyone took an obligatory swig of their drink. The categories were equal parts entertaining and intrusive. First kiss. Worst date. First time getting drunk. Coop recalled the time his date hurled in an alleyway beside his apartment building; Beth told a handful of stories relating to our exploits in college. The next category Matt suggested, First Love, made us all a little uneasy.

"Mine was the same as my first kiss," Matt said, volunteering to go first. "Cynthia."

"The sixth grader on the playground?" Beth asked.

"We had a very special connection," he said.

"You're full of it! No point in playing the game if you're going to make jokes," Beth said. "My high school boyfriend, Tanner. Thank goodness he broke my heart, otherwise I might not be here."

"Good for us both," Matt said, squeezing Beth tighter. "Madison?"

"Christian. We dated for a year in college," I answered.

"That guy was such a douche," Beth said, tossing a pillow at me for even mentioning the name. "I think my entire sophomore year was devoted to playing referee during your arguments."

"He wasn't the best guy," I said, clenching my jaw.

I looked at Coop, waiting to hear his response. He hadn't had many serious relationships: Celia, a few girls in college and me. Inside I worried—feared—he might say that Celia, the enigmatic girl with the tragic ending who had a way of poisoning my thoughts, was his first love. Another woman would be more bearable; at least he chose to separate from his other exes. Celia was taken from him without choice, which must leave him wondering, would he have left her? Had she not died, would he even be here for me to love? Most high school and college relationships fizzle. People change and mature and move on. Life sorts things out, not death.

"Laura," he answered. "We met in college."

I discreetly exhaled the breath I'd been holding. I was relieved his first love wasn't Celia. I needed to believe their relationship was nothing more than a youthful infatuation. I didn't want to play second fiddle to his deceased ex-girlfriend, for him to wonder how his life might have unfolded had she lived. The cycle of love and loss brought him to me. It brought us to each other.

"I change my answer," Matt bellowed, interrupting my sentimental thoughts. "Truth is, Beth is my first love. I just didn't want to say it and sound like a sap. She's my one and only."

Beth beamed, leaning in for a kiss. Beth and Matt had that spark about them. I always knew they'd end up together. We continued drinking and sharing stories until late in the night. Beth and Matt slept on my cratered futon. Coop slept in my bed; in fact, that was the first night he suggested we live together. I remember drifting to sleep in his arms, happy our connection was growing. I wince, looking back. I miss the naïve, uncomplicated elements of young love. Now, our lives seem so tense.

When Coop arrives, he brings Mexican takeout and margarita ingredients. It's his attempt to erase this morning's squabble. Celia and the mysteries of her death still linger in my mind, but I want to push them away and enjoy my time with Coop. Spending the afternoon discussing our wedding has left me elated.

"So, you've found our wedding planner?" he asks, placing a freshly mixed drink into my hand.

"I have." I smile, thinking of Anne's simple ways and how pleased she was to be selected. "She's a nice woman. She has a clear understanding of what I want the day to be."

"I don't understand why having a planner is so important. I think most people could manage organizing one night on their own."

"I could, but I think I'd also be second-guessing every decision I make. Then your mom would be triple-guessing." I quickly sip my drink, hoping that dig wasn't too forward. "In the end, I guess that's why we're paying her. To make me feel like I'm making the right decisions."

"Do whatever you need. I want this day to be perfect for us."

We lock eyes. "I'm sorry about this morning," I say. "I want you to know that."

"You didn't do anything wrong, Madison. I just hate you've had so much anxiety since we moved here."

"In a lot of ways, what you went through explains why I fell in love with you. Why you're guarded and thoughtful. But it's not fair the people here were so cruel."

"It wasn't just the people here. Celia's mother was the worst." He drains his drink and stares at the fireplace. "The woman had a lot of problems, which is why Celia lived with her aunt. She was in no position to raise a child."

"If they weren't close, why was she so awful to you?" I understand she was Celia's mother, but Coop makes it sound like parenting was more of an afterthought.

"Her mother was the queen of revisionist history. Some people gravitate to drama. Raising a young child didn't sound like much fun to her, but grieving the loss of a teenager? That gave her a much-desired spotlight." He takes a sip of his drink, flipping his hand through the air. "I know that sounds harsh, but it's hard for me not to hold a grudge considering everything she put me through."

"What did she do?"

"Celia's mother exaggerated everything already being said. She'd listen to anyone, as long as that person was against me. When chasing down the media didn't work to her advantage, she became more reckless. She started visiting Whisper and vandalized the *Gazette* building downtown. Showed up drunk to my mother's house. It became so intense we took out a restraining order against her."

"That's terrible," I say, squeezing Coop's hand. He's always been modest. It's understandable why such public acts of ridicule would weigh on him.

"That's part of the reason my parents hired their own team to look into the case. If they could prove Celia's death was accidental, maybe her mother would stop harassing us." He looks away, peeling back the layers of armor he's built around the topic. "For a while, it worked. The last time I saw her was the worst. When I graduated college, Mom hosted a party at some Italian restaurant; it's gone belly up since then, but it was the place to be back in the day. Anyway, everyone that was anyone in Whisper was there. Halfway through the night, Celia's mom showed up and created a spectacle."

"Spectacle?"

"She stumbled into the place and interrupted my mother's speech, shouting, 'He's a liar,' and 'He's a murderer.' I'd never been so humiliated in my life. I can only imagine how my parents felt."

"What happened?"

"The police were called. They arrested her, but my parents dropped the charges."

"Why?" I ask, slamming my glass against the counter. "It sounds like this woman deserved a punishment."

"She lost her daughter," Coop says, looking away from me. "That's punishment enough in one lifetime, even if she never deserved Celia in the first place."

I admire Coop's willingness to forgive. It's harder for me to hear these stories and feel empathy. I love Coop. I'd rather someone lash out against me than him. "I'm sorry you had to go through that."

"I was so young then, still wrapped up in what others thought of me. What happened to Celia was a tragedy, but I didn't cause it. Eventually, I realized I knew the truth and that's all that mattered." He pauses and smiles. "My family really stood by me through it all. They still do. At least I walked away knowing I'd always have someone in my corner."

I smile too, having found a greater appreciation for his family. They can be meddlesome, but at least they support him. "And she hasn't bothered you since?"

"It's been years. Celia's aunt doesn't even live here anymore. The more time passes, the more the whole ordeal fades away."

I don't feel that way, but perhaps it's because I'm hearing all this for the first time. I'm just now encountering these places and faces that forever colored Coop's world. In time, maybe Celia Gray will fade from my thoughts, too. I won't always feel connected to this beautiful girl I never met.

"I still worry sometimes though," Coop continues, placing his empty glass on the table. "It's hard not to be paranoid when an irrational person makes it their intent to ruin your life. A part of me worries she'll never really be gone. That these long periods of silence are just her gearing up for her next move."

"It's been years since she did anything," I say, trying to comfort him. "I'd say she's moved on."

"I'd like to think she's off getting wasted somewhere, that Celia and I are nothing but distant memories to her now." He squeezes my hand and looks away. "I guess only time will tell."

CHAPTER 21

June 16, 2006

Regina arrived at the dock with the intention of being alone. When she saw Cooper and Celia, she groaned.

"Afternoon, Gina," Celia said. She always pronounced the nickname with a long I, so that it rhymed with vagina.

Each time Regina heard this, her skin crawled. She wanted to lunge forward and scratch Celia's pretty face, but she wouldn't do that to Cooper. He was her older brother and she respected him. They were Douglases, and she respected that. Still, none of this made being around Celia Gray any easier.

"Don't call her that," Cooper said. It wasn't the first time he'd heard Celia say it, but it was the first time Regina remembered him coming to her defense.

"I'm just kidding around," Celia said, skidding her foot through the water and splashing Cooper. "We're all friends here, right?"

Regina didn't respond. Neither did Cooper. He didn't even flinch when she splashed him with more water. Regina realized then she'd walked in on something. Not necessarily a fight, but something. She always knew Celia had an expiration date, and she hoped it was approaching.

"What are you doing here?" Cooper asked his sister. He wasn't being rude, but there was an edge. She thought it had more to do with Celia than her.

"It's summer," Regina answered. She shrugged. "I like to read by the dock."

"You're so smart, Reggie," Celia said. "Mama Douglas must be so proud."

Regina could speak Celia's language. She knew smart was code for not pretty. And both girls knew Josephine Douglas would prefer a daughter who looked like Celia. Celia, who could flow effortlessly from a string bikini to a debutante gown. She might be white trash, but she looked like a Southern Belle, and Regina hated it.

"I'll just head back to the house," Regina said.

"Ridiculous," Cooper said, swinging his legs away from the water. "Celia was just leaving."

"No, I wasn't." Celia looked straight at him, her stare so hot she was practically steaming. "I'm not going anywhere."

Regina had definitely walked in on something, but she didn't know what.

"Fine," Cooper said, standing. "I'll leave."

He brushed past his sister and walked up the hill. Both girls stayed at the dock and watched him go.

CHAPTER 22

Madison

This weekend was wonderful. Nothing extraordinary happened, but it felt like Coop and I were back in our groove. We spent time together in Whisper Falls Park, enjoying the ideal temperatures and colorful mountain views. Coop wasn't preoccupied with work, and I wasn't bothered by the insecure thoughts that have been plaguing my brain.

On Sunday night, Coop surprised me by announcing he'd arranged for me to join Josephine at the hair salon. Truthfully, I haven't put much thought into my appearance since leaving Atlanta. At first, I was hesitant, seeing as I don't know any hairstylists here, but I didn't want to seem ungrateful. Besides, I'm feeling better about life in Whisper. Perhaps it's time my outward appearance starts matching my new persona.

Josephine picks me up on Tuesday and we make the short drive to Inner Glow, a nail and hair salon sandwiched between a cash advance place and a consignment shop. From the outside, the place is forgettable; all the effort has been saved for the interior décor. The walls are hot pink, the doors are black and there is a collection of animal print rugs (zebra, cheetah and leopard) in front of each workstation. It's like my fourteen-year-old self designed the place.

Josephine introduces me to my hairstylist. "This is Monica," she says. "She's the owner."

Monica does a bizarre little skip while keeping her feet in place, like she can't contain her excitement. I'm surprised to see she's close to my age. She's tall with long black hair that reaches the top of her jeans. In some ways, she reminds me of Regina, only it's clear she puts in more effort.

"Madison," I say, taking a seat and resting my bag on the small table to my left.

"So, Cooper Douglas. Quite a catch, huh?" Monica says. "I was beside myself when Josephine called saying his fiancée needed an appointment."

"I'm happy you could work me in on such short notice."

She flaps the apron over my chest, fastening it behind my shoulders. I feel her cool hand graze my neck as she untucks my hair. "Let me tell you, there's not a better mother-in-law than Josephine Douglas. The woman is an absolute saint around here."

"I've heard." Staring in the mirror, I can see Josephine is leaned back, another technician preparing to wash her hair in the sink. "She's been wonderful. Very generous and supportive."

"Those two words exactly. She's the one who gave me the loan to start this place. This will be my fifth year. I always wanted to do hair, but I never thought I'd be a business owner."

"That's great," I say, feeling a twinge of pride. There's at least a faction of Whisper who sees past the rumors, choosing to focus on the good. Josephine's given a lot to this town, more than people give her credit for.

"So." Monica takes a deep breath and pushes back her shoulders. "What are we doing today?"

"I definitely need a cut," I say, staring back at my own reflection. Back in Atlanta, my hairstylist was Rodrigo. We'd been together so long, I never had to tell him what I needed. We'd built that unspoken rapport where he just knew. Of course, I've not seen him in over six months. I canceled our last appointment after I lost my job at the *Chronicle*. Even now, after months without communication and a move to an entirely different state, it feels like I'm cheating on him.

"What about the color?" she asks, looking at my two-inch roots.

"Lighten it up." I need to appear more put together. I don't want anything too drastic because there'll probably only be time for one more appointment before the wedding. "I'd like something a little softer."

"Your natural color has come in a lot at the back." She claws a clump of hair and lets it fall. "I could bring that out a little more. That's a big look right now, you know. Bronde."

"Right," I say, studying my face in the mirror. "Just a warmer shade of blonde, perhaps?"

"You got it," she says, turning on her heels. "I'll be right back."

Perhaps I need to ease back to my natural color. I'd come across more mature, more respectable. In the city, whenever people hit me with a dumb blonde joke, I'd name drop the *Chronicle*, but I've lost that power chip.

Behind me, I see Josephine is still leaned back, her mouth moving a mile a minute. It's impossible to hear what she's saying with the cacophony of hair dryers and running faucets and southern accents. Monica returns with a bowl full of color and a packet of foil. She gets to work painting and folding my hair. I close my eyes, trying to ignore her gentle tugging and relax.

"So, how did you and Cooper meet?" she asks, interrupting my meditation. "Atlanta, right?"

"Yeah," I say, closing my eyes again. "We met at work."

"Give me more than that," she says, and I can see in the mirror that she's smiling. "Like, how did you meet? What's your story?"

I rarely ponder those early weeks anymore. I'm too busy dealing with the present, moving from one issue to the next. It's almost magical looking back, thinking something so mundane could unfold into one of the most meaningful relationships of my life. Perhaps that's what we all go through. Love at first sight rarely exists; instead, you look back one day and it is suddenly there.

"I was a writer," I begin. "I'd been working at this paper for several years. My schedule kept me busy, so I didn't have much time for dating. Coop was hired, started doing entry-level work. Our paths didn't cross much, but I remember noticing him. He had this confidence about him that caught my eye. This sense of self, but not in a cocky way. I didn't really get to know him until a few weeks later, after our office Christmas party.

"I think we both had one too many drinks. By the end of the night, we'd been at the bar for hours. We talked about everything. Families, friends, career ambitions. He told me all about life here in Whisper Falls, which amazed me because I'd never lived anywhere outside of the city. He told me about his family's newspaper, that the only reason he was in Atlanta was to gain some real-world experience before taking over the *Gazette*. Most guys I'd dated at that point were running the rat race, busy showing each other up. Coop already had his whole life figured out, and that was incredibly attractive."

"I bet so," Monica says, painting the back of my hair.

I think I forgot she was there. I was rambling, almost entirely to myself. It's been so long since I thought of that night. I chuckle when I think about the felt Santa hat sliding off his head and the gross holiday light necklace I wore. Who would have thought such a garish tradition would result in me meeting my future husband? I didn't. Love was the furthest thing from my mind back then, and perhaps that's why it was so easy to find.

"How did he pop the question?" Monica asks.

"We went to dinner with friends. Afterward, he invited people back to our place. I thought it was going to be another night of drinking and throwing darts. Next thing I know, he's down on one knee." I think back to that moment, my surprise. Beth and Matt and some colleagues from the *Chronicle* were there. They all looked so happy for us. Said we were an ideal fit.

"That's sweet he got others involved."

"My best friend, Beth, helped him sort things out. It was very intimate. Perfect, really."

"Your ring is gorgeous," she says. I can feel her towering over me to get a better look.

"Thank you. It's a Douglas family heirloom."

"Very fancy," she sings.

Then there's that, like I'm only along for the purse strings. My interactions in Whisper Falls to date have made me wary of what others think. I never used to care, but I'm not used to this dynamic of people either kissing your ass or cutting you down. It's made me cynical, but Monica genuinely seems interested, and from the praises she's offered Josephine, she must be someone who firmly sides with the Douglases.

"So you grew up with Coop, Roman and Regina, right?" I say, giving her a chance to talk. It would be nice to hear some pleasant memories about Coop's past for a change.

"We all knew them, of course. Regina and I had a few classes together but she was a bit of a loner. I was a late bloomer myself. Didn't get close to any of them until later."

"Yeah?" I ask, thinking there's more. Maybe Regina actually has a friend.

Monica turns around, scoping out where Josephine might be. "Roman and I had a little fling a few years back. Nothing serious." She smiles. "He's a real special guy."

I can see it. Monica and Roman. They're both attractive, although Roman is rough around the edges. I can't tell from Monica's expression whether they were serious or not. Maybe she doesn't even know.

"They're always making comments about Coop being the first one to tie the knot."

Monica laughs. "Yeah, can't say I see the other two getting hitched anytime soon." She smiles as she continues fiddling with the foils. "Roman's a decent guy. Just not big on commitment."

"What about you?" I ask, kindly maneuvering the conversation to a different topic. "Are there eligible bachelors in Whisper?"

"Not really." She laughs again, nervously. "My current boyfriend lives in Knoxville. We see each other on the weekends."

"Nice." I can't imagine why anyone would live here if they didn't have to. I guess I'll truly never understand how a place this small can have such a tight hold on its residents.

"Let's get you under a dryer," she says. "Then we'll wash you up."

I bask in the silence of the heat around my head, then the warm water rinsing over my hair and Monica's nails digging into my scalp. I'm able to relax for the rest of our session. I flip through a magazine as Monica cuts and dries my hair, but I'll occasionally smile when I think about Coop and some of our happier memories back in the city.

"We're all finished," Monica says. She spins me around to face the mirror.

My natural hue is now the dominant color on my head. There's only a few ashy blonde streaks, but they're spread apart, only heightening the contrast. It's like someone poured a bottle of ranch dressing over my head and let it sit. It's not natural in the least, or unnatural in a trendy way. I look like a nineties pop star, and I hate it.

My eyes bounce around the salon, looking at the other patrons. I see this is the same look they all have. Like they're all stuck in a different decade. If only I'd seen this pattern before.

"What do you think?" Monica asks. She must sense my silence isn't good.

"It's different," I say. It's the nicest I can be. The gleam of pride in her eyes tells me she thinks she's done a good job. She's desperate for my approval. I'd readily share my opinion back in Atlanta, where I think people are tough enough to take criticism. Here, the look on Monica's face—I don't have it in me to spoil her confidence.

"The colors should blend after a few washes," she says, stroking the back of my hair. "What do you think of the cut?"

Dear God, the cut is even worse. It's not been this short since college. My hair stops just above my shoulder and curves in. I look like a Stepford version of myself. Or, perhaps, a Whisper Falls version.

"It should grow out some before the wedding, right?" My voice is cracking as I speak.

"Plenty of time," she says. Her smile is back, which must mean she thinks I'm happy with what she's done. "Don't worry. We'll schedule some practice sessions before the big day."

So, it's already decided, at least for Monica, that she'll be doing my hair for the wedding. I don't know if I can trust her to ever touch my hair again. There's nothing wrong with her technique per se, but the final product is just so… not me.

"You look beautiful," Josephine says, standing behind my chair. Her hair looks exactly as it did before we arrived, only a few gray strands removed, and her fingernails have been painted a delicate color of pink.

"You think?" I say, trying hard not to let either woman sense my disappointment.

"Very mature," she says, placing a hand on my shoulder. "I told you Inner Glow was the best in town."

I stare at my reflection in the mirror, at this person who seems to be withering away by the day. *Yeah, you're a grown up now, Madison*, a little voice says inside. *Start acting like one.*

CHAPTER 23

Madison

On Wednesday morning, I return to Whisper Falls Park and run. I should be buying groceries, but I don't feel like fighting off crowds. During my short time in Whisper, I've learned one thing: Walmart is always the busiest place in town. There's no good time to go, and there's no healthy alternative like Whole Foods nearby.

I'm rounding off my fifth lap when Bailey arrives. She occupies the same spot as last time, pulls out her laptop and starts typing. The only difference from last week's encounter is she's using a rock as a paperweight. I still can't believe she had the gall to write such a suggestive article about Coop. After two laps of trying to forget about her and failing, I walk toward the bench.

She lifts her head, fingers still typing on the keyboard. "Like the new look."

As though I weren't irritated enough. I'd forgotten about the hair fiasco. Yesterday, Coop did his best to build my confidence about the whole thing. He swore he thought the style suited me, but that's just him being optimistic. Staring at Bailey, I can't decide if her compliment is sincere. "Why would you write something like that about Coop?" I ask.

"I write about all local events in Whisper Falls." She gently shuts the laptop. "His return is interesting to a lot of people."

"Coop isn't a local event." I say, plainly. "He's not a celebrity."

"Around here he is. Everyone knows the Douglas family, and the Celia Gray case is Whisper Falls' biggest unsolved mystery. People never get tired of reading about it."

"But it is solved!" I put my hands on my hips. Bailey, with her intellect and wit, assumes she knows everything about the Douglases. After speaking with Coop about Celia's mother, I see how much pain he's been carrying as a result of these ugly rumors. Bailey couldn't possibly understand how her article unlocked a Pandora's box of unresolved emotions. "She drowned. It's a closed case."

"Only because the Douglases hired their own PI to close it." She laughs, then continues typing. "Not everyone is so convinced the case is solved."

"The police are. All you're doing is creating drama."

"You're a writer," she says, holding eye contact. "You know you can't just accept what's written on paper. You have to dig deeper. You have to investigate."

I wonder if this is a dig about 'Chrissy', but that's just me being paranoid. The *Chronicle* erased the article as fast as they could. Unless someone had a hard copy in hand, Bailey couldn't know about it. That situation made me all too aware of the dangers in following the wrong story. Bernard Wright and his gang of lawyers actively planted lies to create doubt. People are malicious. They'll take another person's pain and use it to their advantage.

"The things you write affect people. All you're doing is stirring up ghosts."

"I'm not the only person who thinks the Douglas family had a hand in covering this up. They did more than hire an outside examiner. They buried as many stories about Celia as they could. I bet my post on *The Falls Report* was the only article you've even read. Why do you think that is?"

I stumble. "When the *Gazette* adopted their new online system—"

"Yeah, yeah, yeah. They lost a few articles. How convenient that every article about Celia Gray didn't make the cut. The Douglas family has money and power. That makes them suspicious." Bailey tilts her head to get a better look at me. "You don't buy everything they say either, do you? That's why you're so bothered by this."

"I'm bothered because I know Coop. He's a good man, and I hate to see the way this incident has followed him."

"Cooper Douglas seems like a stand-up guy. It doesn't mean there aren't skeletons rattling in his closet."

I'm blushing, but I refuse to cower in front of her. A week ago, I might have been wounded by what she said, but Bridgette's accusation changed things. It forced me to communicate with Coop about his past. Forced him to reveal this town's involvement in his shame. For a while, I drifted through Whisper Falls, unsure of my purpose. Now I understand my role is to support Coop, assure him he no longer has to carry this burden alone. We're in this together.

"I'm sure it's difficult finding entertaining stories in a town this dull but work a little harder," I say, holding eye contact as I take a step back. "And stop writing about Coop."

I jog back to the track, not leaving the park until I've finished my routine.

CHAPTER 24

Helena

I've spent the entire afternoon collecting materials at the local craft supply store. Tomorrow, I'll drive to local florists and snap pictures of various arrangements on display. It's a lot of effort to put into an event I know will never happen, but it's important for me to build a rapport with Madison. To impress her, even. It's the only way I can get close to her whilst steering clear of her in-laws. They'd know me in a second. How could they forget?

When it became clear the police were no longer investigating, I had to do whatever I could to keep my daughter's face out there. I contacted news stations and newspapers, and not just the corrupt *Gazette*. Eventually, even they grew tired of my phone calls. There were bigger stories to tell, more important people than my girl.

That's when I started drinking. I'd always been a social drinker, but now when I imbibed, it wasn't for a connection; I no longer relied on people in the superficial way I once did. The bottle listened to my stories without telling me to move on or accept what had happened. The bottle didn't tell me I was being irrational for placing the blame on Cooper Douglas. He knew something. His wealthy family hired a lawyer to shut him up, but who would do that unless there was something to hide? Why weren't they contacting me, telling what they knew? They didn't even send condolences.

After six months, I couldn't take it anymore. I needed to contact Cooper directly. After several glasses of Merlot, I trekked to Whisper Falls and made my way onto the Douglas estate. I wanted to talk to

Josephine, mother to mother. Cooper was young, after all. Maybe he was intimidated by me. His mother would understand the anguish of not being able to protect a child, and, perhaps, offer her support.

A mindful person would have reached out over the phone, but that would have provided too much time for a reaction. If his mother could only see me in person, she might take me seriously. Finding the house wasn't hard. Everyone in Whisper Falls knew how to reach the Douglas estate. I went there on a Saturday afternoon, immediately mesmerized by the hydrangea bushes lining the driveway and the ominous lake in the background. I walked to the front door, which was opened by a member of the staff—what people have staff these days?—and was directed to the library.

I sank into a velvet armchair by the fireplace, scanning the rows of books between the floor and ceiling. The back window overlooked Whisper Lake. I wondered how many times my daughter might have visited this place. A dozen? More? How close had she and Cooper become? Surely his family mourned her loss as much as I did.

"I'm Josephine Douglas," she said when she entered the room. She wore a lime skirt and blazer, a colorful silk scarf fastened around her neck. Her dark hair sat atop her head, a jeweled hairpin holding it in place. She pushed back her shoulders and smiled, her presence sucking the air out of the room. "How may I help you?"

"I'm Helena," I said, standing to shake the woman's hand. My knees buckled from the nervousness. This wasn't the type of place I belonged, and Josephine wasn't the type of woman I'd ever befriend. "I wanted to speak to you about your son."

"Which son?"

"About Cooper." I took a step closer.

"I thought this was about a charity event."

The man who had let me inside was standing in the corner of the room watching us. She looked at him for confirmation, and he shrugged. Of course I wasn't there about a charity event, but I needed some excuse to get into the house.

"Mrs. Douglas, I need to talk to you about Cooper. You see, my daughter—"

Her face filled with recognition and horror. She knew what I was about to say, but she wouldn't let me finish. "You need to leave. Now." She turned to exit the room.

"Please, if you'd just listen to me." I yanked her arm, pulling her back. I didn't mean to grab her with such force, but the combination of desperation and wine overpowered my manners.

"Let me go," she said, her eyes as deep as the lake beyond the doors. And yet, there was something in them. Fear. I was scaring her.

"I know he was the last person to see her. Maybe there's something he could tell me. Some way he could help."

"Let. Me. Go." Her words reverberated from a place of contempt.

I released her and covered my mouth with my hand. I was mortified by my behavior but exhausted of being rejected at every turn. I started crying, sobbing uncontrollably. "I only want answers."

"Roger, escort this woman out," Josephine said. It was clear she was trying to remain dignified. I'd gone about this the wrong way. She'd labeled me deranged, not worthy of conversation. She thought I'd come here to terrorize her child. All I'd wanted to do was uncover the truth about mine.

"Please, Mrs. Douglas. If you'd just speak with him. Or let me. You can't imagine how painful it is not knowing what happened to your child."

"No, I can't." She stared at me with those deep, cold eyes. "It's a mother's responsibility to know everything about her children. I'm sorry you failed at that, but I'm not going to let you harass my son. The way you've treated him is repulsive."

I felt like I'd been punched in the gut. She thought Cooper was a victim in all this. She'd refused the opportunity for me to show her otherwise. Roger, a little kinder this time, touched my shoulder, urging me to leave. As I made my way to the front door, I saw three heads poking over the banister of the staircase. A young man, a teenage girl and *him*. They all looked scared, even Cooper, but seeing his face forced me into action.

"Cooper!" I screamed. "Cooper, tell me what you did to her!"

Every ounce of self-restraint escaped when I saw his frightened face. My anger and grief and despair flooded my body. I made a run for the stairs, but Roger was holding me back. He had a good grip, despite his age.

Cooper, looking even more afraid, walked away—the second time he'd turned his back on me in a time of need. The other boy followed him. The girl stood there, watching my outburst with tears in her eyes.

"Get back here!" I was screaming, mustering all my strength to wriggle from Roger's grasp. Why did Cooper get to walk away? Why could he—and his entire family—write me off? Refuse me answers? Josephine stood by the staircase, undressing each layer of my emotion with those cold eyes. Her posture never slackened, and she only moved to reposition the scarf around her neck.

"Please, ma'am," Roger whispered in my ear. "I don't want to call the police."

The police. The same people who had done nothing for my precious girl would gladly come to this fancy house and arrest me. They'd love the opportunity, especially in a town like this where alliances are firmly forged. I wiped tears and snot with the back of my hand before marching out the door.

That was the first time my rage overshadowed my grief. I felt an almost animalistic need to lash out at Cooper Douglas. Hurt him. Inflict the pain I was feeling onto him. Until then, I'd been waiting for an explanation, reserving my forgiveness. Now I'm waiting for a moment to strike back. At long last, my moment has arrived.

CHAPTER 25

Madison

I welcome Anne into the house. She carries a large box of flowers.

"Let me help you," I say.

"No need. The box is lighter than it looks." She puts it down and flattens her slacks with her hands, staring at me for a moment before she speaks. "I've brought some candles, too. I thought we could make a few centerpieces. See what works. I'll pass along whatever we decide to the florist."

"Thank you." I'm not sure what I was expecting, but it appears Anne is going above and beyond. "This is great."

She studies my appearance. "You've changed your hair."

My hand grazes through my strands, a useless attempt to wipe away the damage. "Yeah. I'm still getting used to the color. And the cut."

"I think it suits you," she says, but I sense she's only trying to be kind. "Shall we get started?"

I sit while she stands, twirling twine and ivy around candles of various sizes. She shows me some pictures on her phone, all of which are lovely.

"I can tell you've spent a lot of time working on these."

"It's what I'm hired to do. Make the bride happy."

"I've never been part of an event this elaborate before. It's nice, feeling like I'm helping coordinate all of this. Not just pointing at pictures and writing a check."

"Who else is helping you with the planning?"

"Well, Josephine has been incredibly generous. She obviously arranged to get you involved."

"Of course."

"And I've decided to let Regina's restaurant cater the reception. Nectar has the best food around by far."

"That's a big box to check off our list. It must be nice having a chef in the family." She smiles, placing the arrangement on the table. "What about your family? Are they involved?"

My mouth opens, but my voice catches. "I'm not really in contact with my family."

"I see." She starts fiddling with flowers again, nervous she's pushed into unchartered territory. "I think we're more than capable of handling this on our own."

"I've never been close to my family," I say, feeling the need to explain. "I grew up in the system. My most recent foster mother and I were close, but she died not long after Coop and I started dating. Cancer."

"I'm sorry to hear that, Madison." She stops what she's doing and stares, like she wants to cradle me. "It must be hard planning a wedding without the person you love the most there to help."

"I guess that's why I'm so laid-back when it comes to all this. I never had daydreams about my father walking me down the aisle, or dress shopping with my mother." I smile to let Anne know I'm okay, even though I feel like I'm on the verge of crying. "I do wish my foster mother could have been here though. Ginny. That was her name."

Anne drops her gaze to the bouquet in her hands. When she looks at me, there are tears in her eyes. "I lost my daughter some years back. That's why it's been so long since I've planned a wedding."

"I'm so sorry, Anne." I reach for her hands. My instincts want to ask what happened, but I don't. I don't need to resurrect this woman's pain. And I know how difficult it can be trying to answer questions about one's past. "That's a terrible loss."

"I couldn't wait for the day we'd plan her wedding. Once I realized that wouldn't happen, it wasn't much fun organizing events anymore. That's why I've stuck to community functions. I still have bills to pay, but those hurt a little less."

For a brief moment, I try to imagine the anguish Anne must feel. I've never had deep connections with anyone besides Beth and Coop. Before them, the closest bond I had was with Ginny, but the nature of our relationship meant our time together was limited. Even if she were alive, our relationship was always an artificial sort of mother/daughter bond. In the brief moments Anne has spent telling me about her daughter, I can tell they had the real thing.

"It means a lot you're planning this with me," I say, reaching for Anne's quivering hands. It calms her, and she smiles.

"It's like fate, isn't?"

"I suppose." I'm not sure why my wedding is so special, why this is the event that has brought Anne out of her seclusion. It must have something to do with me marrying a Douglas, and all the power and prestige one feels being involved with them.

"Well." Anne wipes tears from her cheeks and smiles. "I've got more to talk to you about than sad memories. I'll pass along your centerpiece decisions to the florist. Now, we need to decide on invitations."

I pull out my computer and show her my shortlist of potential designs. We select one and submit our order, so they'll arrive next week. Afterward, Anne presents various options for entertainment. We select a band that's available, and Anne promises to reserve them. Then we move on to the bridesmaid dress. I tell her I'll go shopping with Regina, since she's the only attendant.

"Will your sister-in-law also provide the cake?"

"I think dinner will be all her staff can handle. We should see if we can find a bakery willing to commit last-minute."

"Between now and our next meeting, I'll sort it out. Maybe I can even organize a tasting."

"Sounds wonderful." I laugh, and Anne does, too. It's nice, feeling assured about the decisions we've just made.

"I must say, this is quite an easy job," she says, holding out her hands. "There's little left for me to do."

"Still, I appreciate your help. It makes me more confident."

She smiles. It's as though she wants to say more but doesn't. "Well, I guess we can meet next week after the invitations arrive. Will Thursday work?"

"That's perfect." I stand, as does Anne. "If you don't mind, Josephine would like to join our next session."

She pauses as she walks to the front door. "Any particular reason why? I know she's a very busy woman."

"I think she's tested her patience in staying out of our hair this long." I laugh. "She says she wants to give me control over the wedding, but deep down I know she wants to be involved. You don't mind?"

"Of course not," she says, pulling sunglasses over her eyes. "It's her son's wedding. It's natural for her to help."

"Great." I smile, not because Josephine will be joining us, but because Anne understands. "I'll see you Thursday?"

"See you then."

She loads the boxes into her car and leaves.

CHAPTER 26

Helena

Shit, shit, shit. Just when I thought things were going my way, Josephine Douglas has to get involved. The poise and power of that woman makes me want to spit. If she were in my position, she'd carry herself better. She'd start a charity. Become an inspiration. But I don't think that woman loves her children the way I loved my girl. She could move on. I can't.

Here I am, sounding all judgmental. I've dealt with my fair share of accusations over the years. People who think I didn't do enough. *If she'd known her daughter better* or *if she'd been around more* maybe this wouldn't have happened. For a time, I thought those comments warranted a reply, then I realized no one really cared to know the truth, they just wanted to make snarky remarks. An outsider could never understand the depth of a mother's love for her child. Whatever mistakes I made, they don't lessen the pain I feel no longer having her around.

I pull my thoughts away from the past and back to the present. To my current conundrum. There's no way I can meet with Josephine. She'll know who I am within minutes. But I'm not ready to tell Madison the truth, either. We aren't close enough yet. We made steps in the right direction during today's session. I didn't plan on opening up about my loss, of course. I need her to see the composed woman I once was, not the vengeful one I've become. It's the only way I can get her, or anyone else for that matter, to help me. When Madison opened up about her own family life, my memories came spilling out.

I've considered the irony a million times. If it weren't for Cooper Douglas, I'd be planning my own daughter's wedding at this point in my life. Maybe I'd even be a grandmother. Sometimes I like to envision that alternate path, how full my life could have been had she not been taken. Now, in some twisted turn of fate, I'm planning her murderer's wedding instead. Of course, that's the role I'm forced to play. I must get closer to his bride before I can expect her to trust me. Just a little more time.

It makes sense why he chose her now. Madison has no family of her own. No connections. That Douglas clan can swoop her up and swallow her whole. There'll be no one left to advocate for her. That's why I have to do this. But first I have to get Josephine Douglas out of my way.

CHAPTER 27

Madison

I've spent the past three hours rotating between cleaning, unpacking and cooking. Coop called me on his lunch break to say he'd invited his family over for dinner. I stifled the immediate urge to strangle him; Lord knows I could have used another week to get the house in order. Maybe I needed a deadline. It's been ages since I had one, and I always work my best under pressure.

"What's left to do?" asks Coop. In the ten minutes he's been home, he's watched me stumble between the living area and kitchen at least a half dozen times.

"The table's set. I just need to move empty boxes to the back porch. They're an eyesore."

"It's handled." He places his hands on my shoulders and kisses my forehead. "Go upstairs and get ready."

I'm reminded I'm still wearing sweats that smell like scented candles and bleach. "Thank you," I say, marching up the stairs.

Josephine, Regina and Roman are due to arrive any minute. I don't have time to shower. I dampen a washcloth and wipe the grime off my naked body, slip into a maxi dress and pull my hair into a low ponytail. I whip on some mascara and lipstick. The doorbell rings just as I'm fastening a necklace around my neck.

I walk downstairs to find the Douglas family sitting in my freshly organized living room. It suddenly feels smaller with them here. Josephine stands to hug me.

"Thank you for inviting us," she says. "I've been dying to see the place."

"Of course," I say. I give Coop a knowing glance as he approaches.

"You've been in this house hundreds of times," he says.

"Yes, but it's different now. This is your home."

"What's for dinner?" Roman asks. He's sitting by the fireplace, an opened beer bottle in his hand. It must have been one he brought, as we don't have that brand in the house.

"Just a casserole I threw together." I look to Regina, who is wearing distressed jeans and a tank top, the most casual I've ever seen her. Her face is scrunched and reminds me of a teenager who is forced to be somewhere against her will. "I'm afraid it won't be as good as anything you'd make."

"It'll be great," Coop says, before Regina can throw her first dig of the night. He squeezes my shoulders, an attempt to relax me.

"Give us the grand tour," Josephine says, taking my hand.

I show them the dining room, which looks especially fancy now that the table is set with new china. I must have scrolled through a half dozen posts explaining the correct way to do it. Upstairs, I give them a glimpse of the bedrooms I finished arranging only hours ago. When we return to the main level, Coop has taken the dish out of the oven and placed it on the table. Everyone gathers around.

"Love what you've done with the place, Cooper," Josephine says.

"Yeah, I feel like I'm in the showroom of a model home," says Regina, unfurling her napkin.

"Be nice, Regina," Roman whispers.

"Madison has done all the work," Coop says, ignoring his sister. "You're right. It looks great."

I smile a silent thank you and begin to eat.

"Managing a home. Planning a wedding," Regina says. "Not working can be a full-time job."

"No more talking until we all have wine." Coop stands. His charm erases the cattiness his sister seems determined to bring into the room. He walks to the kitchen and returns with a bottle of Pinot Noir. He walks around the table with the delicacy of a server and fills everyone's glass. Roman drains his beer—the second since he's arrived—and pushes his glass forward.

"Speaking of the wedding, I'm very excited about joining your next appointment," says Josephine. "It's been years since I've worked with Anne."

"I really enjoy her. I'm happy you were able to set it up." My mind recalls Anne and her daughter, the reason it has been so long since she's organized a wedding. I consider bringing it up, but I'm not sure how close she is to Josephine. My mother-in-law strikes me as the type of person to claim many friends, when in reality she has few. "We've made progress. After we sample cakes, there's not much left."

"I thought you wanted Nectar to cater the food?" asks Regina, clinking her fork against her plate.

"I do," I say, taking a moment to wipe my mouth. "I mean, I'd expected you'd prepare the meal. I thought having you do the cake might be asking too much."

"I'm a professional chef," she says, crossing her arms.

"Exactly," Roman says, stuffing his face with another bite of food. "You're not a baker."

"My mother always said people can either cook or bake," Josephine sings, trying to lighten the mood. "It takes a real talent to do both."

"What does that mean?" Regina asks.

"It means you're a fabulous cook," Coop says. Across the table, Roman laughs.

"It's my brother's wedding," Regina says. "I can bake a damn cake."

"I really wasn't trying to offend you," I say. Already it feels like this night is slipping through my fingers. For whatever reason, Regina has been on edge since she arrived, and her attitude is worsening. "I'd love for you to provide dessert, if it's not too much work."

"No," Coop says, resting his glass. "Madison's right. Having your crew be in charge of the meal is enough."

Regina doesn't respond. She stares at the fireplace in the living room, taking a slow sip from her drink.

"The food is tasty," Josephine says. Mothering this lot for so long has made her an expert at putting out fires.

"Thank you," I say.

"Wait until you try the dessert," Coop says. Everyone snickers at the connection to the previous topic, except Regina. She keeps staring into the other room, as though it's her mission to pretend we're invisible.

"I was wondering if we could pick a date to go shopping, Regina," I say. Her role as the black sheep of the Douglas family is obvious, and partially self-imposed, but I want her to see I'm trying to change things. I want us to become friends. "We still need to find your dress."

"Just tell me when and where," she says, reluctantly being dragged back into conversation.

"You're the only bridesmaid, so it's whenever suits you. My schedule is wide open." I take a sip of my drink, unable to resist a response to her earlier insult. "As you've already pointed out, I'm not working at the moment."

"Why aren't you having more people in the wedding party?" Roman asks.

"We want to keep things small," Coop says.

"But why?" Roman leans on the table with both elbows. "Between your local friends and fraternity buddies, you could have a slew of groomsmen."

"You know how it is. Those friendships are artificial. We want the day to be about family." Coop looks at me, his smile reaching out and calming my nerves.

"Why isn't your family involved?" asks Regina. She's no longer fascinated by the fireplace in the next room; her entire body has turned to face me head-on.

She's not the only one. Everyone at the table is looking at me, waiting for a reply. Regina might have asked a rude question, but they all want to know my answer. This topic has been discussed before. Roman and Josephine's lack of interference proves it.

"I don't have family," I say, hoping my blunt response will put an end to this.

"What about friends?" Regina asks.

"Enough, Regina," Coop says, tightening his hold on the wine glass.

"Don't you have some high school BFF or sorority sister you want standing beside you on your big day?" Regina asks in a false pitch.

"We want to keep things small," I say. "Like Coop said."

"But why? From what I'm hearing, it sounds like *you* want to keep things small," she continues, coiling her neck like a snake about to bite.

"My friends are back in the city," I say. "I don't want to inconvenience them."

"So they're not invited?" asks Roman, his tone slightly less intrusive.

"Yes, they're invited," I say. "My best friend, Beth, is having a baby soon. It doesn't make sense for her to travel. She's the only person I care about being there."

"I'm not sure why this is anyone's business," Coop says, standing and carrying empty dishes into the kitchen. "It's our wedding."

"She's been poking around our business since she got here," Regina says, pointing at me.

"That's not true," I say.

Roman drains the rest of his drink and clenches his jaw. Without saying anything, he pulls the bottle from the middle of the table and pours more.

"You might want to slow it down," Coop says to him, walking back into the room.

"My drinking isn't the problem right now," Roman says, chuckling.

The room is quiet, so quiet I realize the music I'd been playing as I cooked is still on. The soft melody drifts towards us from the kitchen. It's the instrumental version of a popular song I can't quite place. I cling to this unknown tune, trying not to feel the pressure rising in my chest.

"I'm sorry, Madison." Josephine is the first to speak. "I'm not sure what's gotten into Regina. Whatever it is, she's taking it out on you, and that's not fair."

Regina pushes her chair and stands dramatically.

"Will you settle down?" Coop tries desperately to reclaim the evening.

"I'm only saying what all of us are thinking," Regina whines. "She's worming her way into our family, and we know nothing about her."

Is that what they think? That I'm infiltrating the Douglas caste? That I've trapped Coop somehow? The fact no one speaks suggests so. If they only understood how much I've sacrificed to be with him. My city. My job. My hand might have been forced on the last one, but I still chose to move here. And I'm choosing to stay, despite the tension between Coop and his family and this shitty town.

"Why do you have to always start something?" asks Roman. He stares at Regina, and I can see there's a dangerous sheen in his eyes.

"Sorry, I don't take orders like you," Regina says, snidely. "All I did was ask questions."

"And Madison answered them," Coop says, placing his arm on the back of my chair. "She didn't have to, but she did."

"Why can't you be happy for Cooper?" asks Roman. His eyes haven't left Regina, but his face is reddening. "Why can't you be happy for any of us?"

"Oh, I'm happy. I'm the only person in this family who isn't living like a fraud." She pushes in her chair, then stomps to the back porch. It amazes me that even in a horrific display of rudeness, Regina still has manners. She's conditioned. They all are.

Roman stands and puts his napkin over his plate. "Excuse me." He follows Regina out.

"What's going on with them?" Coop asks his mother.

Josephine doesn't reply. She sips her wine gracefully, ignoring the crumbling dynamics around her. Yelling breaks out on the porch. Regina first, then Roman. Coop leaves the table, joining his siblings outside in an attempt to mollify them.

I don't know what to say. I don't even know where to start. There's never been anyone in my life that could pull this level of frustration out of me over something so petty. And yet, I feel like I'm the source of all this. Coop's family is displeased with me, and I don't know why.

"Well." Josephine finally speaks, once Coop has slammed the back door shut. That one word pulls my attention immediately. I'm no longer distracted by the music playing or the raised voices outside. I'm tuned into Josephine, and what she'll say next. "I apologize on behalf of my children."

"I'm not sure what went wrong," I say. It's true. I never predicted this evening could spiral so quickly.

"When my children were younger, I never imagined they'd still behave this way. Become this bothered over the tiniest comments. A lot has happened since they were younger, though. You have to understand that."

"All I want to do is be happy here. I want to get to know all of you," I stutter, thinking of the best way to form the next sentence. "I'm not digging into the past."

She smiles. "It's okay for you to have questions. Regina prides herself for being different, but she's more trapped than she'd prefer to admit. We all are, in our own way. What happened back then, between Cooper and Celia, had an impact on all of us."

This is the first time I've heard her say the name. The first time we've discussed anything deeper than material finishes. "Josephine, we don't need to talk about this."

"Maybe we do." She runs her forefinger around the rim of her glass. "From what I can tell, that's what has set Regina off. Your interest in what happened back then. She's very protective of her brother. Roman, too. It hasn't dawned on my daughter, bright as she is, that you have a right to ask questions."

What has Regina said to them? We spoke about Celia at the lake and at Nectar; I didn't say anything off-color. She's been friendly since, so I don't believe those interactions have brought out her hostility. It must be something else. There's a layer of sweat forming between my skin and clothes. It's like I'm under a spotlight, and I wish one of the angry Douglas children would barge back into the room and end this conversation. "Coop told me everything I need to know."

"It couldn't have been easy for you moving to Whisper Falls and hearing the things people still say about him. It certainly hasn't been easy for us." She looks at me, her eyes searching. Her throat wobbles as she speaks, as though she's trying hard to fight her emotions. That's another skill she must have perfected over the years. "You must understand we've all carried this burden for years. It's made us protective and loyal just as much as it's made us paranoid and bitter."

"I understand."

"Good." She takes a sip of her wine. "Now all I can ask is that you show us a little bit of patience."

CHAPTER 28

Madison

Cooper loads the last of the dishware into the washer and slams the door.

"Do you want to talk about it?" I ask.

"Where should we begin?" He slings a dishrag over his shoulder and leans against the counter.

I copy his stance. "What happened out on the porch?"

"Regina and Roman were having it out like two spoiled teenagers."

"What do you think set them off?" I ask, remembering their bickering outside. "Regina seemed aggravated before they arrived."

"You remember *The Falls Report* article you read last week?" He crosses his arms, as I nod. "Well, Regina and Bailey have been friends for a long time. Mom and Roman must have been giving her a hard time about continuing the friendship, considering what was written about me."

That's not what I was expecting. Regina's vitriol tonight was aimed at me; I thought she was upset about something I'd done. I didn't think everyone was mad at her. It's equally surprising Regina wouldn't take Bailey to task over what she wrote in the article. During our conversation at the lake, Regina said people in Whisper had to choose their sides and defend their stance. Why would she choose to align herself with someone who openly criticized Coop? Her own brother? What side was she really on?

"I'm no longer as sympathetic toward your sister," I say, pouring another glass of wine. "That article was ridiculous. If they are friends, Regina should tell Bailey to back off."

"Regina doesn't have many friends. If she cut ties with every person who made a snide remark about our family, she'd have no one," Coop says, sliding his glass toward me. "Her behavior in general irks me. I mean, how many digs did she make tonight? Saying our house looked like a showroom and pointing out you're not working. Again. Between Regina's bitchy attitude and Roman's excessive drinking, there's a whole pit of drama."

I look down. "Regina doesn't know how to communicate without putting others down."

"She's my sister. I know how she operates." He looks at me and his demeanor softens. He pulls me in for a hug. "What I don't want is you thinking you're the cause of any of this. This is my family. It's how we've always communicated. Sometimes I think they tire of putting on the Douglas front, that's why it all crumbles behind closed doors."

"That makes sense." It's clear why he waited so long to introduce me to his family. Anyone who witnessed this behavior before a certain level of commitment could easily walk out the door. The only reason I don't now is because I love Coop. I see he's the one hurting in all of this.

"It's just embarrassing." He runs his hands through my hair, his mouth close to my ear. "I've been away so many years, I don't think I realized how miserable they've all become. They can't even pull it together for one meal. To hell with the wedding."

I pull back and playfully slap his chest. "Don't say that. Anne and I are hard at work to make sure it's spectacular."

"I just don't want my family to mess up our happiness." He shakes his head as he pours the rest of the wine into his glass. "They really do want what is best for me. They just have the absolute worst way of showing it."

"That's what your mom said."

"Really?" He leans back to get a better look of me. "You two talked?"

"She just brought up what you've been through as a family." I don't want to mention Celia. Every moment between us can't revolve around his dead ex-girlfriend. "She said the hardships have made you protective of each other. And paranoid."

"Quite the psychologist, my mom." We clink our glasses, and Coop takes a sip. "On the porch, Roman accused Regina of being jealous of us. He said she only wants to tear you down because she can't handle a relationship of her own."

"That's mean."

"She went after his drinking. Pointed out I probably would have never moved back to Whisper if he was capable of running the *Gazette*."

"Ouch."

"What they said to each other was hurtful, but true. I tried my best to diffuse the situation."

"Is that your role in all of this? Peacemaker?"

He laughs. "Tonight, I was. With siblings, you're always switching roles."

"You kept your cool tonight. It helped me keep mine."

"The wedding is in eleven weeks," Coop says, pulling me close. "Hopefully my family can avoid killing each other until then."

"Speaking of the countdown," I say, dancing my fingers across his chest. "Are we still going to make our little pact?"

Coop rolls his eyes. "Are you going to make me go through with it?"

Before the move, I'd suggested we agree not to sleep together in the weeks before the wedding. Modern relationships tend to lose the intrigue couples had in previous generations. It would be nice for our wedding night to feel special, different. Coop agreed to the idea, but it's a harder promise in practice.

"Let's give it a try," I say, holding his hand. "Beth and Matt stopped sleeping together weeks before their wedding. Lots of couples do it. At this point, it's one of the few traditions we have left."

Coop smiles, looks down and releases a heavy sigh. "The countdown to the wedding just got a lot longer."

"We still have time," I say, kissing his lips. "According to my calculations, we have a few weeks before we start abstaining."

"Let's make the most of it."

We shuffle up the stairs and push open the door. Within minutes, we're disrobed and celebrating in a whole different kind of way. Afterward, Coop takes a shower. I pull on one of his hoodies, relishing in its masculine smell. All I can think about is how patient Coop is. How understanding. He's the type of man to defend my honor, the type of man to diffuse his family tensions. He sees the best in others. The awful things people have said and written about him over the years couldn't be further from the truth. Those people don't know the real Coop Douglas, and it's their loss.

CHAPTER 29

June 16, 2006

Celia stared at Regina with contempt. "You have the worst timing. Anyone ever told you that?"

"It's my family's dock," Regina said, sheepishly.

"*My family's dock*," Celia mocked. "You think you're special because of your parents? They don't have enough money in this world to make you important in this town."

"That's not true," Regina said, her voice stronger. "I'm important."

"Yeah, right." Celia hopped up, brushing debris from her legs.

"Cooper's my brother. You could at least try to be nice to me."

"Listen here, you little lezzy—"

"Don't call me that," Regina shouted. Why did Celia have to be so mean? Regina had never done anything to her except exist. She hated being labeled while she was still in the process of finding herself. Girls like Celia could never understand. It's like they were born bloodsuckers. Cruelty came naturally to them. "You're such trash."

Celia's jaw dropped, then she did something Regina never expected to be so painful: she laughed. The courage Regina had mustered to say those words had no effect on Celia. It was just another joke.

"Call me that again and I'll knock the class out of you." Celia took a step forward. "I don't care if your brother is my boyfriend."

"Which brother?" This time her words stung. She saw the light leave Celia's eyes.

"What did you say?"

"I know you're not cheating on Cooper with Steven Burns."

Celia backed away from Regina, stepping closer to the dock's edge. "You don't know what you're talking about."

"Yes, I do. You think you can weasel your way into this family." Regina stomped her foot on the dock, casting vibrations through the weathered wood. "I'll never let that happen." She stepped forward, tightening her fingers around the book.

CHAPTER 30

Helena

It took some digging, but I figured out a way to throw Josephine off my trail. If I could only ditch her for this one meeting, I could move on to the next stage in my plan, and this farce of a wedding can be through. I'd prefer more time to build Madison's trust, of course, but Cooper's family, circling like vultures, is forcing my hand.

Here's what I've figured out: Josephine Douglas is a predictable woman. She hides what she thinks. She hides what she feels. But she always wants the world to know what she's doing and gawk with amazement. That's why she attaches her prestigious name to all those charities and causes. There's the Presbyterian Women's Group she meets with every Wednesday. The first Monday of the month, she hands out food at the local homeless ministry. Every other Thursday, she meets for lunch at the local library to host the Read and Roast book club, of which she's a founder. I collected this information by reading the fine print of several community pamphlets and doing what I do best: listening to what the little people of Whisper Falls say about the bigger people. You learn a lot that way.

Luckily for me, this week's Read and Roast meeting is scheduled only hours before I'm supposed to meet Josephine and Madison for our consult. I've thought all week about how to ensure Josephine never lays eyes on me. If she does, she'll know who I am and the whole scheme will be up. But I can't cancel the meeting either. All that would entail is rescheduling, making it that much longer before Madison can hear the truth. Likewise, I don't want to give

Josephine reason to track down the real Anne; it would only take a few phone calls for everyone, including Madison, to realize she's not me.

Josephine has to be the one to cancel. That's why I'm parked outside the library, watching as the members of Read and Roast shuffle down the sidewalk. I wait until Josephine arrives. I know it's her based on her car alone: a two-seater painted an obnoxious fire-engine red. It is just like Josephine Douglas to add her name to the Clean Air Society of Knoxville, which she does, and drive a flashy gas guzzler.

Josephine exits the car, positions her pearls across her collarbone and walks inside. I count to a hundred Mississippis, giving both Josephine and my nerves time to settle. I need her to finish all her waves and air kisses before I follow.

Inside, the library smells like Clorox and lemon. I only spot one other person roaming through the rows of books, but I can hear riotous laughter coming from a back room. That must be where they're meeting, tucked away from all the commoners on the hunt for this week's read.

A woman walks from the back and approaches me. She's dressed modestly with a long black braid. "May I help you?" she asks. She must know I've never been here before.

"Just looking." I smile and grab a book from a stack at the front.

The woman looks over her shoulder, then back at me. "I'm helping with an event at the moment. There's a bell should you need assistance."

"Thank you." I quickly dodge into the next aisle, watching through the gaps in shelving as the woman's feet move away. I'd been hoping the library would be empty and understaffed. It's the only way I can get away with what I have planned.

After another five minutes, two young girls enter through the front door. One is carrying a large tray, while the second carries a sturdy pot. These are the food caterers, and I'd bet my library card they come from that ridiculous restaurant the Douglas daughter owns. The woman with the braid meets them at the front desk, and they follow her to the back.

I'm not sure in what order the Read and Roast crew conducts business, but my plan is fairly simple: I'll sneak into the back, monitor as the servers pass around food and carefully slip something into Josephine's meal. Nothing too damaging or catastrophic. It'd be hard for me to get my hands on anything serious in an unfamiliar town, and I don't want to waste my own medication. After a quick google search, I realized all I needed was a liquid laxative. If I can get to the backroom unseen and add a few drops to Josephine's meal, she'll spend the next few hours on the toilet, forcing her to cancel her upcoming appointment with Madison.

The only other person in the library leaves without borrowing a book. I take this as a sign to make my move. I follow the delicious aromas down the narrow hallway, passing an array of corkboards with community events along the way. There are two open doors leading to the conference room. Several women crowd around the table, the same book in front of them. Of course, the books aren't opened, and it wouldn't surprise me if half the group hadn't read anything at all. Women like Josephine Douglas only bring books into the mix to make themselves feel more intelligent. Food and trash talking is what they're really about. They should change their name to Gossip and Gobble or Chat and Chomp.

No one looks in my direction. They're all too busy talking. Half the women already have a bowl of soup and a sandwich in front of them. Thankfully, Josephine isn't one of them. I'll have to hurry if I want to follow through with my plan.

"May I help you?" asks the raven-haired librarian. We're crammed into the dingy, narrow hallway.

"I'm sorry." I quickly turn on my best dimwitted expression. "I'm looking for the restroom. I didn't mean to disturb you."

"You have to be a library member to use the restroom," she says. A howl of laughter leaves the conference room, and she turns. Whatever is going on in there, the librarian would rather be dealing with them than me.

"I'm new to Whisper Falls. Just moved here from Knoxville." I smile. "I was planning on applying for a card today."

A bell rings at the front signaling someone else has arrived. The librarian rolls her eyes. "Bathroom is the last door on the left. When you're ready for that card, remember to ring the bell." She marches off to deal with her newest customer.

I follow her directions, peeking my head inside the other rooms as I pass. On the right, I see the two servers standing in the doorway, each holding two meals in their hands.

"I'm sorry," I say. "Where's the bathroom?"

"Last door on the left," one says.

I move out of the way to let them pass. When they disappear, I duck inside the room they just left. I probably have less than a minute. There are eight meals remaining on the counter. Enough for half the group. Each tray is plated with a bowl of soup and half a sandwich. I'm not sure which one is Josephine's, and I don't have time to wait around and see. I pull out the bottle, the lid already loose, and pour five or six drops into each bowl. I quickly mix the contents. As long as Josephine hasn't received her food, I'm guaranteed one of these meals will be delivered to her.

I quickly exit the room, passing both servers in the hallway. I keep my head high and shoulders back. As I pass the open conference room, I spy which women already have plates. Nothing sits in front of Josephine Douglas. That means she'll eat one of the contaminated meals, and unfortunately, so will seven of her friends.

I brush past the librarian as I exit. I rush to my car, shut the door and laugh until my belly hurts at the idea of Josephine and her friends shitting their guts out in an hour's time.

CHAPTER 31

Madison

Our appointment was supposed to start a half hour ago, and Anne still hasn't arrived. I'm worried; she's usually punctual and alert, as though our consultations are the highlight of her week. I dial her number.

"I've been trying to call you, but there are so many patchy areas entering Whisper Falls. There's a ton of traffic leaving Knoxville," she says when she answers, her voice breathy and rushed. "I'm sorry for making you wait."

"It's no worry," I reassure her. She's right; reception is unreliable this far out in the country. "We've actually had a change of plans."

"Oh, really?"

"Josephine won't be joining us. She called about an hour ago complaining about stomach cramps."

"That's awful," Anne says, but she doesn't sound completely displeased. I wonder if, like me, she'd been dreading the addition of Josephine. "If you'd rather reschedule—"

"No, no. I'm happy to meet," I say, eyeing the clock. "You've already driven so far. I hope the cakes haven't spoiled."

"They should be just fine," she says. "And we have invitations! Be there in fifteen minutes."

When she arrives, she doesn't seem flustered at all. She's carrying four boxes stacked atop one another. I love that Anne maintains poise even when she's running behind; it gives me reassurance for the big day. She places the boxes on the kitchen counter, turns and sniffs the air. Her eyes catch the pot on the stove. "What's this?"

"This might be our last meeting for a while. I thought I'd make you dinner, as a thank you." Anne strikes me as the type of person who doesn't like to make a big fuss of things, which is why I wanted to surprise her.

"That's so kind." She rolls up her sleeves and peers into the pot. "Now I feel worse for being late."

"It still needs time to simmer. I'd thought we could get the planning stuff out of the way, eat and sample the cakes last."

"Sounds delightful." She walks into the dining room and takes a seat. "It's a shame Josephine won't be joining us."

"More cake for us." I force a laugh. "She thinks she might have suffered food poisoning, and to make matters worse, the food came from Nectar, Regina's restaurant."

"Oh, dear," she says, pulling a package from her bag and placing it on the table. "Should we get started with invitations?"

"Oh, they're here!" I hurriedly open the box, running my fingers over the perforated cardstock. All our details are in print: the date and time and location. This makes the wedding feel real, and immediate. "Anne, they're gorgeous. Thank you for picking them up."

"My pleasure," she says, folding her hands on the table. "We can stuff them, then I'll pop them in the mail on my way out of town."

We organize our own assembly line. I stuff and seal, she stamps and addresses. The final guest list came in at just under sixty people, which mostly consists of Douglas family acquaintances. As we prepare the envelopes, we discuss the remaining details on our to-do list. Anne's booked the band and placed an order with the florist. She's rented a tent for the outdoor reception, too. As I imagine each element, my nerves flutter with anticipation. I can't believe it's all coming together. Only a few weeks ago, the idea of organizing this wedding seemed impossible.

"It's going to be a wonderful day. I just know it," I say, handing over the last of my invitations. "We've accomplished a lot in our short time together."

Anne takes the stack of envelopes and taps them against the table. "Now that these are complete, all we have left is the cake."

I check the time. Coop should be returning home soon. Anne thinks the meal I've prepared is the only surprise for tonight, but I've also asked Coop to join us for the dessert tasting. After all the work she's put into the wedding, it's important she meets the groom. "Let's eat first."

"I am famished," she says, patting her hand against her stomach.

I bring the food to the table.

"This is really too much," she says. "You're the easiest client I've ever had. Half the decisions were already made."

"You've helped me more than you know," I say, folding my napkin in my lap. "I feel ready now. I mean, I've always known Coop was the right man, but the stress of the wedding and moving here took its toll. I'm in a much better place, and you've helped with that."

My jovial demeanor drops when I see the look on Anne's face. I'm not sure what I've said, but it must have been wrong. She looks different now, as though I've insulted her.

"Madison, there's something I've been wanting to talk with you about," she says, her voice shaky and her eyes watery.

"Are you okay?" I reach across the table, placing my hand over hers. I've never seen her this emotional, even when she talked about her daughter.

Before she can answer, we're both distracted by the sound of Coop's car pulling into the driveway.

"What's that?" asks Anne.

I smile. "It's another surprise. You deserve to see the groom." I hope introducing her to Coop will lift her spirits again, but instead she looks like she's seen a ghost.

"He's here?" she asks, as the front door opens.

"Madison?" Coop is calling from the foyer. "Can you help me?"

I excuse myself from the table. By the entrance, Coop's balancing the bouquet I'd ordered for Anne in one hand and a bottle of champagne in the other.

"Sorry I'm late. Got held up at the office," he says. "Is she still here?"

"In the dining room." I grab the flowers, picking at the pieces so they're just right.

"Where's Mom?"

"Couldn't make it. She isn't feeling well." I lean forward and kiss his cheek. "We're just now sitting down to eat."

"Hopefully there's still cake."

"Plenty." I pull away, holding the flowers in front of me as I walk back to the dining room. I'm hoping Anne will be in a better mood now that Coop has arrived, but when I approach the table, she isn't there.

"Where is she?" Coop asks, his eyes bouncing around the room.

"Maybe the bathroom." I place the flowers on the table. Only five minutes ago, Anne and I were giggling about the wedding. Now she's gone. I can't shake the feeling something is wrong. The back door clacks against its frame. When I walk into the kitchen, I find the patio screen is open wide.

"Anne?" I call, but she's not on the porch. She's gone.

At the front of the house, I hear a car engine start. Coop follows me as I race to the front porch. By the time we're both outside, I see Anne's taillights pull onto the main road.

"Did she leave?" he asks. "What happened?"

"I don't know." I think back to our conversation, to everything that was said and done before Coop arrived. "I have no idea."

CHAPTER 32

Madison

"I don't understand," Coop says. He's sitting on the sofa, his palm against his forehead. The scent of gardenias—the one's from Anne's bouquet—fills the room.

"It's like she ran away once she knew you were here." I keep looking out the window, thinking she might come back to offer an explanation. I still don't know why she took off the way she did.

"Why would she leave so abruptly?"

"No clue." I sit beside him on the couch and pull both legs onto the cushion. "She got emotional out of nowhere before you arrived. I've never seen her act that way. Even when she talked about her daughter."

"Her daughter?"

"She mentioned during one of our previous appointments that her daughter had died. That's why it's been so long since she's planned a wedding."

Coop looks confused. "This was Anne Richards. Her company is based out of Knoxville, right?"

"Yes. Have you met her before?"

"Ages ago. I'm not sure I'd remember her face, but I used to play baseball with her son. He was one of three boys. He didn't have a sister." He sits up, resting both elbows on his knees. "You're sure the woman's name is Anne Richards?"

"Yes, I'm sure. Your mother gave me her information."

"Has Mom met with her?"

"She was supposed to join us today before she fell ill."

"Did you look into this woman before you hired her?" He stands, pacing between the sofa and fireplace. "Do any research?"

"Of course I did. I looked up her website and everything. She's completely legit."

He pulls out his phone and types in the business details. As I did, he scrolls through galleries of various events, but there's no picture of Anne on her website.

"What are you doing?" I ask, craning my neck to get a better look at his phone.

"I don't want to startle you." He slides his phone into his pocket and looks at me. "But what if the woman in our house wasn't Anne Richards?"

"What do you mean? This is our third meeting this month. She delivered our wedding invitations today. Who else could she be?"

"Look." He pulls out his phone again and types Anne Richards, Knoxville, TN into the main search bar. Various women pop up. He scrolls through several, until he finds an advertisement for a local sponsor. He holds up the phone. "This is the Anne Richards I remember. It may not be a recent picture, but it's good enough. Is this the woman who was in our house?"

I stare at the woman on the screen. She's short and squat with auburn curls and a wide smile. She looks nothing like the Anne I know. Nothing like the woman I've allowed into our home.

"That's not Anne," I whisper.

"This *is* Anne Richards, an event planner in Knoxville." He stuffs the phone in his pocket and resumes pacing. "The woman you've been meeting with is someone else."

I shake my head, my thoughts bouncing between the picture of Anne on Coop's phone and the image of Anne in my mind. "I don't understand. Why would a woman pretend to be someone else?"

"You said she talked to you about her daughter. And she started acting weird once she knew I was here, right?"

I nod. "It's like she didn't want you to see her."

Coop closes his eyes and rubs his forehead. "Madison, I think I know who the woman was."

"Who?"

"Celia's mother."

"What? Why would Celia's mother want to pose as our wedding planner?"

He sighs. "I think she's trying to disrupt things. That's what she does."

"It doesn't make sense." I remember the antics this woman pulled in the wake of her daughter's death, but according to Coop, she's not harassed him in years. "After all this time, she can't still have it out for you."

"She thinks I killed her daughter. That's a hatred that never goes away."

I return to the window, hoping against hope 'Anne' will return and make sense of all this. "The way you described Celia's mother, she's unstable and erratic. Anne's never struck me as off. She's always been level-headed."

"Pretending to be another person isn't very stable."

"But why?" I'm crying now, hot tears rolling down my cheeks. I feel vulnerable and taken advantage of all at once.

"Can you think of any other person who would want to fool us?" He sits beside me, stretching his arm over my shoulders. "It must have been her. She vowed to make sure I'd never be happy. I just didn't think all these years later she'd keep her promise."

"I welcomed a complete stranger into our home." I lean over and cry into Coop's arms. "What was I thinking?"

"She wasn't a stranger to you. Mom gave you her information. Who knows what kind of tricks this woman pulled? She's clearly sick."

I've been deceived by more than just Anne; I've fooled myself. Again. I lowered my guard, and it backfired. I feel like I did the day I learned 'Chrissy's' story was nothing but a lie. Like I've been manipulated, yet somehow deserving of shame. Coming here was supposed to heal me from that embarrassment. Instead, this situation has further highlighted that my gut is not to be trusted.

"She said she booked a florist and band," I say, playing back every detail of my conversations with Anne. "Was that all bullshit?"

"We'll have to look into it." He sounds nervous, like this is the first in a series of disappointments he expects to face.

I walk into the dining room. The stack of invitations is gone. The only evidence of Anne's presence is a pen she's left behind. I walk into the kitchen, staring at the boxes on the counter. There's a different slice of cake inside each, which only adds to my confusion. The actions Anne must have taken to keep up this ruse!

"You can't blame yourself," he says, walking behind me and placing a hand on my shoulder. Those are the same words he used when I told him about the 'Chrissy' retraction, when I admitted I'd lost my job.

"That stupid bitch." I lift a slice from its box and throw it, missing the trashcan and splattering icing against the wall.

"Madison, what are you doing?" Coop asks, taking a step back.

"No telling what that psycho did. The food is probably poisoned." I take another slice and throw it too. I discard the desserts and curse and cry. Coop lets me. He sees that I'm ashamed and embarrassed, and he knows he has some fault in this. This is our life together. Our future will always be impacted by his past.

CHAPTER 33

Madison

I can't ignore the flutter of intimidation I feel every time we drive past the iron gates leading onto the Douglas family property. We are going to Josephine's house for Sunday brunch, her latest attempt at making us feel better. It's been three days since I learned the woman in our home claiming to be Anne was an imposter. Several questions linger, and the answers I have received are disappointing. Josephine immediately reached out to the real Anne Richards—something she's apologized profusely for not doing earlier—who confirmed no one in her company had anything to do with the Sharpe/ Douglas wedding.

We contacted the florist and the band and the baker 'Anne' alleged to have arranged. None had our wedding on the books; in fact, they were reserved with other engagements, so there's no chance of getting them. We lost precious time pretending. All the samples brought into our house were ploys, bait to keep me hooked. She probably got the cakes we were meant to sample from the Walmart bakery. The invitations we addressed are gone, likely already trashed. Not only did 'Anne' deceive me, she ruined our wedding in the process.

Josephine has gone to great lengths to ameliorate the situation. She's contacted friends, asking them to pull strings, but there's only so much that can be done for a wedding date fast approaching.

"I can't believe someone would go to such lengths to ruin your wedding," Regina says. Even she's outraged by this. I've figured out she likes being the antagonist in her family, and anyone who tries to usurp that role pisses her off.

"It doesn't make any sense," I say. Sitting on Josephine's back porch, staring at the lake in the distance. The sun is beginning to set, stretching its mirrored image across the still waters. It looks so peaceful here, yet all I feel inside is upheaval and uncertainty.

"I blame myself," Josephine says. "I should have been more involved. I should have contacted Anne myself."

I fear this event is setting a precedent for others moving forward. Josephine went against her nature in letting me organize the wedding on my own, and it turned into a complete failure. I don't want his family to think I'm incapable.

"We wanted to handle this," I say. "I was handling it. I didn't realize another person could be so deceptive."

"How could you know?" Josephine reaches over to pat my hand.

Regina lifts a heavy pot off the porch planks. There's a pack of cigarettes and a lighter underneath. She takes one.

"Darling, don't smoke," Josephine says. "It makes you look so trashy."

"They are your cigarettes," she tells her mother.

"Only in times of stress," Josephine says, looking over her shoulder.

Regina puffs a large plume of smoke in Josephine's direction. She turns to me and smirks. Witnessing my upset in the past few days has softened her, at least toward me.

Roman and Coop join us outside. Coop is carrying a cardboard box. He places it on the table and pulls out a sepia-tinted newspaper.

"What's that?" I ask.

"I've been trying to find a picture of her," he says, flipping through pages. "I want to be sure it's her."

"Who?" I ask.

"Celia's mother." He scans the newspaper. "She should be in one of these articles."

"Has anyone looked online?" Regina asks.

"She doesn't have any social media," Roman says. "To be honest, I figured she'd drunk herself to death ages ago."

"I already looked through anything I thought might have her photo," Josephine tells Coop. She looks at me. "Bless her heart, the woman wasn't an upstanding member of society. Very forgettable."

"This is the box with all the Celia articles," Coop says. "Surely there's a picture of her in here."

My body tenses as I rock back in the chair. It's strange Josephine would keep articles about such a traumatic incident—articles I can't even find online because they've been wiped clean.

"Unfortunately, that woman wasn't much of a mother." Josephine closes her eyes. "I think that's why she always had it out for Cooper. She needed someone to blame other than herself."

"If she'd spent more time caring for Celia when she was alive, maybe all this would have turned out differently," Regina says. Leaning against the porch banister, she flicks her cigarette butt toward the lake. It lands in a patch of weeds by the water.

"Here." Coop walks closer to me, holding the paper in his hands. "This is the best picture I've found."

The headline reads: *Whisper Falls Remembers Missing Teenager.* The picture appears to be taken at a vigil, as there's a large crowd standing in front of an altar of candles and flowers. The smaller picture is a close-up of a woman. She's covering her face with one hand, clinging to a teddy bear with the other. She's crying.

"Is that her?" Coop asks.

I stare at the picture, trying to see past the black and white pixilation. The woman's frame matches 'Anne', and they both have dark hair, but her jaw is the only visible part of her face. And the photo is thirteen years old.

"It could be her," I say, feeling all their eyes on me. "I'm not sure."

"I'll keep looking." Coop folds the paper and stuffs it back into the box. I wonder what other words and pictures are in that box. What other secrets.

"There's no point in driving yourself crazy. There's nothing we can do," I say.

"There's a lot we can do," Roman counters. "We can charge her with fraud, identity theft. If she deposited the check you gave her, that's even better."

"Let's just move on," I say, walking closer to the water. "This woman has already ruined enough."

"This is a setback." Coop stands behind me and rubs my arm. "We won't let her ruin the wedding."

"We have two months. The vendors I thought we booked are unavailable," I say.

"We can push back the date until spring. That will give us plenty of time to plan," says Coop.

"I don't want to push back the date because of her."

"Then don't." Regina walks closer, still smelling like tobacco. "You have a dress. You have a location. I'm doing the food. This woman didn't plan the whole wedding, just parts of it. We can find you a florist and entertainment."

"For once, my daughter is right," Josephine says. "It might inconvenience people to commit to something last-minute, but I can be persuasive."

At least her checkbook can be. They're right; the idea of having to book things months in advance and hire out every detail is a millennial concept. We're planning a party, and I can do that in the remaining weeks.

"I'm in if you are," Coop says, kissing the top of my head.

"I'm all in." I place my ear against his cheek, watching ripples dance in the lake.

CHAPTER 34

Helena

I think I left in time. I think. I got a quick glimpse of Cooper's profile as he stood in the foyer, but I snuck out the back door before he could see my face. After I went to such great lengths to throw Josephine off my trail, I can't believe Cooper arrived when he did. And right when I was on the verge of telling Madison everything!

I hadn't planned on exposing my true motives during our conversation, otherwise I wouldn't have wasted a week's worth of motel money on those gaudy invitations. Or visited two different bakeries ordering slices of cake. I did that because I hoped for a little more time with Madison. I'd planned to call her up later in the week and instruct her to meet me outside of the house. I'd have her alone without fear of being interrupted. And yet, hearing her pine over Cooper and how wonderful he was—I couldn't stand one more minute of it.

Madison must have enjoyed our visits more than I realized. The meal she provided proves that. If I'd had only another half hour, this entire mess would be over. Now the mess is multiplying. She's called six times since I left, but I'm too afraid to answer. My nerves are still rattled from my close encounter with Cooper.

It's now been four days since I darted out of the house without explanation; I make the decision to call Madison myself, hoping I can salvage the connection we've made. I'll tell her some emergency arose and I had no choice but to leave when I did. I know she'll have questions, but if I can only convince her to meet me one last time, I can finally finish this. Maybe it's not too late for her to know the truth.

"Anne?" she barks into the phone when she answers. Her voice still carries all the worry and concern she must have felt when I left.

"Madison, I must apologize—"

"I know you're not Anne Richards." This time when she speaks, her voice lacks emotion. She's severed the bonds I'd spent weeks trying to create.

"I… I don't know what you're talking about." I smile, alone in my motel room, an attempt to sound at ease. "Let me explain—"

"I don't know why you did this to me," she says, a discernible quiver in her voice, "but I never want to speak with you again."

She hangs up. For a moment, I hold the phone in my hands, hoping this is a mistake and Madison will call back. But she doesn't. I scream, throwing the phone against the yellowed walls. My anger consumes me now. All my plans had fallen into place effortlessly until this point. Until Cooper ruined everything. Again.

Maybe I was wrong. Maybe Cooper did see me and now everything has been revealed. What if they've pieced the rest of my story together? That means Cooper has had four days to get into Madison's head and fill her with his lies. There's no way I can make amends and convince her to meet me, if that's the case. I don't know how to rebound from this disaster.

All I know is I've made it this far. I'm not leaving Whisper Falls until Madison knows the truth. I'm not leaving until Cooper gets what he deserves.

CHAPTER 35

Madison

It's been a week since I learned Anne Richards isn't who she said she was. Coop is scheduled to attend a press awards dinner in Nashville tonight. It's a bad time for him to leave town, but I don't want to be the scared woman who begs him to stay. He needs to know I can handle myself, which is why I declined his offer to cancel his trip.

"It's only one night," he says, zipping his suitcase. It sounds like he's reassuring himself more than he is me. He clenches his jaw and lowers his eyes in defeat. "Are you sure you'll be okay?"

"I'll be fine. Roman and Regina are coming over for dinner."

"Good." This seems to relax him. He picks up the suitcase, and I follow him down the stairs. "I could always drive back tonight."

"You wouldn't get home until close to two a.m. There's no sense in you spending the whole day in the car."

"It would be worth it to know you're safe."

"That woman only called once. I don't think she'll try it again."

"I could reach out to Jimmy at the police station. It only takes one phone call to get him involved," Coop says, tightening his grip on the suitcase. "I want this woman to be punished for what she did to you."

I look away. "What she did wrecked our wedding, but there's no use in pursuing it. If she's still this disturbed by something that happened thirteen years ago, she's already being punished."

Something that happened. The woman's daughter died. I know grief doesn't have an expiration date, and it must be excruciating to think you know who's to blame. The facts remain: there's nothing connecting Coop to Celia's death, and if she knew the man I know, she'd see he's not capable of violence. Her sorrow may be warranted, but it doesn't give her permission to ruin Coop's life.

"What time are Roman and Regina coming over?" he asks, as I follow him to his car.

"Around eight. Regina is bringing food from Nectar. It should be an easy night all around."

"I hope so." Coop bends to give me a kiss. His lips linger longer than they should, signaling the fear he feels in leaving. "I love you."

I squeeze his neck, a cue that all will be fine. "I love you too."

I didn't think I'd have so much fun with Roman and Regina. Maybe it's because I'm tipsy. In the two hours they've been here, we've drained the pitcher of cocktails Roman insisted he prepare. The Stromboli Regina brought struggles to soak up our buzz, and we're all talkative and giggly. The unfortunate predicament with Celia's mother has brought us closer somehow. Maybe they feel sorry for me, or guilty because being part of the Douglas family has left me damaged.

They've shared a handful of stories about Coop's childhood, all embarrassing but harmless. After much pushing, I tell them about the early days of our relationship and what our lives were like in the city.

"We're just happy Coop is taking the plunge and getting hitched," Roman says. "It takes the pressure off us. I think Mom was afraid she'd never be a grandmother."

"That's not true," Regina chimes in. "You're just more likely to give her a grandchild before a daughter-in-law."

"Hush," Roman says, tossing back his drink.

"I mean, really," she continues. "It's a wonder you haven't had a kid yet. You've only slept with everyone between here and the tri-cities area."

I expect Roman to act bruised, instead he grins. It's not a positive description, but clearly he'll take it. "I don't see you burning up the dating scene either," he says to his sister. "You have plans of giving Mom grandchildren?"

"Only time will tell," she says. They exchange a doubtful look, sip their drinks in unison and laugh.

This is what siblings do, I've learned. They poke and fight, but they forgive and love. Regina especially. Her persistent rib-jabbing might as well be a hug. It's just her way of showing affection.

Another hour passes. We've skidded away from the topic of relationships and are back to discussing the pros and cons of this place we call home.

"There are a few things you need to know about Whisper Falls," Regina says, her words beginning to slur. "The town is quiet, but the people are loud."

I agree with her on this point. I always thought the city and its people were loud. Now I know people there are quieter than they appear. They stick to their huddle, their group. It only seems loud because there are so many groups. Whisper Falls is the opposite; everything is wide open. When people here talk, everyone hears.

"Don't listen to Regina," Roman says, taking on a slightly more serious tone. "She's a pessimist."

"I am not a pessimist," she says, making a poignant pause between each word. The statement is so untrue, even she laughs.

"You won't give this town a chance," Roman says.

"Me?" Regina stands unsteadily. "This town doesn't give me a chance! They don't take a chance on anyone unless they act like everyone else. There's no room for diversity or growth. This place—" She stops talking, suddenly frozen. She sprints to the downstairs bathroom and slams the door.

Roman and I can't help but laugh when, minutes later, there's the unmistakable cry of a person getting sick.

"This is a new one," Roman says.

"What?"

"Usually Regina is the one taking care of me when I've had one too many." He sips his beer, but he can't seem to shake his sister's comments from earlier. "She's always beating up on Whisper, and I get it—life here hasn't been the easiest for her. But Regina only focuses on what this town lacks. Whisper has some nice people. They might talk shit from time to time, but they're also on their knees praying when the bad times hit. Like when Dad died."

He pauses, reflecting on the words he's said and the life he's lived.

"It's definitely a tight-knit community," I say. It's odd to see the contrast between how Roman and Regina view their hometown. From what I can tell so far, I tend to side with Regina.

"There's good here," Roman continues. "We've got some of the best carpenters in the south. They might make a tenth of what your people in the city make, but they're a lot better at the job. People here care about things. They garden and they fish. I'm not trying to convince you to love Whisper Falls. I guess I'm just saying you and Cooper can be happy here, if you want to be."

I finish the rest of my wine, thinking about what he's said. "You two didn't have to come over here, you know."

"It felt like the right thing to do," he says, leaning into the headrest. "Coop would have done it for us."

"The three of you are very close."

"We might fight, but we'll always have each other's backs."

"I think most families are like that," I say. "The good ones, anyway."

"I worried we might have scared you off after your first few dinners with us." He laughs. "I know we take some getting used to."

"Maybe a little." We both laugh. "You've all really been there for me ever since the incident with Celia's mom. That means a lot."

"It's not fair what that woman's put him through over the years." He puts down his beer and crosses his arms. "She really did a number on him after Celia died, and Cooper didn't deserve any of it."

"That's been the hardest part to understand." I look at Roman, who has moved closer to me. He wants to hear my take. Tonight is the first time we've really talked. "Whenever I was around 'Anne', she never seemed spiteful. She never made it seem like she wanted to ruin the wedding or Coop. It's like she just wanted to get to know me."

"Maybe she picked up on the fact that you're new to Whisper Falls, new to this family. That was her way of isolating you."

"Oh." I think back to my interactions with 'Anne' with a renewed sting. She predicted my insecurities and used them to her advantage. It hurts more because her plan worked. Our appointments were the only time I felt I was making decisions as Madison Sharpe, not Madison soon-to-be Douglas. "Based on the way your family has described her, I didn't think she'd have the patience for that."

"To be honest, I thought the same thing." He opens another beer and takes a sip. "Every time I saw that woman, she was either crying or yelling. She was drunk a lot, too. Must have been her way of coping."

"It would be an unimaginable thing to live with. The thought someone murdered your daughter."

"Thing is, no matter what people told her about Celia's death being accidental, she refused to listen." He shakes his head, his brown curls falling over his forehead. "She had her version of what happened, and that was all that mattered. That's what made her dangerous."

"Coop wants to have her arrested for fraud, or whatever. I'm not sure it's worth the hassle."

"She's been in and out of Cooper's life for more than a decade now. He wants to make sure she won't do this type of thing again. You want to know the saddest part in all of this? None of this is about Celia. Her mother was barely around when she was alive. She didn't give a damn about her daughter until after she died."

That's another detail that doesn't make sense about the 'Anne' I knew. The one time she brought up her daughter's death, she didn't make Celia sound like a pawn in a game. She sounded like her whole heart had been ripped from within her. I felt her pain. Not once did I see a bitter woman desperate for revenge; I saw a grieving mother.

"Time does things to people, I guess."

Roman nods, but this time he doesn't smile. "Sure does."

CHAPTER 36

Madison

The bathroom door slams against the wall, startling us both. Regina stumbles into the living room with one of our new washcloths pressed to her forehead.

"Are you okay?" Roman asks her.

"I need to go home," she slurs.

He looks at me, then his sister. "I'd thought we'd stay a little longer. At least until Madison is ready for bed."

"No, please," I say. "I'll be fine."

"Are you sure?" he asks.

Regina sways in between us. "Of course she's sure. You're a big girl, aren't you, Maddy?" She lets out a painful laugh, then speaks sincerely. "Will you be okay?"

"Stop worrying about me," I insist. "I'll probably be asleep before you make it home."

Roman takes Regina's arm and swings it over his shoulders. She's only putting weight on one of her legs and humming a wobbly tune as they make their way to the car.

Roman buckles his sister into the passenger seat and shuts the door. "Promise you'll call if anything weird happens, okay?"

"I promise."

I walk inside the house and lock the doors. I'm always alone during the day, but there is a different aura at night. Each creak in this old house is a little louder, and the room feels hollow. I carry our dirty dishes into the kitchen and wash them off in the sink.

There's more drinking glasses than anything, and I laugh when I think of Regina being so drunk. She puts effort into her tough exterior; it slipped rather quickly after one too many drinks.

By the time I've finished washing, my fingertips are pruned. Without the water running, the house is eerily silent. I walk through the house blowing out candles. For a moment, I wish Regina or Roman had stayed, or that Coop hadn't left at all. That's just my tired, paranoid mind, I know. By morning, I'll feel better about things and braver for having gotten through the night.

Just as I'm about to walk upstairs, I notice a phone sitting on the coffee table. It's locked, but I know it's Regina's because the home screen is a picture of Nectar. Man, she was drunk. She didn't even remember to take her phone.

There's a knock at the front door. I open it, assuming Roman has returned for the phone, but when I swing open the door, no one is outside. All I hear is the hushed sound of wind rustling leaves.

"Hello?" I call out.

"Madison."

It's her. The woman who claimed to be Anne Richards. She's standing to the left of the front door, as though she knocked and lost her nerve. Like she was about to run away again.

"I'm calling the police." I try to close the door, but she moves closer, stopping me.

"Madison, please. Just hear what I have to say."

"I don't care what you have to say." I push her scrawny arms away from me. "My brother-in-law will be back soon. You need to go."

"I watched them pull onto the main road and waited," she says, dropping her hands by her sides. "They're not coming back."

I weigh my options, whether what she's said is true or not. Even if I were to call the police, it would be another twenty minutes before they arrived. I'm alone with this woman, surrounded by nothing but darkness and barren fields. Fear rises, beckoning me to react, but forcing me to stand still.

"I know who you really are," I say, as hatefully as I can.

"Please, just listen," she says, calmly. There's not an ounce of urgency in her voice. She's the 'Anne' I remember. Calmed and poised and sincere. "You couldn't possibly know who I am."

"You're Celia's mother! The Douglases have told me everything you've done to try and hurt Coop over the years, and now you're trying to hurt me!" I shout. Anger pours out of me. Although this woman looks like she can be trusted, I know she's a fraud.

"This isn't about that—"

"I don't care what you say." I cut her off before she can finish. "I know Coop did not kill Celia."

She looks down, like she's already lost the battle. Without moving, she takes a deep breath. Then she speaks:

"I know everything about Celia Gray. Her height. Her weight. Even her zodiac sign. I know how long her body was allegedly in that water before the police fished her out. I have her whole file memorized. But she's not my daughter." She looks up, a gleam in her eyes. "My daughter's name was Laura Price, and Cooper Douglas killed her."

CHAPTER 37

Helena

It feels like forever since I've said her name. Laura. My beautiful, sweet Laura. Speaking of her brings her back, and for a moment, it's like she's here with me, giving me the strength to continue.

Madison stands in the doorway, one hand on the knob, but both feet are outside. She's staring at me, as if she misunderstood what I said. After several seconds, she speaks.

"Who is Laura Price?"

"She's my daughter," I say, letting out a controlled breath. I move forward, and she doesn't tremble, which is a good sign. "I'm Helena Price. I'm sorry I couldn't tell you that earlier."

Madison pinches the bridge of her nose and shuts her eyes. "I don't understand. Why are you… how are you…"

"All I ask is that you hear me out. I'll tell you everything, then if you want me to walk out of your life, I will."

She looks down, like she can't trust her own judgment in this bizarre moment. "My fiancé… Coop is—"

"Cooper is out of the house. That's why I waited until tonight." After some digging, I found out he was expected to attend a press function in Nashville tonight. I'd have made my move earlier, but his siblings stayed later than I expected. I waited for them to leave so I could have Madison all to myself.

"I don't even know you," she says, dropping her hands by her sides. She's struggling over what to do. Over whom to trust.

"You're following us around. And throwing out names I've never even heard before."

"Let me in," I say, gently. "I'll tell you anything you want to know."

Madison looks me up and down, assessing the potential threat. My hands are bare, and only a small handbag hangs from my shoulder. She walks inside, holding the door open for me to follow. She still won't look at me, like she's an opponent defeated in a match. The point of this has never been to beat her. I'm trying to beat Cooper, but in order to do that, Madison needs to know things. Things that will hurt.

We walk into the living room. She pulls her feet onto the sofa and holds a pillow between her knees and chest. "Who is Laura?"

I clear my throat and smile. Despite the intensity of this moment, I finally get to talk about her again. That makes me happy. "She's my daughter. We lived in South Carolina, a good distance from here. She attended college in Tennessee. The same one as Cooper."

"And that's where they met?"

"Yes. They started dating during their sophomore year. She told me a lot about him. He made her so happy." I stop. I always struggle juggling my happy memories of Laura against the painful reality that Cooper gave her those elated feelings. "As I said, I didn't live close enough to visit often. I never met him when they were together."

"How long did they date?" She's trying to compare every detail I provide against her own knowledge of events. Searching, hoping for an inconsistency.

"Several months. She was in love, there's no doubt about that. At the beginning of the year, she was very homesick. When she met Cooper, her whole outlook changed; I'd never heard her more excited. We'd talk on the phone every day, and she'd share about their studies and their dates. Their campus wasn't far from here, so she was no stranger to Whisper Falls. His family had the pleasure of meeting her, too." I tighten my jaw, wishing desperately the story could end here with my daughter's happiness, but I must continue. "The last time we spoke, she sounded different. Upset. She said she'd heard a rumor. Something bad."

"What was it?" she asks, jumping in.

"I don't know. We got off the phone just as Cooper arrived at her apartment. She promised to call back that next day, but never did. No one had contact with her after that night. She was just gone. I did everything I could to find her. I visited the campus and handed out flyers. Social media wasn't what it is today, but several of her friends reached out to help. She had so many friends, my Laura." I smile briefly, then my stare hardens. "Do you know who never once offered assistance?"

"Cooper." His name leaves her lips in a whisper. She's hesitant to say anything else because she's unsure about what she knows. That helps.

"The first time I met him was at a vigil her friends organized. He didn't know who I was, and when I told him, he retreated like he'd seen a ghost. Refused to speak with me. I told the police he was the last person to see her. He cooperated with them, but he actively avoided me. Who does that to the mother of their missing girlfriend?"

"I don't know." She cracks her knuckles and looks away. She's aware something doesn't add up. "What did the police say?"

I hadn't wanted to tell her this part; I know it won't help my case, but I promised Madison the truth. All of it. "The police had this ridiculous theory she took off to some music festival and something happened to her there. But they didn't know my Laura. All college kids are a tad rambunctious, but she would never leave the state without telling me. We were close."

She'd badgered me for weeks about that festival, but I'd refused to give her permission to go. Imagine my surprise when the police showed me a receipt of her ticket purchase. They believed that was proof she'd left town, that something had happened to her while she was gone. But I didn't believe that. Laura would never leave without telling me.

"So the police never found her?"

"No." I bite my lip and look away again. "She's never been found. She's one of the thousands of people who disappear off the face of this grand earth, never to be seen again. No one knows what officially happened, but I do. I know Cooper was involved."

"But how could you know that? This music festival—"

"The music festival theory wasn't taken seriously until after the Douglas family hired a lawyer to represent Cooper," I cut in. I'm trying to keep her focused. I don't want her to start doubting me. "All efforts to find Laura ended after that."

"It's been, what, over ten years since anyone has heard from her?"

"Eleven years and some odd months." I know down to the day how long it's been since I last saw my girl, but I don't want her to think I'm obsessed. "She never would have cut off contact willingly. We were best friends."

"Why didn't she tell you what she'd found out about Coop?"

"We were best friends, but I'm still her mother. Girls at that age—at any age—don't want to worry their parents unnecessarily. I believe she had every intention of telling me her problems, but Cooper didn't give her the chance."

Madison shakes her head. "What could she have possibly uncovered that made him want to kill her?" Clearly she doesn't like the idea of her fiancé being a murderer, but that's exactly what he is.

"I wondered that for a long time. I kept going over it and over it again in my mind. Just like I kept wondering why Cooper, her wonderful boyfriend, didn't want to assist in discovering her whereabouts. Laura had been missing for two months when I hired a private investigator to examine her disappearance—and him. That's when I found out about Celia Gray."

Madison leans deeper into the couch, pulling the pillow tighter to her legs. Finally, she's making connections. She's piecing together the same image of Cooper I made years ago. "You think she found out that Celia had died?"

"It makes perfect sense. It explains why her enthusiasm about Cooper changed so suddenly. And it explains why she wouldn't have wanted to tell me about it. She didn't want me to worry." I wish every moment of my life she'd told me what she learned that day. I wish she'd stayed on the phone with me instead of turning her attention to him. I could have talked her through her heartbreak. I could have protected her. I feel the familiar wave of grief and regret rising and swallow hard to keep it down.

"Wouldn't she have already known about that?" Madison jerks her head at me, like she wants to prove me wrong. "If they were as serious as you say, surely he would have brought up the fact his last girlfriend died."

"Did Cooper tell you that his college girlfriend went missing?"

She hugs the pillow tighter and looks away. She whispers a defeated, "No."

That's what I've been waiting to hear. That Cooper Douglas hasn't changed his spots. He still has secrets, and if it makes me question his morals, surely Madison is thinking the same thing.

"You can imagine my shock to find out not one, but two girls in Cooper's past had died." I clear my throat and steady my hands, which are starting to shake. "Laura's body has never been found, but if she were alive, she would have contacted me by now. I know she's gone."

Madison is nibbling at her nails from the anxiety. I've never seen her do that before. What I'm saying is working. She's thinking. Really thinking about what I've said and what it means about the man she's about to marry.

Then the phone rings.

CHAPTER 38

Madison

My cell phone's happy chirping scares me. I jump, then look at its lighted screen on the coffee table. Helena hasn't changed position, but she looks worried now. I lean forward and grab the phone.

"Who is it?" she asks.

"It's Roman." My voice doesn't sound like my own. I'm not sure what's mine anymore. Everything Anne—Helena—just told me has my mind jumbled.

"Madison, please listen to what I have to say," Helena says, moving slightly in her seat. She knows it's awfully late to be receiving a phone call.

I hold up my finger to silence her before answering the call. "Hello."

"Madison, it's Roman. You okay?"

"I'm fine." Does he have a reason to think something is wrong? I clear my throat, hoping he won't pick up on my nervousness.

"I finally got Regina into the house. She can't find her phone. You seen it at your place?"

"Yes, I found it when I was cleaning." I turn and look toward the bookcase, where I left it. "Does she need it?"

"Nah, she'll be out until morning. I don't mind running by to get it, though."

Across the room, Helena is watching me intently. She must be wondering why he's calling. She must be afraid I'll tell him the person he wanted to protect me against is inside my house.

"No need for that," I say, turning away from Helena so she can no longer see my face. "I'm almost asleep as it is. She can stop by in the morning."

"Everything else okay with you?" There's a protective edge in his words.

I smile, hoping that will make the words flow easier. "Nothing going on here. Thanks for stopping by tonight."

"No problem. I'll leave you alone." He hangs up.

Slowly, I lower the phone from my ear. I'm not sure if I made the best decision in telling Roman to stay put, but I want to continue my conversation. A week ago, this woman frightened me, but that's back when I thought she was Anne, then Celia's mother. Now I know she's someone else entirely, and she's reaching out on behalf of her daughter who I never knew existed. The person she's convinced Coop killed.

I place the phone back on the table. I look at Helena. She's at ease again, knowing I ended the conversation with Roman. I'm not sure where to resume ours.

"When do you expect Cooper to return?" she asks.

"In the morning."

"That should give you enough time to pack some things."

"Pack things?"

She scoots to the edge of her seat. "Madison, you don't need to be here. It's not safe."

The world as I knew it is unsafe now; if what Helena says is true, my whole life is nothing more than a fabrication. The person I was an hour ago seems so different from the person I am in this moment. I don't know how to digest everything Helena's told me. It doesn't line up with the person Coop is. The person I love.

"I'm not leaving Coop," I say, firmly. "Not until I've had a chance to speak with him."

Helena stands, leaving her bag on the chair. She walks closer, but not in a threatening way. More like a mother who is afraid for her child. "You can't confront him about this, Madison. I'll never know for sure, but I believe that's what got Laura killed. She asked him about Celia, and he lashed out."

I close my eyes. Looking at Helena is painful. Her grief is obvious, and I pity her. Still, in the back of my mind, I wonder if this woman is delusional. She might not be Celia's mother, the woman the Douglas family has warned me about, but the same threat exists. Her allegations come from a place of hurt.

"I don't understand. I've known about Celia Gray for a long time. Since before he proposed. He told me because he wanted me to know." Although, an inner voice whispers, he was less forthcoming about the rumors connecting him to her death. I shake those thoughts away. "Why would he hurt Laura over information he so readily provided?"

"I don't know." Helena returns to her seat and crosses her legs. She suddenly seems angry, as though she senses she's losing this battle. "I never had the opportunity to ask."

"I'm sorry about what happened to your daughter. I can't even imagine…" The appropriate words don't exist. I can't relate to this woman's pain; perhaps it's the endurance of that pain that has led her to target Coop in the first place. "You have to understand. The man I know… I can't see him harming anyone. He's kind and loving. I wouldn't be marrying him otherwise."

"Laura said those same things. Then she was gone."

"But you have no proof Coop did anything." I stand and pace the narrow tract of space in front of the fireplace. "All you're able to tell me is that they dated, and that he didn't act appropriately in the weeks following her disappearance. As if there is a proper way to act. He was twenty. Practically a child!" I'm rambling now. Helena has an advantage in that she's had years to prepare for this conversation; I'm laboring to process everything I've been told.

"The odds of anyone having two significant others die or disappear under suspicious circumstances is tremendous. You must see that."

"I see it. It's concerning, but it doesn't make me think the man I love is capable of murder. He told me everything about Celia. What guilty man would do that?"

"He didn't tell you about Laura."

That's the detail that bothers me more than anything. Coop framed the incident with Celia as a tragedy he was wrapped into because of circumstance. More than that, he'd recounted all his previous relationships to me at one point or another. I recall him mentioning an ex-girlfriend named Laura, and yet he never told me she'd gone missing. The fact he didn't tell me is unsettling.

Still, what Helena is asking me to do is unthinkable. I can't believe a stranger's story over my fiancé's—a stranger who has already spent weeks lying to me. As disturbing as this conversation has been, it's not enough to make me abandon my faith in Coop. He deserves a chance to tell me what happened. And I'm craving the opportunity to ask.

"Do you have a picture of her?"

Helena rummages through her bag. She stands and joins me by the fireplace. She's beaming now, with the pride of a grandmother sharing photos of her grandchildren. Of course, Helena will never have that opportunity. Her only daughter is gone.

"She was so beautiful," she says, handing over the picture. "You know, I really was an event consultant years ago. That's why I thought it was a natural way to grow close to you. Laura was like an honorary flower girl at every event I hosted. The sweetest little thing."

My eyes fill with tears when I realize I've seen this girl before. I've seen this exact picture. That photo I'd found stuffed in the box of old newspapers was Laura. I've often wondered who she was, this girl who captured Coop's heart in such a way he felt the need to carry her photograph. Now I know. She's Laura.

"You don't need to stay here, Madison." Helena recognizes my fragile emotions and is hoping she can make one last plea for me to leave.

I hand back the picture. "She is very beautiful. I'm so very sorry."

"He's dangerous," she says, taking a step closer.

"He's my fiancé. I deserve the chance to find out if that's true, and I can't do it in the middle of the night."

Helena slumps back to her chair and rummages through her bag. She takes out a pen and scribbles something on the back of a receipt. She hands me the paper.

"This is my new number. I'm staying in Whisper Falls." She opens then shuts her mouth, surely wondering how much she can trust me. "Call if you need me. Please."

I take the paper, balling my hand into a fist. I follow her to the door, and she doesn't say anything else before entering her car. There is nothing left to say. The only person I need to talk to now is Coop.

CHAPTER 39

Madison

It's near 2 a.m. The wave of sleepiness I felt before Helena's visit has disappeared. Now I'm fully awake, my adrenaline making me desperate. How I wish Coop was here this instant! I want to attack him with questions, unleash my thoughts and fears. I need his deep voice to tell me that Helena Price is a sad, deranged individual. That this is all an unfortunate misunderstanding.

In my gut, I know all that can't be true. As with any story, bits and pieces have accuracy. I realize these hours I have with Coop out of the house are a gift. They give me time to think. They give me time to control myself and decide how I should move forward. Like Helena did with me in the weeks she posed as Anne, I must wait for the right moment. I need to think like a journalist, not his fiancée, and follow the facts.

I thunder upstairs and do something I haven't done since Coop first moved into my apartment, something I'd promised myself to never do again. I sling open our closet and start rummaging through every box, scanning every shelf and upturning every item. There must be something here. Some token from his past that can either validate or dismiss Helena's story. Coop isn't a hoarder, which makes it difficult. He doesn't keep yearbooks and pictures. Everything's digital now. The only sentimental items I find are in a box under his shoe rack, and they all relate to me: a ticket stub from the first baseball game we attended, his key to my old apartment and the empty box he used to store my engagement ring. That jewel twinkles from my finger but feels heavier now.

I haven't found anything related to the life he had before me. Unfortunately, he took his laptop with him to Nashville, so I have no chance of sorting through it. I know the position of every item in this house because I'm the one who unpacked. Now I'm losing my mind trying to find all these secrets some woman I barely know claims my fiancé is hiding. I want to collapse from the stress of it all.

The only other place Coop might store belongings would be the garage. He had several boxes he left there, and I didn't touch them. I storm outside and wait as the door opens, pulling on the dangling overhead light once inside. There's not much here. Half of the boxes are mine, seasonal décor and clothing.

Finally, I reach a stack of boxes I haven't seen. The first box is filled with items from his old cubicle back in the city. I flip through his address book and desk calendar but find nothing of interest. The second box contains old copies of the *Gazette*, probably the same newspapers I found the last time I decided to go snooping. Unlike last time, there's no pictures. That's a good sign. Maybe in the process of moving he found that same picture and tossed it. Maybe Laura was some girl he went on a few dates with and he has no sentimentality toward her. Maybe Helena Price is a despairing person grasping for any excuse to make her daughter seem real again.

The final box is a time capsule of his college years. There are a few textbooks, and several spiral-bound notebooks with illegible scribbles. I flip through the pages; there's not enough time in the week to read each line. Something falls loose and lands face down on the cement floor. I bend down and turn it over. Laura Price's face smiles back at me. I can't breathe. I can't cry. All I can do is look at this picture of Helena's missing daughter. I flip to another page and find a second picture tucked into the crease. This one has Coop in it, too. His arms are wrapped around Laura as they stand in front of a brick wall.

I hold the notebook, letting the pages dangle, and give it a good shake. Pictures fall to the floor, raining down around me. I grab the other notebooks and do the same. Tucked between every fifty pages or so is another picture of Laura. They float down to the ground until there's two dozen photos of her—some with Coop, some without—staring at me, asking for answers. Answers I can't provide.

CHAPTER 40

Helena

I've done it. I've told Madison what she needs to hear, even if she's not yet ready to act on the information. It's easy for an outsider to look at her situation with contempt and cynicism. *He's a murderer! Get the hell out of there!* I must admit, that's been my reaction more than once. It's what I wish Laura had done.

However, I realize my urgency stems from knowledge I've carried for more than a decade. Madison knows Cooper in a way I never will. She's not going to turn her back on the man she loves so suddenly, especially when I can't give her much in the form of proof. My only hope is she won't make the same mistake Laura did. I don't want her to end up the same way.

At least she's considering what I told her. Madison's a smart girl. Laura was smart too, but younger. If only she'd told me her concerns about Cooper without confronting him. But no, she was trying so hard to be mature. She attempted to tackle issues like an adult, never realizing adults enlist help all the time. Adults still turn to their mothers in times of crisis. Madison can't do that. She doesn't have a mother, but she has me. Even if she rejects my help, I'll be here for her. I know what is best. Thank goodness I made the choice to get involved. Because now I'm no longer defending my daughter's past, but Madison's future, too.

CHAPTER 41

June 16, 2006

Celia was burning from the inside out. She'd never felt such rage, such desire to strike back. Worse, she'd never felt so embarrassed. It didn't matter what barb she slung next, in this moment Regina Douglas was untouchable, and Celia wasn't used to being the one who was touched.

"I'm not sure what's more ridiculous," Celia said, after several awkward seconds. "Your accusation, or the fact you think Cooper would actually believe you."

"You're a nasty person, Celia. Maybe if you were nicer, I'd feel sorry for you." Regina threw her book against the dock, which made a loud smack as it hit the wood. "You should leave."

"I don't have my car." The words came out unintentionally, making Celia feel even more inadequate than she already did.

"Then fucking walk!" Regina stomped up the hill.

Celia started breathing fast and heavy. To the left of the dock, Regina's book had landed beside a huge boulder with a gilded plaque bolted into it. The plaque read: *The Douglas Family. Whisper Falls Lake*. Underneath the words, there were the painted handprints of each family member. Seeing this emblem of unity added salt to her wounds. Celia grabbed the book and dropped it into the water, smirking as she watched it sink.

She couldn't believe Regina freaking Douglas just got the best of her. At least no one was around to see. Still, Regina knew her secret, and that left Celia exposed. She sat on the dock and started

crying. It was like everything had hit her in one hour. She blamed
her phone conversation from earlier. Celia always got a little teary-
eyed when she spoke with her mother. It was the only time Celia
felt like a little girl instead of Queen Bee.

She was about to leave when she heard a motor rumbling. She
blocked the sun with her hand and squinted at the horizon. As
the boat got closer, it slowed, preparing to dock. She could spot
Roman's toothy grin before he killed the engine.

"Celia?" He waved both hands wide in the air. "I didn't think
I'd see you here."

"This is a pleasant surprise then." She didn't want him to see
she'd been crying, but it was too late.

"What's the matter?" He hopped off the boat and marched down
the wooden planks to where she sat. "Did Cooper leave you here?"

She nodded, grabbing his calloused hand to help her stand.
Roman was as handsome as his younger brother, but his features
were darker, like the rest of the Douglas clan. His hair was cut short
and a layer of stubble covered his chin and cheeks.

"Come here." He wrapped her in his arms, looking across the
yard to make sure they were alone. "Talk to me."

"There's a lot on my mind." Everyone flashed in front of her:
her mother and Cooper and Regina.

"Let's take a ride. We can watch the sunset over the water."

Roman's eagerness tended to turn Celia's stomach, but the
truth was, she had nothing better to do. Cooper had no interest
in talking to her, and she was too unnerved to attend the bonfire.
If she returned to her aunt's house, she'd spend the night bickering
with her cousins over the TV remote. She pushed a strand of hair
behind her ear and smiled. Taking Roman's hand, she followed
him to the boat.

He waited until they were in the center of the lake to pick up
speed. The wind blew Celia's hair, slicing the heat from her skin.
She sucked in several deep breaths until she felt rejuvenated. They

kept riding for several minutes before Roman stalled the boat. They sat together, his arm over her shoulders, watching as the sun sank behind the mountains.

"What happened?" he asked.

She didn't want to go through it all, so she told him the worst part. "Regina knows about us."

"What?" He spun his head, searching Celia's features for a reaction. "There's no way."

"I don't know how, but she does." She thought back to the dock, how humiliated she'd felt. "I could have snatched that black mop off her head."

Roman's posture stiffened. "Don't say that. She's still my sister."

Celia rarely revealed her distaste for Regina around Roman. Cooper didn't like her catty comments toward his sister, but Roman wouldn't stand it. He was much more loyal in that respect.

"Now I'm all worried she'll tell Cooper about us." She leaned her head on his shoulder. "He's been paranoid ever since he found your shirt in my car. He thinks I'm cheating on him with Steven Burns."

Roman laughed, kissing Celia's forehead. "Maybe it's a good thing. I think it's about time we tell him the truth."

"Are you crazy? Why would we do that?"

Celia and Roman had different versions of the truth. Celia's fling with Roman started out as a game. She'd noticed the stares he'd shot across the dinner table. One night, after a fight with Cooper, she surrendered to temptation. She was attracted to Roman for all the ways he differed from his brother. He was charismatic and confident and fun, but he lacked the potential Cooper possessed. Roman was a wild card. He'd never provide the solid future she hoped Cooper might. In her mind, her trysts with Roman were nothing more than stolen moments when no one else was watching.

Now Regina had seen too much. All Celia could think about was how this decision had blown up in her face. Most of the girls in Whisper would kill to have one of the Douglas boys; she had them both wrapped around her finger, tangling up the world she was used to controlling.

Roman kneeled in front of Celia, holding her hands in his. "I'm crazy about you. I know Cooper will forgive us. He's still a kid. Once he understands what we have together, he'll move on."

Celia blushed. Poor Roman was the one misunderstanding. All day she'd been sorting out which of the esteemed Douglas boys would be the better catch. She might not know what the future held with Cooper, but a life with Roman was far too predictable. He'd treat her like a queen for a few years, then he'd get bored. He'd either develop a drinking problem or find a mistress. That's what all the bad boys in Whisper ended up doing eventually. Roman was too feral to commit to anything long-term, even her.

She leaned forward and gave him a forceful kiss on the lips. "It's getting late. Take me back?"

She couldn't wait to be away from Roman, but she was afraid to walk alone in the dark. She needed him to give her a ride back to her car, and then she could finally be rid of the Douglas family, at least for the night.

CHAPTER 42

Madison

My alarm goes off at nine. Within the hour, Coop will be home. After finding the pictures, I stayed up researching Laura Price's disappearance on the internet. I couldn't find much, but I think my brain was too scrambled to evaluate anything properly. I'm not sure how long I slept after that. Maybe an hour, maybe two.

I check my phone. Coop sent a text when he got on the road. Everything is according to schedule. The schedule we had before I knew of Laura Price's existence. Now I'm not sure about anything, and I won't feel better until I've talked to him. I brush my teeth and wash my face. These things I do to feel human, to feel capable of handling what's next. I arrange Laura's pictures on the bed and sit in the leather armchair by our window. I wait.

"Madison?" Coop calls from downstairs, making my stomach flip. The front door slams. I sit in silence, waiting for him to find me.

I've had enough time to calm myself and go over what I want to say. It's like I've uncovered he's having an affair and I'm confronting him about it, but this is worse.

He walks into the bedroom and drops his bag on the floor. "Madison?" The smile on his face drops quickly; my silence must signal to him something is wrong. "Are you okay?"

"We need to talk," I say, my knees curled in front of me for protection.

"What's wrong?"

I nod toward the bed.

He takes a step forward and looks. When he sees the pictures scattered atop our comforter, he freezes. He doesn't look shocked or angry. If anything, he's sad. He picks up the photo closest to the edge and holds it between his fingers.

"Who is she?" I ask.

"Why are you going through my things?" he asks, calmly.

"Tell me who she is, Coop!"

"Laura," he murmurs. He sits on the bed, and a collection of photos slide closer toward him. "We dated in college."

"Why haven't you told me about her?"

"I have. Here and there. When we've talked about our past relationships."

"Why do you have all these pictures hidden in a bunch of old notebooks?"

"I don't know." Finally, he puts the picture down, but he won't look at me.

"Come on, Coop. You're not sentimental. I didn't find pictures of anyone else, but over twenty of this girl."

"I'm sorry. Okay?" He gets up and walks toward me, his face scrunched. "She's an old girlfriend. These pictures don't have anything to do with my feelings for you."

"I'm not jealous," I say, flicking his hand away when he tries to touch me.

"Then what is this?" He holds out his hands, trying to decide what exactly it is I'm upset about.

He's rejected the opportunity I gave him to share the full story behind his connection to Laura. Instead of telling me about her disappearance, he assumes I'm insecure. He's already failing this test. I bite my lip and look out the window.

"The woman posing as Anne Richards wasn't Celia's mother. She was Laura's mother." I look back at him. "Her name is Helena."

I wait for him to say something, but he doesn't. He returns to the bed and sits, resting his head in his hands.

"Helena told me you dated Laura in college. That you were dating her at the time she went missing," I say. "Why wouldn't you tell me about her?"

"It's been so long," he says. "I didn't want to upset you."

"You told me about Celia. That didn't scare me away."

"I've had one girlfriend die and another go missing," he says, his tone biting. "It's not exactly great first date material."

"We're well beyond a first date," I say, placing my feet on the carpet and leaning forward. "I'm your fiancée. When were you going to feel comfortable telling me?"

"I don't know." He exhales and stares at the ceiling, then me. "I don't like talking about either of them, but I knew if we were going to build a life together here, you'd have to know about Celia."

"Well, now I want to know about Laura," I say, holding eye contact. "Tell me everything."

He cracks his fingers and stares ahead. "We dated during our sophomore year. We'd been together maybe six months when she disappeared. She was supposed to go to some music festival and wanted me to go with her. I didn't, and she was never seen again."

Helena had mentioned a music festival. At least that lines up, but I need more. I need to believe Coop is telling me the whole truth. "And that's it? She went to some festival and was never heard from again?"

"I don't know." He stands and paces between the bed and the bathroom. "I spent a good chunk of my college years trying to find out. My family hired private investigators. We tried to track her down. She was just… gone."

"Did you cooperate with the police?"

"Of course. She was my girlfriend. She… she was the first girl I really loved, you know? Not like what we have, but I cared about her. I couldn't stand the idea of her being in danger." His cheeks are red and he's on the verge of crying. Coop never gets emotional, and yet this conversation is bringing it out of him.

"Why wouldn't you tell me about her? If she was this important to you, why wouldn't you mention her?"

"Because at some point, I had to let go. It was driving me crazy. Thinking about her. Where she was. Where she might have ended up. I had to move on with my life." He takes a deep breath and bites his fist. "I like to think she just walked away from me and everything. That she's out there happy, living her life somewhere."

"Is that what you think happened? That she just walked away?"

He stops walking and stands with his arms crossed. "No. I think some monster scooped her up from the music festival. Or maybe grabbed her from a gas station she visited on the way there. Maybe she had car trouble, and someone took her then. Or maybe she was hit by a car and someone panicked, got rid of her body." His eyes are cold. "Trust me, Madison. Any sick scenario you can imagine happening, I've thought of it. I simply *prefer* to think she walked away from her life. That she's alive and happy."

It's hard to see Coop grieve like this, to hear the unlocked possibilities that have tortured him over the years. I can't imagine what that must be like. I don't know what I'd do if one day Coop, the person I loved, failed to come home and I was never given a reason why. But he could have told me about this, just like he'd told me about every other major event in his life. Celia's death. His father's death. His love/hate relationship with this stupid town. Why hide Laura?

"You should have told me about her. We can overcome anything together, but only if you let me in."

"I didn't tell you because I didn't want you to look at me the way you're looking at me now!" he shouts, stretching his arms in front of his body. "You think I had something to do with her disappearance."

"I didn't say that." Not with words, at least. But this entire confrontation has been geared toward finding out if Helena's suspicions about Coop are true. I can't be sure. Because while I love the man standing in front of me, I don't know the Cooper Douglas who once dated Laura Price. He didn't give me that chance.

"It's like I'm cursed. First Celia died. I thought I'd found happiness again with Laura, then she went away, too." He's crying now, not even attempting to shield his tears. "I just wanted the past to stay in the past."

I understand that, wanting to walk away. It's how I felt in Atlanta when my 'Chrissy' story was exposed as a lie. Or how I felt here when I learned people still believed my fiancé was responsible for Celia's death. I'm about to attach my life to this person and all his prior indiscretions. Be his partner. Bear his children. I need to know everything I'm getting into, the good and the bad.

"I shouldn't have found out about this from Laura's mother. You should have told me."

"I'm sorry for that," he says, walking toward me. "I should have been upfront from the beginning, but it's been so long since I thought about her. And I've not seen Helena in years."

I scan the collection of pictures on the bed, finding it hard to believe he no longer thinks about Laura. I look at him and pull my legs closer to my chest. "Helena didn't just tell me Laura went missing. She thinks you had something to do with it. She thinks you killed her."

He rubs both sides of his face with his hands. "I know she thinks that. She's no different from Celia's mother. She's grasping at straws, trying to find someone to blame. Any mother would be desperate for answers, and they think it must be the boyfriend, right?"

I look away. Most people would blame the significant other, especially if there's a pattern. That's what Helena sees, and I see it, too. "There's nothing else you can tell me? Nothing else I need to know?"

"I never thought Helena would go to such lengths to try and destroy me. She was persistent in the years following Laura's disappearance, then she just went away."

"She didn't go away! She's inserted herself into our lives, and now I'm forced to defend my fiancé, not about one woman, but two!"

I'm angry with Coop and Helena and everyone involved in this situation. I deserved all this information before I uprooted my life.

"I'm sorry, Madison. I'm sorry for what you must endure by being with me. But I love you. I love you more than anyone I've ever met." Coop kneels in front of me. I try to wrestle away, but he won't let me. He grabs my hands and holds them. "I hate myself for putting you through this, but you have to believe me. I didn't harm Celia, and I don't know anything about Laura. I love you, Madison. I'll do anything to prove it."

From downstairs, we hear banging on the front door. Coop stands quickly and looks out the window.

"Who is it?" I ask, afraid Helena has returned to confront Coop herself.

"Regina," he says, annoyed. "She can wait."

"No." I stand, walking away from him and to the packed bag I'd hidden in the closet.

"What are you doing?"

"I'm getting out of here."

"You can't do that, Madison. You can't leave."

"I need time to process everything. Give me that." I hold my hands in front of my body, trying to keep my distance. Downstairs, the banging continues. "She left her phone here last night. She's not leaving until she gets it."

Coop clenches his fists. "Just wait," he tells me, then marches downstairs.

When he's gone, I slide the knife I'd hidden under my chair into my bag. I'd sat on it during the entirety of our conversation, just in case. Then I follow him.

"Morning, sunshine," Regina says, clearly not having picked up on the mood between us. Or maybe she has and is just glorying in it.

"Madison, don't leave," Coop says, grabbing my arm. I pull away from him and get into my car. As I back away, Coop and Regina stare, both wondering what I'll do next.

CHAPTER 43

Madison

I'm not sure where to go. All my connections in Whisper Falls are through Coop. I drive, following the signs to I-40, then eventually Knoxville. People in Whisper always refer to it as 'the city'. It's not my city, but that's okay. I just need different scenery, so I can think.

An hour seems to have passed in twenty minutes. My brain has been preoccupied, replaying every syllable of my conversations with both Coop and Helena. I pull off the interstate, following the rows of cars in front of me. I've driven past four red lights when I spot a familiar restaurant chain and park. I request a seat on the patio and order a drink. Sorting this situation on my own hasn't produced results. I need someone else's thoughts, and the only person I can trust is Beth.

"You miss the hustle and bustle of the city?" she asks when she answers my phone call.

The sound of her voice makes me burst into tears. "More than anything."

"Madison, what's wrong?"

"You remember what Coop told me about his ex-girlfriend who died? Celia?"

I tell her everything. How the people in my new hometown act as though Coop is responsible for Celia's death. How Helena deceived me for weeks in an attempt to turn me against him. That part of what she'd done worked because I no longer trust him. I tell her about the pictures I found and our angry confrontation.

When I finish, I'm out of tears and Beth is something she never is: speechless.

"What do you think I should do?"

"Honestly," she begins, then waits. "I think it's bullshit."

"Which part?"

"The part where Coop is some girlfriend-killing madman. He's a standup guy. The type to nurse injured cats back to health and help old ladies across the street. Could he put on that image and still be violent? Sure. Tons of people do it. We only show one facet of ourselves to the people around us. Very few see underneath the mask."

"Is that supposed to make me feel better?" I ask, wondering if I've seen the wrong side of Coop this whole time.

"If you need a Hallmark card, I'm sure there's a Walgreens down the street." She snorts. "What I'm saying is you're one of the few people Coop has let in, from the sounds of it, ever. These angry simpletons and grieving mothers only see what they want to see. You have the full picture. Do you think he's capable of murder? Of hurting these women?"

"No. I don't. But I can't very well trust my emotions on something like this. People are content in relationships all the time only to find out their spouse has a secret family or a lover or worse."

"Yeah, but there's usually a lot of heads in the sand before those revelations are made. You're not like that, Madison. Hell, I'm surprised you made it this long without snooping through his things."

"I did look once before. I felt so guilty I vowed never to do it again."

"Okay, so that's the lesson in all this. Some good can come from being nosy."

"Do you search Matt's things?" Their relationship is perfect; I can't imagine him giving her reason to be suspicious.

"Are you kidding me? I have all his passwords memorized. I know where everything is in our house, even the things he thinks he's hidden from me. But he knows all my stuff, too. Our lives are together. We should be able to go through each other's things on a whim and not find anything."

"That's what bothers me," I say, wiping the tiny droplets sliding down my glass. "I'm afraid he has something to hide."

"Coop's past isn't the cleanest. You have questions and he can't fault you for asking. Honestly, I can see why he didn't tell you about girlfriend number two. The idea two of his relationships ended under mysterious circumstances would scare a lot of people off."

"Should it scare me off?"

"You're the only person who really knows. Do you think the man you're about to marry is dangerous? Or are you considering walking away because everything is too coincidental?"

"Anytime we've talked about Celia, he's seemed genuine. When I asked him about Laura, he was upset, but I believed him. I think he was more scared of losing me."

"There's your answer. Take some time. Think about it. Then go home and decide whether to make this relationship work."

Beth must have more faith in Coop than I do. She wouldn't encourage me to go home to a potential murderer otherwise.

"The way Helena speaks about Laura and Coop... she seems so convinced. It's so real to her."

"It *is* real to her. She has no other outcome, so she copes with her daughter's disappearance by finding someone else to blame. It doesn't mean she's right."

"You possess this unique gift that keeps me from jumping off the ledge." I smile. Beth is working her magic.

"That's just the maternal wisdom starting to show."

"No. It's been there all along."

"I can't tell you what to do or who to believe. Listen to your heart. It knows Coop better than anyone." She pauses, releasing a deep sigh. "I must say, I've never been more disappointed about missing the wedding. Sounds like Whisper Falls is full of shit starters."

"You have no idea."

By the end of our conversation, the anxiety in my chest lifts and my stomach grumbles. I order a sandwich, plus another drink. What I need to do is get back to a state of normal, physically and mentally.

I text Coop, *I'm getting a hotel for the night. We'll talk in the morning.*

I google Yelp reviews for nearby hotels. A night apart will be good, for both of us. Plus, it provides a small taste of the independence I've been missing since moving to Whisper Falls.

I check into my room and spend the first hour re-reading the articles I bookmarked last night relating to Laura's disappearance. The available information is a web of miscommunication. Leads with no end, problems with no resolution. At least four or five people at the music festival claimed to have seen a girl who looked just like her. A few people traveling along the highway said the same thing. Eyewitness testimony is the most unreliable kind. Like most missing people, Laura was forever seen but never found. Still, with every article I read, there's nothing that would make me think Coop is to blame. He was never identified as either a love interest or a suspect, but, in my mind, I can still hear Helena's voice insisting he's a murderer.

I give up. I place my phone on Do Not Disturb mode, expecting to spend several hours mindlessly watching television. Instead, within minutes of crashing on the bed, I'm asleep.

CHAPTER 44

Helena

Still no word from Madison. It's been a full day since we spoke. On a whim, I drive by their house. The winding roads are scarier at night; the darkness and woods surround my car as though I'm on the brink of being swallowed whole. I approach their driveway and spot Cooper's car, but Madison's is gone. That's a good sign, isn't it? Maybe she left him. But then, why wouldn't she call me? Why wouldn't she reach out for help?

There's nothing more unpredictable than the human heart. To me, Cooper Douglas is the vilest creature on this earth, the monster who stole my girl away. But to Madison, I remind myself, he's something more. Madison doesn't strike me as the type to hop into bed with the first man who dangles a ring in front of her face. She's sacrificed for this relationship. Her feelings are developed and mature. A single conversation with me may not be enough to turn her. Yet.

Everything in this town closes by ten. Thankfully, I visited the liquor store earlier in the week. I have a bottle waiting for me in my motel room's mini fridge. Drinking has been my crutch ever since Laura died. I know it's not healthy or good for me. Booze does to my emotions what scratching does to a scar; it makes me feel better in the moment but negates any real healing.

I stopped drinking for several years. Before returning to Whisper, my life was nothing more than an intermission from one meeting to the next. Missing children support groups and Alcoholics Anonymous and grief counseling sessions. It helped for a while, but no community can guide me through this. That's why I'm compelled to drink. It's a way to come down from my mania.

Shady Lane Motel is an accurate name if I've ever heard one. My neighbors here are scoundrels, usually booking the room next door only for the night. I imagine most people here are on the run or in between vices. This revolting place has been my temporary home for weeks, and I don't plan on leaving until I know Madison is safe.

Overgrown weeds cover the sidewalk leading to my room. There's a water fountain in the courtyard just outside my door: a swan with an amputated wing, the aftermath of roughhousing between previous guests. The pool at the bottom is filled with cigarette butts and the stone needs a good pressure washing, but if I sit close enough to my window, I can hear the fountain's tinkling through the walls.

I like to close my eyes and imagine I'm back home. My real home in South Carolina. Back then I was married, not to a particularly good man, but a partner nonetheless. My days were spent planning weddings and parties and celebrations. I was the type of person people trusted with control. And I had the most beautiful daughter. It feels like a lifetime ago, and it was. Never did I imagine my life could fracture the way it has.

We didn't live far from the beach and would spend every spare moment visiting the water. I was amazed Laura wanted to leave our sunny shores behind to attend college in Tennessee, but I remember that age. You're yearning to experience something different from what you've always known. I wanted that for her, too. For her to experience the world.

Now I wish I'd pushed back harder. I should have demanded she attend school closer to home instead of sending her so far away. Cooper would have never met her. And yet, she always seemed happy when we spoke. She shone during our visits. My girl was happy that last year of her life, and I try to cling to that.

The air conditioner kicks on, eliminating the sound of the water fountain and halting my happy memories mercilessly. I retrieve my bottle from the mini-fridge and pour a drink. After a few sips, I feel better. Calmer. I've missed Laura all these years. I'll always miss her, but now I'm putting forth my last effort to bring her justice. Maybe I can bring justice for Celia, too. If more had been done to punish Cooper for her death, my Laura might still be alive. There must be some good in what I'm doing, otherwise I'll have lost all reason to live.

I lean against the stiff mattress I've called my bed. When I leave this town—if I ever leave this town—I'll need to scrape together enough money to visit a chiropractor. Just another sacrifice I'm willing to make in the name of catching Cooper.

For peace of mind, I pull out the nightstand drawer. Inside there's a Bible, and beside that, my gun. I sleep better knowing it's there. I sleep better knowing that if my appeals to Madison fail, at least I have some options left.

CHAPTER 45

Madison

When I wake, it takes me a few minutes to recalibrate. Everything is different. My hotel room is white and cold and superficial. The bedside clock reads 5:21 a.m. I guess that's what I get for crashing as early as I did. It takes mere seconds for the past two days to come flooding back. Helena and Coop. My conversation with Beth. I'm as unsure after a hard sleep as I was before.

Coop has sent several text messages during the night. He left a voicemail around three o'clock.

"Madison," his voice starts, slow and tired. "It's me. Again. I just want to make sure you're okay. I understand you need space right now. I just… just…" There's a pause and I can't tell what he's doing. The slight slur in his voice makes me think he's shared one too many with Roman, or maybe he drank by himself. "I want you to know how much I love you. I hope you believe I wouldn't do anything to hurt you. I wish I could go back to the beginning of our relationship and tell you everything. Anything I held back was only because I didn't want to lose you. I still don't want to lose you. Come home. Please. And we can talk."

He didn't send any messages after that. It wouldn't be too difficult for him to find out where I am. In the rush of everything, I didn't take the time to disable the location app on my phone. He could track my credit cards to find out which hotel I'm in. Knowing all this, I take comfort in the fact he's giving me space. He's allowing me time to process. He knows that's what I need.

Even in these moments of anger, I miss him. I miss Coop. More than a day has lapsed since my conversation with Helena. Despite everything she said, as convincing as she sounded, she wasn't able to erase the love I have for him. As Beth pointed out, Helena sees a skewed side of Coop. I see all of him, and I know he's good.

I stand and stretch. There's no chance of going back to sleep. It's like my body gave me rest, then provided this placid window of time where I can do nothing but be alone and think. I pull back the curtains from the window. Knoxville is dark except for sporadic glimpses of light in scattered buildings. The view certainly isn't like the city, but it's not Whisper Falls either.

I fear my overall anxiety about our new location has impacted my decisions. I'd never imagined living in a town so small, in a place where everyone knows each other's secrets. I wouldn't be there if it weren't for Coop, and sometimes I resent him for that. I wanted to be Madison Sharpe, a writer and key player in my own life, not a supporting role in someone else's. I wanted to be more than Mrs. Cooper Douglas. It's easy for me to blame him for my change in pace, but my own faults led me to where I am today. My ambitions pushed me too far, and now I'm mourning both the person I was and the person I lost the chance to become.

How can I fault Coop for what's happened in his past when I've made bad choices myself? The way I fumbled the 'Chrissy' situation didn't only halt my career; it had the potential to discredit other women. Real victims whose lives could have been ruined at the hands of an over-zealous journalist. Thankfully, that didn't happen, and Bernard Wright received punishment for his crimes. But what if he hadn't? I'm not sure I'd be able to live with the guilt. My brush with scandal changed my outlook. It's not fair Coop lost both Celia and Laura in equally mysterious ways. Likewise, those losses have made him the man he is, the man I fell in love with. He's guarded, with good reason.

The only grudge I can hold against Coop is that he didn't tell me about Laura sooner, and he withheld key details about Celia, too. He lied to me, in his own way. After having a small taste of what his upbringing in Whisper must have been like and seeing the lengths women like Helena would take to punish him, I can't say I blame him. I understand why he keeps me and everyone else at a distance. When we uncovered Helena's deception, his first reaction was anger *for* me. He was mad at himself for having dragged me into his past. He relinquished his own pride and ego years ago. My happiness is his main concern.

The hours tick by. I shower and change clothes. As I'm eating the hotel's in-room offering of scrambled eggs and toast, I google wedding boutiques in the area. While I'm in Knoxville, I might as well shop for a bridesmaid gown. When I check out of the hotel, I plug coordinates into my GPS for a shop called Chiffon and Champagne. I arrive just as they open and tell the woman at the register I'd like to see bridesmaid gowns.

"How long until the wedding?" she asks. She has platinum curls and red lips.

"About nine weeks," I say, pushing my sunglasses on top of my head.

"Oh, heavens. That limits our selection." She's probably afraid her commission will be cut if there's not something I like.

"As long as it's white and available, I'm easy to please," I reassure her.

She pulls out four or five dresses and hangs them on a rack. "Will someone be joining us for a fitting?"

"No, but I've got her measurements. I'll pick something and be on my way."

"I wish every bride was this easy to please," she says, fluffing the skirt of her first selection.

I choose the third dress. It's elegant, but not too bridal. It's a different style from my dress entirely. The fabric is loose and flowy with a sheer overlay covering the neckline. It will look gorgeous on Regina with her pale skin and dark hair; her slim figure could pull off anything.

I fill out the paperwork and follow the saleswoman to the counter. As this particular style is discontinued, she allows me to take the dress home today.

"Anything else we can do for you?" she asks.

"I've got everything I need."

I mean that. I'm back on track.

It's dark when I arrive home. The sun sets about twenty minutes earlier every night. Part of me expected to arrive to a full house. I thought Coop might recruit Regina and Roman to sit with him until I returned. Instead, it's quiet. Coop is standing by the fireplace. He doesn't budge, even when he hears me walk inside.

"I'm home," I say, placing my bag on the floor. I stand there, waiting for him to turn.

"Where did you go?" he asks, putting his drink on the hearth.

"Knoxville." I walk toward him, slowly. This is our first big argument, and the wounds are fresh. "I just needed space."

"What took you so long getting back?" he asks. His face is red. I can tell he's been crying since before I arrived. My absence took more of a toll than I realized.

"I decided to make use of my trip by going shopping. I bought Regina a dress for the wedding."

When he hears this, his solemn mood drops. He hugs me so hard my feet almost leave the ground. He'd been waiting for reassurance. I'm still with him. Not ever leaving his side again. I begin to cry, thinking about how I almost let mindless gossip tear us apart. How I almost gave this up for a history I'll probably never truly understand. And I don't need to understand it to love him with every ounce of my being.

"I'm sorry," he says, pulling my hand to make me sit on the sofa. "You're so good to me, and I've not done right by you."

"You should give yourself more credit," I say. The soft glow from the fireplace dances across his features, accentuating his handsomeness. I don't think I could go the rest of my life without his face.

"I know being with someone like me isn't easy."

"It's worth it," I say, kissing his forehead. My own tears fall, landing on his hand.

He stands and walks back to the fireplace. He finishes his drink, holding the empty glass as he watches the fire. "I've thought a lot about what you said. How we can overcome anything together. I know that now. I never want you to feel blindsided again."

"I'm sick of talking about the past. Let's just be happy together. We were so happy, weren't we? Before all these stories got the better of us."

"Unless we accept what's happened in the past, we can't move forward. That's why I need to tell you something."

"Coop, I know who you are. I don't need explanations—"

"No," he cuts me off. "You need to hear this. I owe it to you, before we go any further."

"Okay." I'm uneasy again, not sure I can take any more indecision. "What is it?"

"You need to know the truth about Laura." He turns to face me. "You need to know why I killed her."

CHAPTER 46

Madison

The room is spinning. My heart is racing, but my body is frozen in place. Did I mishear him? Is this his idea of a joke? No one would joke about something so sinister. Especially Coop. Especially after I've left town to think things over. He's serious, his face red and his chin trembling.

"You did what?"

"I killed Laura."

I expect Coop to run at me. Instead, he slowly walks toward me, puts his hand on my shoulder. This man I love, who does so much for others—even now he's trying to calm me—just admitted to killing someone. I wriggle away from his touch, attempting to dart for the door. His grip on my arm isn't aggressive. It's gentle, but I see the desperation on his face.

"Madison, listen. Everything you said was right. You deserve to know what happened. I'll make sense of this. I promise."

I don't understand. Coop is admitting to killing a woman I didn't even know existed until two days ago. I can't make sense of what he's saying, and yet he looks like the man I love. I start hyperventilating. Coop dashes to the kitchen and comes back with a glass of water and a washrag. I take the water but dodge his attempts to place the towel on my forehead.

"Did you murder Celia, too?"

"No." He throws the towel onto the floor. "I told you that."

"Yesterday, you said you didn't know what happened to Laura Price. You whined about the unfairness of being accused of two crimes. Everything you told me was a lie."

"Not everything. When you mentioned Laura, I didn't know how to react." He stands and walks back to the fire. "Everything I told you before yesterday is true. I did not kill Celia. I left her at the lake, and to this day I don't know how she died. Losing Celia that way, so suddenly… it changed me. The way I was treated in the wake of her death made it worse. People turned on me. Spread rumors and filled my head with lies. That first year of college was a blur. I hardly have any memories, but I'll never forget how I felt. It was all anger and paranoia and outrage. After a while, I started to believe those horrible things people said about me. I felt like a monster, not because of what I'd done, but because of how they made me feel."

The light I'm accustomed to seeing in his eyes is gone. His pupils are black, his mind back to that dark part of his past, when he was first labeled a murderer, and there was nothing he could do to prove his innocence.

"Then I met Laura," he continues. "She was innocent and fun. So very beautiful. She had this glow about her that pulled me out of the dark place I was in following Celia's death. With her, I thought I might have a shot at happiness. A normal life."

"What happened?" I ask, my throat dry, despite the gulps of water I chug.

"She found an article online about Celia's death. One of those snarky ones suggesting I'd killed her. I'd never told her anything about Celia, so she didn't know how to react. I'd fooled myself into thinking I could be with Laura and all the bad stuff from the past wouldn't be able to hurt us.

"She couldn't understand why I hadn't mentioned Celia before. The night she confronted me, she hammered me with questions. Some shitty rumors were more believable to her than the time she'd shared with me. I was so angry she wouldn't listen. I no longer felt like the boy she fell in love with. I was back to being that monster all those people made me out to be. We fought, and she tried to leave her apartment. When I tried to pull her back, she clipped her head against a nightstand." He pauses, struggling, all these years later, to say the words. "She died. Bled out right in front of me."

As I listen, I picture everything he tells me. Coop's desperation and Laura's fear. How quickly their argument had turned fatal. "You're saying what happened to Laura was an accident?"

"An accident I caused. Yes."

"Why didn't you call the police?"

"You have to understand. Back in Whisper, I was still considered a suspect in Celia's death. All those people already thought I'd killed one girl; I couldn't very well have a second girl turn up dead on my watch."

"So, what happened?" I want him to quit talking almost as much as I want answers, but the latter prevails. I try to stabilize my breathing, counteract the nausea rising. "What did you do with her?"

He hesitates. "I drove home and left her in Whisper Lake."

"Her body has been in the lake all this time? The same place Celia was found." It's all too coincidental. All too connected. New patterns are arising, dizzying my thoughts. "Wouldn't she have turned up by now?"

"This has nothing to do with Celia! She drowned and it was an accident, and if people had believed that, none of this would have ever happened! I know this lake like the back of my hand. I made sure Laura wouldn't be found." He exhales shakily and looks away in shame. It's difficult for him to say these words. I wonder if he's ever said them aloud before. "I cleaned Laura's apartment and tossed her personal items. I used her credit card to buy a ticket to that music festival she'd been wanting to attend. I thought that might help establish an alibi."

"Do your siblings know about this? Your mother?"

"No. Regina was still in high school. And Mom... Mom would never look at me the same if she knew what I did, especially after she defended me when it came to Celia. I've carried this secret a long time."

"What about your dad?"

"He never knew what happened either. No one in the family knew anything until Laura was reported missing. That's why my parents hired their own private investigator to re-examine Celia's case. They realized that any time something bad happened in my life, Celia's death would be there coloring the way people viewed me."

"Why are you telling me this?" I ask, placing my empty water glass on the table.

"I figured I'd rather tell you this one horrible truth than carry on a lifetime of lying."

"You've been lying to me our entire relationship!" I scream. I stand but feel too weak to take a step. From the time I first met Coop, he's been a murderer, and I never knew.

"When we met, I'd been hiding the truth about Laura for years. I forced myself not to think about her. To pretend she never existed. That's the only way I was able to move on."

"Move on from murdering someone?"

He takes a step closer. "I'm ashamed of what I've done, but I can't undo it! If I hadn't been so tortured with all those lies about Celia, I wouldn't have lashed out the way I did. She would have never been angry with me."

"You have dozens of pictures of her hidden away."

He looks down. "Sometimes it's nice to remember the good times. I pay respects, in my own way."

"And you think telling me will clear your conscience?"

"I'll never atone for what I did to Laura, but I try. I've been nothing but an upstanding individual. I help with charities and the community. I'm good to you."

I shake my head and laugh. Our whole relationship has been a pit stop on some apology tour. "None of that changes the fact you killed a woman."

"I know it doesn't, but I'm more than the worst mistake I made. You know me better than anyone. Would you continue this conversation if you didn't think I was a good person?"

"You're one of the most wonderful people I've ever met." I begin crying. "But you did a horrible, horrible thing. Poor Helena still doesn't know what happened to her daughter!"

"Will telling her the truth ease her pain? Knowing what happened won't bring her daughter back." He touches my arm. "I'm asking you to forgive me."

"I... I don't know what to do." I walk to the front door. My head feels like it's about to burst, and a wave of dizziness makes me stop.

"Maybe you should sit."

I shrug him off. I try to sit on the sofa, but stumble and nearly miss. "Did you put something in my drink?"

"It's just something to help you sleep. I didn't want to worry about you running off again while you're this emotional."

"Oh my gosh, Coop. What are you doing?"

He lifts my legs and puts them on the couch. He takes the washrag and folds it over my forehead. I'm too weak to push it away. "You just need rest. I promise, you'll feel better about things in the morning." Coop sits in the armchair across from me, the shadows from the fire dancing across his face.

CHAPTER 47

June 16, 2006

Cooper squeezed his truck in between two poorly parked cars. Music and laughter echoed in the distance. He left the gravel lot and marched down the steep hill leading to the south bank, brambles and twigs slicing at his shins. Partying was the last thing on his mind. He wished he'd had the opportunity to finish his conversation with Celia, perhaps arrive at the truth.

He was sick of her and the cruel impact she left on those around her. Watching her toy with Regina was the last straw. His sister already had it rough; although it was only her second year in high school, she hadn't risen to the levels of popularity he or Roman had. Being a Douglas wasn't enough for her. Maybe it's because she was a girl. Having only lived in the small radius of Whisper Falls, Cooper didn't understand a lot about social dynamics. This much he knew: guys stuck together, while girls tore each other apart.

He reached flat ground and immediately inhaled a big whiff of campfire. It made his eyes and throat dry, but he enjoyed that in a nostalgic way. Two girls skipped by him, waving as they passed. He was used to receiving attention from girls, but that changed when he started dating Celia. Girls still flirted if she wasn't around, but they were also cautious. The only thing that could ruin the thrill of a hookup with Cooper Douglas was having to deal with the wrath of Celia Gray the next day. Cooper would never cheat anyway. That wasn't him. He was loyal.

That was why he was so bothered with the idea Celia would betray him for the likes of Steven Burns. Part of him still didn't think it was possible; Cooper had his own sense of invincibility, too. His parents sponsored most sporting events, making sure poor kids, like Steven, would have uniforms and anything else they needed to play. It would be a slap in the face for any of his friends to betray him for a girl, even if that girl was Celia. She wasn't wrong about her special effect on the town. Like her or not, no one could deny it.

"Coop Dog! You made it." Jim stumbled in Cooper's direction. He looked red and slimy from hours of drinking in the summer heat. "Bring any booze?"

"No, I couldn't get a hold of Roman," he said, although he hadn't even tried. Roman was in for the summer, but he never hung around with Cooper and his friends. That was beneath him now that he was in college.

"Aw, poo," he whined, leaning against Cooper's shoulder. "Where's your lady? Ce-li-a."

"Couldn't make it."

"Did you talk to her about Steven?" For a brief moment, Jim sobered up. He was interested in how Cooper would reply.

"Didn't really get much out of her," Cooper said, kicking the dirt. He was embarrassed Celia had such a hold over him, making him look weak in front of his friends.

"She's probably stunned you called her out. You deserve better, my man," Jim said, his words beginning to slur again. "If she were my girlfriend—"

"I got it, okay?" Cooper didn't care to hear how Jim might act in his situation. Jim couldn't get with a girl like Celia if he tried. It was easy for him to boast about what he'd do, what treatment he wouldn't tolerate. "I'll get to the bottom of it."

"I've got your back. Whatever you need." Jim slapped Cooper's shoulder, a lazy smile across his face. "Come grab a beer."

Jim swaggered away, wrapping his arm around the hips of a bikini-clad girl nearby. Cooper still didn't know why he'd come. Perhaps it was better than being alone. Usually, he only attended parties at Celia's request. She loved the atmosphere, walking around like they were king and queen of Whisper Falls.

With Cooper leaving for college soon, all that would change. Maybe that's why Celia had grown distant, kept doing things to rile him up. She wanted to remind him who he'd be leaving behind, take back the control she felt she was losing. Cooper didn't want to get married as quickly as Celia did, but he was willing to stay with her. Do long distance, if they must. He saw potential in Celia, something she always pretended to have, but deep down never believed about herself.

As night fell, the flames from the bonfire blazed larger and the chatter from the crowd increased. It was the first time Cooper realized how out of place he felt in the midst of this small-town revelry. For most of his peers, this would be the highlight of their lives, sad as it was. Cooper always knew he'd achieve better and was willing to take Celia with him on that journey. Would she really leave him for the likes of this?

By the lake, he saw Steven Burns. He was sitting on the ground, his trunks wet and dirty, with a girl on either side of him. For a second, his eyes met Cooper's, and he winked. A jolt of electricity went off inside Cooper. He couldn't take it anymore, the uncertainty of whether these rowdy rednecks were getting the best of him. It made him clench his fists and grit his teeth. He had to get to the bottom of things. He had to know who was on his side, and who wasn't. He had to talk to Celia.

He marched away from the noise and left.

CHAPTER 48

Madison

Sunlight beams through the window, waking me. I'm in our bedroom, still wearing my clothes from last night. Coop sits across from me. When I see him, it takes a few seconds to remember all the awful things he told me. About Laura. Inside, I feel disgusted. Deceived. And yet, he still looks like the man I love.

"How are you feeling?" he asks, uncrossing his arms.

"You drugged me." I sit up in the bed, resting my head against the headboard. There's no way I can make it out of this room without an altercation with Coop, and I'm still too weak to try. "How do you think I feel?"

"I'm sorry about that." He crosses his legs, cupping his knee with his hands. "I didn't want you to leave without having the chance to talk."

"What else is there to say?" He's already told me the worst of it.

"I want to talk properly. Now that you're calm."

I look away. How I wish I hadn't gone digging into the past. Then I wouldn't know any of the horrible truths he told me. Of course, then I'd be marrying him in the dark, but that seems like a worthwhile alternative right now. I do feel calm though. Perhaps it's the aftermath of whatever drug he gave me, but my mind is clear.

"I'm not going to hurt you, Madison, if that's what you're thinking."

I notice my overnight bag sitting by the door. The knife should still be inside. I'd put it there when I first got the nerve to confront

Coop about Laura. Before I knew he'd killed her. Could I really use it on him? Would he provoke me to do so?

"Where do we go from here?" I ask.

"I'm going to go on living like normal. I'm happy with our life, Madison. I'm happy with you."

"What you told me about Laura… what you did…" I struggle to find the right words. I'm appalled by what he's done, but he's still the man I love. Since the first day I met him, he's been a murderer. Yet all I saw was his kindness and maturity and dependability. I'm conflicted. "I'm not sure I know you anymore."

"You do, Madison." He kneels in front of the bed, resting his hands on my legs. "You know me better than anyone ever has. That's why I told you. I trust you to accept what I've done and love me regardless."

"I can't accept what you've done, Coop."

"You have to understand the person I was back then was different from the person I am today. I was jaded because of Celia, and I was too young to properly process it all," he continues. "I've never been a violent person. What happened with Laura was a huge mistake. I live with the pain of what I've done every day. You don't know how many times I've thought about turning myself in."

"Then why haven't you?"

"A confession will only hurt the people I love." He looks away and clenches his jaw. "Besides, it won't change anything. My confession won't bring Laura back."

"Why tell me any of this?" I ask. "There must be some part of you that wants to admit the truth."

"I've carried these secrets long enough. It wouldn't be fair to marry you without giving you the chance to walk away."

"Is that what this is?" I ask, sitting up straighter. "My chance to leave you?"

"If that's what you want. Turn me into the police. We'll call off the wedding and you can move back to Atlanta." He pulls my hand and holds it against his chest. "Or you can forgive me. You can accept that I did a horrific thing over a decade ago. A horrific thing that, in some ways, made me a better person. And we can move forward."

"Move forward." I laugh over the pure lunacy of the suggestion. The idea we can keep living our lives like nothing happened. In the back of my mind, there's a tingle of fear. That this whole conversation is a trick, and if I give the wrong answer, I'll be punished.

"You don't have to decide right now." Coop stands and returns to his chair. "And you don't have to be afraid of me, Madison. I'll accept your decision, whatever it is."

I don't know what to say to him. I'm afraid to leave the bed. "Does your family know about Helena?"

"They still believe Celia's mother was posing as Anne. They know we had an argument because Regina saw you storm off, but I didn't tell them what it was about."

I picture the beautiful faces of the Douglas family. Each one with their quirks and secrets. There are more people involved in this decision than Coop and myself. I think of Helena's face, too. Her desperation to be proven right. I could give her that, if I had the strength.

"How can I trust you?" His confession aside, he drugged me last night. Yesterday revealed a side of Coop I never knew existed. "I don't know how."

"Do you love me?" He looks at me. There's no anger in his face.

"Yes," I answer, honestly. "But I'm scared."

He looks out the window, leaning against the wall. "No one can do what I did and be proud. But I know I love you, Madison. I love you enough to tell you the truth, despite the fact it can ruin everything I care about."

"Can I take a shower?"

"You don't have to ask my permission. Do what you want." Coop chuckles, then turns serious. "I'm sorry for slipping something in your drink. I only did it to protect you. I wanted to have a calm conversation. Not react on emotion."

I exit the bed slowly, walking closer to Coop to cross over to the bathroom. I'm afraid he might grab me, but he doesn't. He keeps staring out the window. In this moment, he's at peace.

"I'm sorry," he says. "If you leave me, I'll understand. It won't be easy, starting over again. I'm sure you'll move back to the city and piece together the life you had. Maybe one day you'll be happier. It's obvious you've never been very happy here."

I close the bathroom door and lock it. I lean against the frame and release a deep breath. It feels like I've been holding it in for days. I can't decide what my next move should be. I still very much love the man standing on the other side of the door. Those feelings haven't disappeared, despite what he told me.

I stay in the shower for a long time. I think about what he said about my return to the city. It wouldn't be an easy transition. I've not worked in months, and I insisted on pouring a big chunk of my savings into the wedding. I'd be starting off in a far worse position than I left, not to mention the added emotional turmoil of knowing my fiancé is a murderer. Ex-fiancé. Ah, I don't know what to think. Deep down, I know what should be done, but acting on that decision will be difficult.

Eventually the images of the Douglases and Coop and Laura fade away. The one face that remains in my mind is Helena. All these years she's suffered from not knowing what happened to her daughter, and yet, she's known the truth all along. She tried telling me Coop was involved. She was right. But like Coop said, knowing the truth won't bring Laura back. And turning Coop in won't erase the love I have for him. In some ways, it would be easier if he was a madman with threats and danger. But he's not. He's just my Coop.

CHAPTER 49

Madison

Coop is very much the same person. Has been for the past two days. Nothing feels different, and yet everything has changed. At least I don't feel like I'm in immediate danger. We never discuss Laura or Celia. We don't talk about the wedding either. I think we're both waiting on the other shoe to drop, neither of us knowing what that means.

"Are you okay with having my family over for dinner on Monday?" he asks.

I'm sitting away from him on the couch, flipping through a magazine. The news is on the television, but neither of us is watching.

"Sure." This is the first normal exchange we've had since the weekend. It's the first sign that we're going back to normal.

He's pleased with my answer because he smiles. "Regina wants to know all about her dress."

"She'll have to try it on. Surely your mother knows someone who could do speedy alterations."

He smiles again, like he's unwrapped a present. This is the first signal I've given him that the wedding is still on. "What about the other decisions? You know, the ones you'd thought were made by... Helena."

Hearing her name hurts. I don't show it though. I flip the page of my magazine. "Your mom is arranging the last-minute details. She's the one with the connections. I trust her judgment."

"Good to hear." He stands and walks into the kitchen. "Would you like a glass of wine?"

"Sure."

He comes back with two glasses, placing mine on the coffee table.

"By the way, I stopped by the post office and rented a P.O. Box. I don't want to run the risk of Helena sending anything to our house. I've gone through our phone records and blocked her number from both our phones, too." He takes a sip. "I'll make sure she doesn't bother you again."

For the first time during our conversation, I look up. I hadn't expected him to be this proactive, but it makes sense really. He trusts me, but only so much. "Good," I say, reaching for my wine glass.

Coop doesn't know Helena has a different number, and that it's written on a piece of paper I've hidden in the desk drawer.

He sits beside me, rubbing his hand through my hair. "I love you so much."

I look at him, and don't flinch when he leans in for a kiss.

The next morning, Coop leaves for work. I get my cell phone and use it to call Helena. I can't tell her everything I know. Helena very much runs on emotion, and, in her position, I can't blame her. My emotions are certainly involved, but I've tried to remain practical. I must, in order to protect myself and everyone else involved.

She answers after the first ring. "Madison?" she barks into the phone.

"Yes, it's me."

"Are you okay?" She sounds desperate. Scared.

"I need you to do something for me."

"Have you talked to Cooper? What did he say—"

"Helena, please. Just listen to me." I give her clear instructions, all the while knowing she has no reason to follow through with what

I say. She has no reason to trust me. I'm struggling to even trust myself. To know the difference between what is wrong and right.

"I can do that." The connection turns fuzzy, likes she's moving around. "But why?"

"I can't talk long. Just do what I say."

"Then tell me why!" She's frustrated. It's been almost a week since our last conversation, enough to test anyone's patience. "I've poured my heart out to you—"

"Just trust me. Please." I take a deep breath. It's hard talking to this woman, hearing her pain. If she'll only do what I ask, life can return to its new normal. "And don't call this number again."

I hang up, and for what feels like the hundredth time this week, I have a good, long cry.

CHAPTER 50

Helena

I did exactly as Madison instructed. I try not to be too critical of her, but I can't help being frustrated with the fact she hasn't left Cooper. I've driven by their house every day this week, and her car is still parked in the driveway. Its presence worried me at first. What if he'd done something to her? Hearing her voice over the phone alleviated that stress, but I'm tired of waiting for what comes next. I've spent the last decade of my life waiting. Telling Madison about Cooper was supposed to put an end to all of this, not drag it out further.

Each day, I wait for a sign from Madison. A call. A text. She told me not to reach out, but I don't think she's stopping to think about how excruciating that is for me. It's been days since I did what she told me to do.

I dial her number, my heart sinking after each unanswered ring. When it goes to voicemail, I'm defeated. Doesn't Madison understand I'm already in purgatory, that she's now the person deciding my fate? I press redial, intending to leave a message. Instead, the line connects.

"Hello?" she whispers into the phone.

"Madison?" I'm so happy to hear her voice again. "Are you okay?"

"You can't call me. I told you—"

"I did as you told me." I can hear her scurrying around on the other end of the line. "I only want to know what all this means."

"You have to leave me alone," she says. This time her volume is louder, and her tone is sterner. "I have nothing more to say to you."

"What are you talking about? Madison, please don't do this to me now. Just—"

There's more turmoil on the other end. I panic, thinking maybe I've put her in a dangerous position by calling. How selfish of me! My need for understanding outweighed her safety. Then, the activity finishes. I hear shallow breaths puffing into the receiver.

"Madison?" I ask.

"This is Cooper."

His voice pierces through my skin, jolting fear into my heart. I almost drop the phone. This is our most direct interaction in years. Our first real communication since the vigil. I want to lunge through my device and scratch him. I should have known better than to go through Madison, expecting a different outcome. I should have gone after him.

"Helena? Are you there?" he asks.

"Yes," I say, my voice shaky.

"Helena, you need to leave us alone now," he says, calmly. "You've done enough damage."

"*I've* done enough damage!" The outrage of such a statement! Coming from the man I know killed my daughter. "You've never taken accountability for what you've done. Cooper, you—"

"We've tried to handle this civilly," he continues, cutting me off. "If you try to communicate with either one of us, we'll be seeking a restraining order. Again."

The phone clicks off. I fall to my knees, melting into the stained carpet of this God-awful motel room. Anguish leaves my body in a medley of moans and tears. I can't believe I've just talked to him. That he knows I've talked to her. I can't believe I'm no closer to achieving the justice I came here to find.

CHAPTER 51

Madison

Coop places the phone on the kitchen counter.

"Why did you have to get involved?" I ask. I'm angry. Ever since he told me about Laura, he's been inserting himself more into my life. I don't like it, this sense of losing control. I don't let him see my disappointment; I continue cooking dinner like nothing is wrong.

"How long has she been calling you?"

"She called once a few days ago. I called back, not realizing it was her."

"What did she say?"

"It wasn't a long call. When I realized it was Helena, I told her not to call back."

"And yet here she is. She's changed her number." He slaps a palm against the refrigerator. "The woman won't stop."

"I'm sure she will now that you've talked to her." I walk past him and return to the chopping block. I resume slicing carrots.

"Are you angry with me?" he asks, his voice delicate. I think of how I treated Coop when I first learned people suspected him of killing Celia. I was reluctant to admit it then, but now I know I was watching him, analyzing his every move as a sign of whether he could be trusted. That's how he watches me now.

"I'm fine," I say, clacking the knife against the wood. "I can handle Helena on my own. I don't need you interfering."

"It's my fault she's bothering you." He leans against the refrigerator and raises his hands to his head. This is where I need him:

guilt-ridden, not distrustful. It's bad enough he's sorting through the mail and asking questions about where I go during the day. He doesn't like losing control either.

"She's a sad, lonely woman. She doesn't have anything tying you to Laura." I stumble over her name.

"Maybe we should get a restraining order. Get ahead of this thing."

I turn and face him, the knife dangling from my right hand. "Do you really think that's our best move right now? Involving the police?"

"You're right." He paces around the kitchen with his arms crossed. "I just wish there was a way we could keep her away."

"I told you. Hearing your voice probably spooked her." I turn and start chopping. "Don't worry so much."

Coop walks up behind me and kisses my neck. "I'm so lucky to have you."

"No," I say, rubbing my cheek against his temple, tightening my grip on the knife. "I'm the lucky one."

CHAPTER 52

Madison

Coop was supposed to be home more than an hour ago. His tardiness worries me, just as every deviation from routine makes my pulse race these days. I'm wearing a pencil skirt and blouse with nude heels. I must appear like a Douglas family wannabe, regardless of how I feel inside. I don't want anyone picking up on the shift in our relationship, and I'm already anxious because Coop mentioned they know about our fight.

I hear the door slam and Coop's steps thundering up the stairs. By the time he enters our bedroom, I'm standing in front of our mirror perfecting my lipstick.

"My family should be here any minute." He throws his briefcase on the bed, refusing to look at me. Something is off.

"What's wrong?"

"I don't want to get into it right now." He brushes my shoulder as he enters the bathroom. I hear the faucet running and the sound of splashing. When he walks out, his face and neckline are damp.

"Talk to me, Coop." I touch his forearm to try and calm him. I'm nervous.

He stares at me for a minute, deciding whether to bend. "I checked the bank account earlier today. You've moved some money out of our joint account."

"Money for the wedding," I say, quickly. "I told you that."

"What's the money going toward exactly? Mom is paying off the last-minute bookings."

"I know, but I moved some money over before that."

"In the last week, you've been making small withdrawals. Where's that going?"

I sit on the bed and inhale through my nose, trying to appear relaxed. "I've been trying to pay myself back for money I've spent along the way. My personal checking account is getting low, and I obviously don't have any form of income."

"Right." His tone is sarcastic and cruel. He unbuttons his shirt and slings it onto the bed.

I walk to him and press my hands on his shoulders. "I've also been setting aside funds for our honeymoon, when we get around to planning it, that is. What's the big deal?"

He slides his arms into a new shirt, staring at my reflection in the mirror. His gaze tests mine, trying to decipher the truth.

"What's going on?" I ask, soothingly.

He sits on the bed. "I worried you were trying to move money around without me knowing."

"Why would I do that?" I ask, raising my arms and dropping them at my sides.

He starts to say something but stops. "I don't know." He turns and continues buttoning his shirt.

He does know, as do I. He thinks I'm collecting some type of emergency fund for when I leave him. Coop has been spiraling since he told me the truth about Laura. He's used to being in control, confident. He'd thought confessing might bring us closer together, perhaps alleviate the guilt he's been carrying alone all these years. But that part of him that craves order is crumbling. He's not convinced about what I might do.

"You have to trust me, Coop." I rest my head on his chest. "The way I trust you."

He looks at me for a second, and I can see the regret he feels. I'm thankful for this conversation, though. It provides insight into what I can and can't do.

The Douglases arrive ten minutes later. Regina marches straight to the refrigerator and places a pie inside. Roman stands behind her, waiting for her to move so he can deposit his beer. Josephine peers into the oven and spies our entrée, then turns to me.

"I feel like it's been ages since we've seen you, Madison." She smiles, then looks at Coop. "And you."

"It's been one of those weeks," he says, taking a seat at the table. "I'm happy everyone was free tonight."

"Nectar has been slammed lately. There was a slow period after someone started that rumor about food poisoning," Regina says, rolling her eyes. "I'm happy things are back on track. Guess it makes sense you went dress shopping without me."

"I'd planned on only window shopping," I say. "When I saw your dress, I knew it was the one. I hope you agree."

"Speaking of the wedding," Josephine says, taking a seat at the table, "I've got an idea I wanted to run by the both of you."

Coop and I share a look before sitting beside each other. "What is it?" I ask.

"How would you feel about moving up the date?"

"Moving *up* the date?" I ask, my voice strained.

"I've worked my magic and asked around. Apparently, there's a wedding that's been canceled, and if we act fast, we can book all their vendors," she says. "The cake, the entertainer, the florist."

"How soon?" Coop asks.

"One month." She holds out her palms and smiles. "I know it sounds crazy, but since the original invitations never went out, we could change the date and still have time to let people know. Lord knows the people around here would drop anything to be there. We'd have everything exactly as you wanted."

I feel all their eyes on me, and I'm trying hard to hide my angst. I can't help wondering if they're speeding up the wedding to protect Coop. What if he whispered this suggestion into Josephine's ear?

"I think we can pull it off," Coop says, looking at me for an answer.

I take a sip of my wine and smile. "Sure. Everything else is already sorted."

"Regina and I can help you get the invitations in the mail. I've already spoken with the entertainment. If you could get me a list of songs for the reception, that would be great." Josephine places both palms together. "It's just perfect."

"We've started on a playlist," Coop says. "We still can't decide what our first dance song should be. Unless, you've found one, Madison?"

"Not yet," I say, grinding my teeth.

Roman catches me staring at him across the table. I quickly smile and lift my glass. "Yours looks empty? Would you like more?"

"Sure." He slides his glass forward, never breaking eye contact.

I return from the kitchen with the last of the wine. "Help yourself."

"I'm stepping out for a cigar," he says, taking the bottle. "Join me, Cooper?"

Coop leaves the table and follows Roman to the back porch. Inside, Josephine and Regina ricochet ideas about the new wedding date. I watch the two brothers outside. I'm left wondering what they're talking about. Wondering how much Roman knows.

After everyone leaves, I begin rinsing dishes off in the sink. Coop walks behind me and kisses my cheek. "Thank you for tonight. It was wonderful."

"Just a simple meal," I say, taking a small step to the left.

"I think they were worried about us," he admits. "They should feel better now."

"Hope so." I pat my hands with a towel. "What were you and Roman talking about outside?"

"This and that. Nothing important."

They must have been discussing something, and Coop's not telling me. That's not a good sign. He steps forward and kisses me, this time on the lips. When I back away, he pulls me in closer, sliding his tongue into my mouth, then moving to my neck.

"What do you say we break our little pact?" he asks. "Just for tonight."

"Now that the wedding is moved up, it won't be much longer," I whisper, giving him a playful push.

"Tonight reminded me of the old us. It made me realize how much I've missed you." He leans in again, nuzzling my neck and rubbing his hands atop my skirt.

I pull his head close to mine and give him a passionate kiss. Enough to make him think I'm longing for intimacy the way he is. "Some things are worth the wait."

He backs away slowly and smiles. "As you wish, Mrs. Douglas."

He walks upstairs. I stay in the kitchen doing mindless chores for the next twenty minutes. When I enter the bedroom, I'm happy to see Coop is fast asleep.

CHAPTER 53

June 16, 2006

As they bumped over the water, Roman thought about Celia. He'd always had his eye on her, even when he was still in high school. When Cooper made his move, he backed off, but he couldn't ignore his feelings. Sleeping with his brother's girlfriend was the most dishonest thing he'd ever done, but he believed, in time, his brother would forgive him. Cooper would understand she wasn't just some girl. She was Celia. Cooper would move on and find another; Roman wasn't sure he ever would.

Roman wanted to tell her how he felt, but he knew a debate with Celia could last hours. For whatever reason, she wasn't ready to commit to a relationship yet. That was okay. She was young, too. He knew eventually she'd come around. She'd have to. After the few weeks they'd spent together that summer, he could no longer imagine a world without her.

It was now completely dark. The dock posts were decorated with lights, but they weren't enough to combat the black skies. Roman turned on the boat's overhead strobe and eased closer to the bank. Celia sat with crossed arms at the stern. Roman didn't speak, but his aggravated maneuvering of the boat said enough. The way he threw down the anchor, stomped from one end to the next. He couldn't stop thinking about the one thing he couldn't have, the only person who didn't want him back. And yet, Celia looked so beautiful; the light falling on her features at the perfect angle made him want her even more.

"I love you, Celia," he said, against his better judgment. He'd never been so forward with another girl, so desperate. Maybe if he could make her understand the lengths he'd go for her love, she'd change her mind.

"Don't say things you don't mean."

"I mean it. I do." He kneeled in front of her, rubbing from her knees to the fleshy tops of her thighs. She felt slick from suntan lotion and lake water, but he didn't care. He wanted all of her.

"I don't need you to love me," Celia said, pushing him away. "I'm with Cooper."

"Cooper is a follower. He's my brother, and I love him, but he's never going to be with you the way you want."

Celia started to tear up. She had to know parts of what he said were true. Roman knew that's why she'd slept with him in the first place. Being with Cooper felt like work. She must be tired of trying to mold him, show him the way. With Roman, she could just be.

He kissed her. She gave his shoulders a light nudge, but eventually relented. Celia could never turn down a good kiss, and this was one, in the comfort of Roman's arms at the dark dock. They were so lost in that moment, they didn't hear the crunch of footsteps on grass. They didn't see the flashlight's glare. They didn't realize they weren't alone until they heard a voice.

"What in the hell is going on here?" a person shouted.

Roman and Celia froze in fear.

CHAPTER 54

Madison

After Coop leaves for work, I slide into leggings, a sports bra and jacket. I slick my hair into a ponytail and drive straight to Whisper Falls Park. This is the first time I'd describe the weather as cold. According to the weekly forecast, it's probably just a spell. Winter won't fully arrive for another month or so. Today it feels like a different season. Something about the gray sky and stiff grass. I jog toward the running track and then my phone rings. It's Cooper. Adrenaline shoots up my neck, hot and sharp. Does he know I'm here? I answer.

"Are you still at the house?" he asks. He must know. He probably checked my location on our phones. Does he do this every morning now? I wonder.

"No," I say, keeping my voice steady and calm. "I decided to go for a run in the park."

"In this weather?"

"It's not too bad, once I break a sweat." I can hear phones ringing and the copier going in the background, so I know he's at the office. I try to shake off the feeling I'm being watched. "What's up?"

"I left my lunch at the house. I was wondering if you'd bring it to me."

"I'm almost finished here. I'll have it to you by noon."

"Don't bother. I'll walk across the street and eat at Nectar." He retreats too quickly. This was an attempt to figure out where I am. "You could join me there, if you'd like."

"I would, but I promised Beth we'd video chat this afternoon. She wants to show me what they've done with the nursery." I pause, trying to gauge his response. "I can call her later tonight, if you'd like."

"No. Catch up with her. I'll see you at the house tonight, okay?"

As I slide my phone into my leggings, I see a car pull into the parking lot. Much to my delight, it's Bailey. I give her a head start before I approach. She sits on her familiar bench, but this time she doesn't have a laptop or notebooks. She's waiting.

"Morning," I say. "Mind if I sit?"

"I'm expecting someone." She looks away, her mind thinking about other things.

I sit beside her on the bench anyway. "I'm the person who wanted to meet you here."

She turns, a look of confusion on her face. Last week when I called Helena, I'd asked her to write down everything she could about Laura and her disappearance. I told her to include what she knew about Coop's involvement. Using the mailing address on *The Falls Report* website, I instructed her to send the information to Bailey. I'd sent my own anonymous message shortly after, telling Bailey to meet me in the park.

"You're the person who sent over the information about the Laura Price disappearance?"

"Technically, Laura's mother did. Helena." I take another look around the park, making sure we aren't being watched. "I told her to write down everything she knew and send it to you."

"But why? What am I supposed to make of this?" she asks. She shifts to better face me, like she's shedding her skin. "Cooper Douglas is connected to the disappearance of Laura Price?"

"Helena seems to think so," I say, staring ahead at the empty park. I still can't shake the feeling someone is watching.

"And you've actually met this woman?"

"She posed as our event planner the first several times we met," I say, rolling my eyes. Even now, I feel foolish about the whole ordeal. "She eventually confessed her true intentions and told me everything about Coop and Laura."

"Do you believe her?"

I look down. I'm hesitant to come forward with what Coop told me until I know I'm completely safe. I don't think he would hurt me, but it's hard to say what a person might do when the possibility of punishment lingers so close. I know how things ended up for Laura.

"I think Helena's story is compelling. That's why I'm coming to you. We must think alike, even if we disagree at times. Right?" I look down. I know Bailey is blindsided by my presence, trying to figure out my motive in all this. Last time I saw her, I berated her for what she wrote about Coop. Today serves a different purpose. "You see, I lied to you the first time we met. I didn't leave my job to come here. I was let go. I got caught up in chasing a story over facts, and it cost me a career I loved. I'm not doing that this time. And I don't want you to do it either."

Bailey's posture relaxes. She leans into the park bench, staring at the empty jogging track before us. She looks drained and defeated. "Why did you have to tell me all this?"

"I knew you'd investigate. And you clearly have it out for the Douglas family. I thought you'd enjoy the opportunity to take Coop down."

"It's just…" She stops talking and looks away. Something is weighing heavy on her, and I'm afraid I've made a mistake. "I don't want to hurt Regina."

Coop had mentioned Bailey's friendship with his sister, but I wouldn't think that would be enough to interfere with her chance to break this story. "You didn't seem to care when you wrote that Celia article last month."

"I know. She was angry about that, but she understands what I'm doing with *The Falls Report*. I'm shattering the glass ceiling built around her family and all these other Whisper Falls fakes."

She looks down and cracks her knuckles. "This is different. I don't know if she'll forgive me."

"If Regina's your friend—"

"She's more than my friend." She looks at me and hunches her shoulders. "We're together."

"Oh." I wasn't expecting that. All the snide remarks about Regina and her love life take on a new context. If I'd known they were involved romantically, I'd never have roped Bailey into this. "She never told me."

"We're discreet. I can't say our relationship is a secret, but we don't broadcast it. Josephine's not keen on her only daughter being a lesbian."

"I see." The longer I'm around this family, the more secrets come to light. I lean back and pinch the bridge of my nose. We've reached an impasse, and I'm not sure how to proceed. "Have you told Regina about any of this? What you've been looking into?"

"No. I feel guilty enough researching Cooper behind her back. Celia's case is different. The whole town has talked about that for years. If Cooper is involved in something else… it will break her heart."

"Have you talked to anyone else about this? Learned anything?" I ask, trying to steer the conversation away from emotional attachments. Back to the facts.

"Here's what I've found so far," Bailey says, leaning forward. "Cooper Douglas and Laura Price were enrolled at the same university for their freshman and sophomore years. Laura was reported missing, by her mother, in May. Detectives believe she went missing either en route to or during a music festival about three hours away from campus. She'd sent some text messages to friends saying she wanted to meet up. She never did."

I'm sure those messages were sent from her phone. Coop had it, and he had her credit card that bought the ticket. Everything she's told me thus far aligns with Coop's fabricated version of events.

"Did police ever search her apartment?" I ask, hoping something there might indicate foul play.

"They did a week after she last spoke to her mother. I've even seen pictures of the place. Everything looked in order, but they did find small amounts of blood and bleach. Something was cleaned up, but not enough to warrant an investigation."

"Why not?" I ask, frustrated at the unknown reach of the Douglas clan. "And how did you see pictures?"

"I write about our sleepy little town primarily, but I've done my fair share of networking over the years. I've got a friend in every police department between here and Memphis. My buddy pulled the cold case file and let me take a look."

I knew Bailey would be relentless, especially if she thinks she can finally nail Coop. She's convinced he got away with Celia's murder, too. Having all this information about Laura dropped into her lap strengthens her conviction.

"If there was blood in her apartment, it should have been classified as a crime scene."

"It's tricky when there's no body. If Laura was found in a sewage drain a month later, then they would have gone back and torn the place apart. Considering her age and the circumstances, it's harder to prove she didn't just walk away."

"Helena's convinced Laura would never do that." And I know she didn't do that.

"It's been more than ten years since anyone has heard from her. I don't know what else can be done. We have minimal blood in an apartment and Cooper's connection to Celia's death. That's it. In our eyes, it's a lot. In the eyes of the law, it's not enough."

I lean my head back, looking at the blue sky above. The clouds drift and birds fly and leaves fall. The serene setting juxtaposes the ugly topic we're discussing, the grisly decision I'm about to make.

CHAPTER 55

Helena

It's been too long. If Madison had any intention of leaving Cooper, she would have done it by now. I really thought things would be different this time. I suppose all desperate people think that. Insane people, rather. Is that what I've become during all these years without Laura? Insane?

I thought reading about Cooper's engagement was my lowest point. The idea of spoiling his wedding and telling his fiancée the truth gave me some hope. After meeting Madison, I convinced myself this would be the closest I'd ever come to getting justice. She was so different from what I expected: smart and independent and thoughtful. I fooled myself into thinking she might believe me. Now I feel worse than ever. I've exhausted all my options; irrational thoughts are all I have left.

I strap protective eyewear to my face and fasten the bulky headphones on my head. In all the years I've owned this gun, I've never used it. I bought it during those blurry months after Laura's disappearance. It's a natural reaction for people who've lost a loved one to violence, or so I've read. The weapon provides a false sense of security, becomes a symbol I'm still in control. I've never had control of this situation, I realize. No matter how much I prepare and scheme, Cooper Douglas is always one step ahead of me. And I'm tired of losing.

Removing the gun from its case, I check the ammunition chamber, careful to follow the protocols provided by the range instructor. Several meters in front of me hangs a paper with a series of circles. Planting my feet, I pull back my shoulders and stretch both arms in front of me, aiming for the target in the distance. My finger rubs against the trigger, yet even in this contained environment, I don't have the strength to pull it.

I close my eyes and try to forget where I am. I try to forget who I am. Years ago, I was a happy person. I reminisce about all those summers at the beach with Laura, her dark hair dripping over sunburnt shoulders. I remember how small she'd felt sleeping beside me as a toddler. I remember the scraped knees I'd bandaged and splinters I'd pulled during her youth, how I always vowed to protect her when times got hard. I see her smiling face as a young woman, the pride she felt embarking on a new life. Then I think of what happened to her. The terror she must have felt when the boy she loved turned against her. I wonder how many minutes she was in that fearful state. Did she cry out for me the way she had as a child? I couldn't hear her then, but I hear her now. Her strained voice echoing all around me.

I open my eyes and pull the trigger. My shot is way off, but I shoot again. And again. Each shot skids closer to its intended target, until the chamber clicks empty. I reload and repeat the process. After a while, my stance is sturdier, and my movement is less doubtful. I've obliterated the piece of paper, but in my mind, I've finally destroyed Cooper Douglas.

Afterward, I approach the Whisper Falls Range counter, deciding to restock the ammo I just used. The store owner hovers over the register, carrying on a casual conversation with the customer ahead of me.

"Did you hear the Douglas boy is getting married next month?" the customer asks the owner.

I whip my head in their direction, listening to every word.

"The older one?" the owner replies.

"Whichever one runs the paper. Cooper, I think," the other man says. "Sissy name, if you ask me."

My mouth drops. So, the wedding is still happening? Worse, they've moved up the date? I got all this wrong. I was foolish to think Madison would believe the words of a stranger over her own fiancé. I was foolish to think she'd see the truth. I stare at the rows of weaponry tacked to the wall, realizing I could have saved myself years of regret and hurt if I'd reached this conclusion sooner.

"Ma'am?" the owner asks. I look up. "Can I help you with something?"

"Ammo," I say, sliding my shaking hands into my jacket pockets.

CHAPTER 56

Madison

It's been days since my conversation with Bailey in the park. I'm waiting, unsure what the next step in all this will be. My phone rings. It's the last person I expect: Roman.

"Is Cooper home yet?" He sounds aggravated.

"Not yet. Is everything okay?"

"Just tell him to call me. Fast."

He clicks off. I'm still staring at the phone in my hand when Coop enters the front door. He's smiling and appears happy. Too happy.

"Get dressed," he says. "We're meeting everyone at Nectar for dinner."

"Everything okay?"

"We're celebrating your new job," he says, squeezing my arm.

I smile a broken smile, unsure by what he means. "I'm a little lost here, Coop. Tell me what's going on."

"There was a scuffle with one of the staff writers today. He's been turning in assignments late and not following my suggestions. I just had enough of it and told him to pack up." He holds my hands. "Which means there's now a place for you."

This isn't Coop. He's not the type to fire someone because they made a mistake. He'd give them chance after chance. He's loyal to his staff, which is why he insisted it would be a while, possibly years, before I could guarantee a job at the *Gazette*. He's making unsound decisions. Trying to regain control of his situation. Control of me. I've come to realize *this* is who Coop is. For most of his life, he's been in a position of power. He's been a Douglas. When things don't go his way, he starts acting off. That's why he lashed out at Laura, and I can sense he's turning that erratic behavior on me. He's trying to create reasons for me to stay. He's abandoning his own sense of right and wrong to keep me here.

"Didn't you think we should talk about this first?" I ask.

"What's there to talk about? You've been missing your job. It won't be like the *Chronicle*, but at least you can get back to doing what you love. You'll have a greater sense of purpose here now."

His phone rings, and I'm quickly reminded that Roman had called earlier sounding agitated. Coop answers the call, stepping into the kitchen to put distance between us. As he speaks, his features morph from curiosity to worry to defeat. When he hangs up, he doesn't say anything. He stands still, staring ahead into the living room.

"Something wrong?" I ask.

"That was Roman." He takes a seat at the desk. His jovial demeanor from earlier has disappeared.

"He called me, too," I say, taking a step forward. "What's going on?"

"He said there are police boats at the lake. They've brought a dive team." He looks at the time on his phone, then stuffs it in his pocket. "They're looking for something."

"Looking for what?"

"I don't know." His eyes connect to mine, searching for answers. "Do you think they're looking for—"

"After eleven years?" I interrupt before he can finish the sentence. I take a step closer, soothe him by rubbing my hand against his arm. "I think you're being paranoid."

Coop refuses to look at me. Finally, he says, "You're right. It's probably nothing."

He starts tapping into the laptop, and my insides feel all jumpy.

"What are you doing?" I ask.

"Trying to find more information before I visit the scene."

"Are you crazy? You don't need to go there. We're supposed to meet your family at Nectar."

"This is news," he says, still staring at the computer. "I need to go for the *Gazette*."

I sit beside him, placing one hand on his lap while the other reaches over to gently close the laptop. "You're the editor. Send someone else. We need to get ready for dinner."

"Roman sounds nervous," he says. "He can be rowdy and quick-tempered, but he's rarely nervous. I don't know what to make of that."

"You said Roman doesn't know about Laura—"

"No, no, he doesn't." He strokes his jaw. "All this just worries me."

"Let's get dressed," I say. "We don't want to make your family wait."

I stand and walk toward the staircase. Coop remains seated. "Would you tell me if there was something I needed to know?"

"What?" I say, my pitch a tad too high. My own nervousness is starting to show.

"I'd understand if you turned me in. I just want you to tell me."

I walk over to him slowly. My phone is sitting beside him on the coffee table. I pick it up, not sure what to do. Should I call someone? Should I run? Should I be honest?

"I think I found it," I say, scrolling through my music library.

"What?" Coop sounds grief-stricken.

"The perfect song for our first dance at the wedding." In recent days, this has been my fail-proof tactic. Force Coop to stop thinking about the past and worrying about the present by reminding him of what's to come.

I press play. It takes a few bars, but eventually the music fills the nervous chambers of my heart and calms me. I think the same magic is working on Coop. He smiles. He needs reassurance I'm not going anywhere.

"I've always liked this song," he says.

"We both do," I say, closing my eyes. "That's why I picked it."

Coop stands, placing both hands on my waist. "Will you dance with me, Madison?"

I nod. He wraps an arm around my lower back, and I lay my head on his chest. Alone in our living room, we sway to the music. I try my best to push Laura and the search party and all the other ugly parts of our reality from my mind. I try to focus on only him. This man I love, despite his faults. His crimes can't diminish the love I've felt for him through the years, and the sadness I'll feel when he's no longer in my life.

I think he senses it, too. That the end is near. "I love you," he whispers.

"I love you, too."

I really did.

CHAPTER 57

Helena

I finished my liquor last night, promising myself, no matter how the day unfolds, I won't drink again. The habit was hard to kick last time but has been a necessary accompaniment to this process. I'm unsure what this day will bring for me, but I know how it will end for Cooper.

My plan to approach him as he left the *Gazette* didn't pan out. I waited outside headquarters until well after four. When he still hadn't exited the building, I went inside. The woman behind the counter—Misty, I think was her name—said he'd already left. Defeated, I got into my car and drove to his house. I'd rather not involve Madison in any of this, but she's had more than enough time to walk away.

I drove past their house once, wanting to gauge if anyone else was present. To my surprise, Madison and Cooper were walking to his vehicle. I turned around in time to see them merge onto the main road. I followed them along the same path I'd just driven, until they entered downtown and parked their car in the Nectar parking lot.

Whisper Falls is surprisingly busy tonight. Heads turn as the charismatic couple enters the restaurant. Cooper shakes hands with a few people he passes, still upholding the charade he's spent an entire lifetime perfecting. I'd not intended to confront Cooper in such a crowded venue, surrounded by all these nosy people. On second thought, maybe it's better this way. Once the real story gets out, no one will question what I've done. His family won't wonder why their son and brother met such a gruesome fate. They won't search for answers, as I did with my own daughter. At last, the truth will be revealed to all.

I park a few blocks away. I walk along the sidewalk, detouring at the Whisper Falls Memorial Gardens I visited my first day back. I stop at the bench dedicated to Celia and kneel. Last time I was here, I was determined to find resolution for her. This girl lost her life in the same way my daughter did, at the hands of Cooper Douglas. I whisper a prayer, promising both girls I won't let him get away again. I return my hands to my pockets and tighten my grip around the gun.

CHAPTER 58

Madison

Nectar has never been more packed. There must have been a ceremony at the local high school; all the well-to-do families and trendy teenagers are here, ordering overpriced appetizers and artisan sandwiches. There's a line of patrons waiting to take pictures in front of the chalk wall. Regina walks from behind the register to greet us, her face full of pride.

"Busy night," I tell her, my fingers still intertwined with Coop's. He's been tense since we left the house, despite my attempts to calm him.

"Tell me about it," she says, looking around the room approvingly. "No worries. I've set up our table in the back to give us more privacy."

We follow her through the narrow rows of tables to a pair of sliding doors. She opens them, revealing a large round table. Josephine sits alone, swirling a glass of red wine in her hand. When she sees us, she stands and offers Coop a hug. They embrace a second longer than expected, then she looks at me and nods.

"Congratulations," she says. "You must be happy to return to writing."

"It's come as a bit of a surprise," I say, glancing around the room.

"Where's Roman?" Coop asks.

Before Josephine can answer, Regina jumps in. "He took off with something last-minute. I mean, it's no wonder he couldn't run the *Gazette*. He gets overwhelmed enough being Mom's errand boy."

"That's unnecessary, Regina," Josephine says, returning to her seat. "Let's not ruin tonight with petty banter. We're supposed to be celebrating Madison."

A waiter enters the private dining space. Josephine flicks her finger, signaling she'd like another drink.

"Are you working?" I ask Regina, trying to appear less nervous than I am.

"I think my staff can handle it. Lord knows they'll come get me if they can't." She turns to the server. "Bring out something red. The good stuff."

"You got it," he says, nodding at the table before walking away.

The far wall is lined with windows providing a perfect view of downtown Whisper Falls. I watch as people meander and the streetlights flick on. Everything appears calm and quaint, a stark contrast to the emotions I feel rumbling inside. Across the street, I see a person dressed in dark clothing walking toward Nectar with extreme urgency; it's so opposed to the slow pace of the other walkers. As she comes closer, I see her face and recognition sets in. It's Helena.

I stand, pushing my chair back. I'm not sure what Helena is doing, but she's staring right at us and she's not changing direction. The last thing I need is for her to try and confront Coop here.

"What is it?" asks Regina, irritated I interrupted the toast she was preparing to give.

I stumble through the crowded dining hall, trying to reach the sidewalk before Helena gets close enough to do anything irrational. As I'm exiting the front door, a short man with thick hair stops me. I try to move him out of my way, but he won't budge. He grabs my shoulders with both hands.

"Are you Madison Sharpe?" he asks.

Hearing my name rescues me from my trance. I no longer see Helena. All I can see is this man standing in front of me, and the badge he holds in his hand.

CHAPTER 59

Helena

Madison spots me from inside the dining room. She rushes away from the table, which only encourages me to pick up my pace. No one, not even her, can stop me this time. I'm about to lift the gun when I see Madison halted on the sidewalk.

I pause long enough to see she's talking to a member of law enforcement. There's a slew of officers marching inside Nectar. In a panic, I stuff the gun into my waistband and scurry across the street, ducking behind a trio of people who have stopped in their tracks. My first thought is someone must have reported me, but that doesn't make any sense. No one knows what I planned for today, and I hadn't yet shown my gun.

I wait, trying to make sense of what I'm seeing. Madison is standing on the sidewalk beside a uniformed officer, her face scanning the crowds gathering on the streets. Maybe she's looking for me. Then I see him. Cooper Douglas is being escorted out of Nectar by two officers. They usher him to a police car and instruct him to sit in the back seat.

Like everyone else on the sidewalk, I'm staring at the scene in confusion. I'm so caught off guard, I stumble and lean against the brick building behind me. Is this what I think is happening? Is Cooper being arrested? At the very least, questioned? I watch as the remaining members of his family, Josephine and Regina, exit the restaurant. His mother looks distraught while the sister stomps around with her arms flailing. They're clearly upset and as confused as everyone else.

The car containing Cooper pulls onto Market Avenue and drives away. Madison is being escorted to a second car. Now that the spectacle is over, people resume walking and, I'm sure, talking about what they just witnessed. I'm still leaning against the building, shaken and out of breath. My heart is pumping with adrenaline and excitement. Is Cooper finally being held accountable? Has all my scheming these last few weeks amounted to something?

I take a deep breath and stand upright. I feel the hard barrel of the gun pressed against my gut. The sensation frightens me. I'd come so close to doing the unthinkable, to putting Josephine Douglas through the same pain her son had caused me. I sprint to my car, shoving the gun into the glove compartment. My body exhausted from the range of emotions I've just felt, I lean against the steering wheel and cry.

CHAPTER 60

Madison

I must look a mess. My fringed dress and heels don't complement the coat the officers gave me to wear. It's freezing inside the interrogation room. So different from the warm atmosphere inside Nectar.

A woman walks in. She's slim with red hair slicked back into a ponytail. She drops a folder onto the table between us and takes a seat. "Madison Sharpe?"

"That's right," I say, sinking deeper into the jacket.

"You're engaged to Cooper Douglas?"

I nod.

She pulls out a recording device. "I'm Detective Jensen. An informant gave us this recording earlier in the week." She pushes a button, and I listen to a snippet of my conversation with Bailey in the park. I imagine I hear the birds flying above and the leaves crinkling at my feet. I wish I was back at that beautiful day.

It was right after Bailey had told me there was nothing we could do.

"What about a confession?" I asked, avoiding eye contact. "Would that be enough?"

"Do you think Cooper might have told someone what he'd done?" Bailey asked, her brow wrinkling as she tugged a strand of hair behind her ear.

"Coop told me he killed Laura."

Bailey's mouth opened, and she leaned closer. Whatever she expected me to say, it wasn't that. "What? When?"

"He told me last week after my conversation with Helena. That's why I reached out to you."

"Why didn't you go to the police?"

"I'm not in immediate danger, but I don't have the resources to leave. Josephine has half the town in her back pocket. Coop's best friend is the chief of police. If I come forward and they stall on arresting him, or word got out I was trying to pin him for something… then I would be in danger. That's why I came to you."

"Are you sure you're safe?" Her tone was unconvinced, scared even.

"I am now because Coop thinks I've forgiven him. He thinks I'm on his side. But he's become possessive since he told me. If he gets the idea I'm turning on him, I don't know what he'll do. And I don't have anywhere else to go. His family has more connections than we do combined. I can't walk away in constant fear he'll come after me."

Bailey turned quiet, no doubt contemplating what a confession from Coop meant. For him. For me. For her own relationship with Regina. But like me, Bailey must have gauged the magnitude of wrong and right.

"My detective friend in the county where Laura went missing is intrigued by what I've told her so far. If you tell her what Cooper said, she'll make an arrest. I can arrange a meeting—"

"I already told you: I can't. He's watching my every move. Checking our mail and scanning my phone records. I can't sit down with a detective and go home that same night."

"Then tell me," she said, pulling out her phone. "Tell me everything Cooper told you. I'll record it and pass it on."

"Will that be enough?"

"It's worth a try. What do we have to lose?"

I had everything to lose. Bailey had proven reliable, but how much could I truly trust her? Especially knowing the depth of her relationship with Regina? Coop, the person I trusted more than anyone in this world, turned out to be a murderer. But Bailey was right about one thing. After eleven years with limited evidence, this was our best shot.

"Start recording," I said.

Detective Jensen stops the tape, pulling me back to the present. I'm now living the aftermath of what I've done. "Is that you speaking, Ms. Sharpe?"

"Yes." I clear my throat and sit up straighter. "I told Bailey to give you the recording."

The officer takes a pen out of her pocket and hovers it over a writing pad. "I'm going to need you to tell me everything you know. Start from the beginning."

"Where's Coop? Is he—"

"He's speaking with another detective," she says, raising her hand. She has to remain professional and objective, but I see a glint of sympathy in her eyes. Or perhaps it's judgment? My words are what brought us here. I turned on Coop. I take a deep breath, praying this ordeal is almost over.

CHAPTER 61

Helena

An hour ago, I received a phone call from a woman named Detective Jensen. When she introduced herself, a series of images flashed through my mind: the gun tucked inside my waistband, my mad march to Nectar, the crime I'd almost committed on a crowded street. Then Detective Jensen spoke that sweet name: Laura. She was calling me about Laura, my darling girl I thought this world had forgotten.

Now, I'm sitting at the Whisper Falls Police Station, waiting to meet Detective Jensen. She'd assumed I was back home in South Carolina. When I informed her I was in Whisper Falls, she suggested a face-to-face meeting.

Like me, Detective Jensen is visiting Whisper Falls on business. Given her job, it can't be often she's in the position of spreading good news. Regardless of how tired she might be at this hour, she's excited to share an update.

"We've made an arrest related to your daughter's case," she says, after taking a seat. It could be the overhead light or the lack of sleep, but I see a glimmer in her eyes. "His name is Cooper Douglas. He was your daughter's boyfriend at the time she was reported missing."

I know Jensen is set to list off a trail of evidence, but I'm not ready to hear it. I quietly weep, resting my head on the cold tabletop between us. I've waited so long to hear those words. I surrendered to the idea I might never hear them. Eleven years. That's how long I've been searching for answers. Even when I saw him escorted to the police cruiser, I wasn't sure I'd get to this moment. I'd been waiting to see what fancy lawyer his family ushered in this time around. I'd thought of a dozen ways he might weasel out of the charges. But Detective Jensen is telling me that didn't happen. At long last, he's been arrested.

When I raise my head, Detective Jensen is smiling. She must have an idea about how long I've waited to hear this. I wipe my swollen cheeks and attempt to compose myself. This wasn't how I'd thought tonight would end. "Have you found her?"

"Not yet," Jensen says, opening a file in her hands. "We received a tip that her body is in Whisper Lake. Dive teams will continue their search in the morning."

All these years Laura has been in Whisper Lake? Her body hidden beneath the scenic centerpiece of the Douglas family's estate? It makes sense, I suppose. That's where Cooper disposed of his first victim. At least I can stop envisioning all the places Laura might be. I can know.

"If you still haven't found her, why make an arrest now?"

"I hate to ask you to bear with me, but you must understand there's sensitive information I can't share yet. We'll be prosecuting this case in my local jurisdiction, where it's believed the crime took place. I'll provide more information when I can." She pauses, gauging my reaction to everything that has been said thus far. "We're still piecing together what we know, but I'd be happy to answer your questions."

When I speak, my voice is scratchy from my stifled emotions. "After all this time, what urged your department to reconsider Cooper as a suspect?"

"We received a credible tip. Cooper shared some of what happened with this informant, and they contacted us."

An informant? Could it be Madison? Everyone else has been in the Douglas family pocket for years. No one else would have wandered in telling their story now. She must have uncovered something; my far-fetched plan to get her on my side worked.

Detective Jensen answers more of my questions, although she's not willing to provide any specifics that could hinder their investigation. At this point, I probably know more details than they do. They've revisited this case in the past week. I've been imagining different scenarios for over a decade, all which led me back to Cooper Douglas. Finally, the police have reached the same conclusion. He's in handcuffs, and I've been set free.

I make the short walk from the police station to my car. Light rain sprinkles over my skin, setting my senses ablaze. I breathe in the cool, damp air, rejuvenating my exhausted being. The only thing worse than losing a child is believing that loss will never be acknowledged. The world isn't as bright as it was when my Laura was alive, but it's no longer as dark. There's at least some justice, some closure on the horizon. Laura is not forgotten.

For years, I've been my daughter's only advocate, but tonight would not have happened without the help of at least one other person. I'm not sure what Madison said or did, what lengths she must have taken to make the police believe her, but I must thank her for what she's done for me tonight. For what she's done for my daughter.

CHAPTER 62

Madison

I unlock the door to our empty house and collapse onto the couch. My time at the police station was exhausting, both mentally and physically. After I told the detective everything I knew, she left the room for what seemed like hours. I sat there alone, trying to predict all the ways this situation could turn out. What if they didn't believe me? What if Coop was released and I had nowhere to go? Josephine probably already had a lawyer fighting in Coop's corner, and who did I have? No one.

Before the woman left the room, I gave her Helena's most recent phone number. I wasn't sure what information they'd obtained at that point, but I knew they'd want to at least speak with Laura's mother. She's the one who got me involved with all this, and she's the person who cares most about the outcome.

After what seemed like hours, the female officer returned to the room and told me something I wasn't expecting to hear: Coop had confessed.

"Confessed?" I repeated the word as though it were a foreign addition to my vocabulary.

"Yes," she said, tapping her pen against the table. "He corroborated almost everything you told us. The only thing he wouldn't confirm is where he put Ms. Price's body, but we've had boats on the lake for hours."

That part surprised me. He told me where he put Laura's body. Why wouldn't he tell the police?

"Have you found her?"

"Not yet," she said, emphasizing the last word. "We're going to keep looking."

"I thought Coop had a lawyer?" I couldn't believe he had confessed so easily. He didn't even put up a fight.

"Your fiancé refused counsel." The woman shook her head. "I think he's been carrying this guilt for a long time. I think he wanted the truth to come out."

My bottom lip quivered. "Does he know I'm the person who turned him in?"

"Probably." The woman extended her hand, gently tapping her fingers against the tabletop. "But you did the right thing, Madison. It would have been better if you'd come to us sooner, but you're safe and that's all that matters."

"Will I be able to see him?"

"That wouldn't be a smart move at the moment. There's still a lot we need to sort out." She leaned back. "Cooper did want us to tell you that he loves you. I'm not sure how I would take that, but I said I'd pass along the message."

I'm crying now, as I think back to everything that's happened tonight. It was a necessary betrayal to respond to the crime he committed so long ago. I look around this house that I've spent the past two months trying to make a home, something it will never be now, at least for me. I start a fire, knowing this will be what I miss most, and listen to the crackling as it blazes. After several minutes, I go upstairs and pack an overnight bag.

Back downstairs, my phone rings displaying an unknown number. Unsure whether it's someone from the police department, I answer.

"Madison?" I immediately recognize Bailey's voice.

"Yeah, it's me," I say, slumping onto the sofa.

"Is it true?" she asks, her voice low. "Did he confess?"

"Yes. I don't know much beyond that."

"Are you okay?"

"I'm getting there," I say. "I'm leaving town. Not sure when I'll be back."

"Can't say I blame you." She lets out a deep breath. "Have you talked to anyone else?"

"Just you. That's why I'm leaving. Not sure I'm up to dealing with his family just yet."

"Tell me about it. Regina is on her way over here right now. As you can imagine, she's a wreck."

"I'm guessing she doesn't know you were involved in any of this?"

"It'll be an ugly conversation when she finds out. She loves Cooper, but she also has a clear sense of right and wrong. She'll come around."

I hate that the Douglases will be hurt in all this, but these are repercussions of Coop's actions, not mine. At least that's what I'm telling myself.

"Thank you for helping me," I tell Bailey, ending the conversation.

There's a knock at the door. I look out the front window and see Josephine. She's swaying from side to side, rubbing her face with her hands. Seeing her grief reminds me of Helena. They've both experienced the unthinkable, losing their children in drastically different ways. As much as I want to ignore her, I can't.

"Oh, thank God," she says when I open the door. She runs into the house. "I didn't know where else to go. Roman took off and Regina's not answering her phone."

"I'm so sorry, Josephine." I'm not sure how much she knows, but none of it can be good. She breaks into sobs. I sit beside her, rubbing her back.

"I don't understand any of this. They think he killed some Laura from college? I barely remember her." The sorrow in her voice is audible. I'm in pain just listening.

"I'm sure we'll get more details in the weeks to come."

"They're saying someone turned him in," she says, jerking her head. Her makeup is smeared in the creases around her eyes. "It doesn't make sense. This is like the Celia fiasco all over again. They're framing him."

There's much to this story she doesn't know, and I'm not the person who should tell her. Still, I think she needs to understand the arrest was based on more than just speculation. "I'm sorry to tell you this, Josephine," I say, genuine tears forming. "Coop confessed tonight."

"Confessed?" She scoots away and looks at me like I just called her a slur. This doesn't make sense to her. "He confessed to killing someone?"

"That's what they told me when I left the station." I stand and walk toward the fireplace; it's too painful being close to her.

"There must be a mistake. I sent a lawyer—"

"He turned down representation."

"Then that shows he's clearly not in his right mind. Confessions are coerced all the time. I'll have to get the right people on it, but I'm sure we can get it thrown out. Once I find out the details—"

"What if he's telling the truth?" I ask, cutting her off. I'm sorry that she's mourning her son, but I think it would be cruel to let her create these impossible scenarios in her head.

"Madison," she begins, calmly, "he can't be telling the truth. This is Cooper we're talking about. He's not capable of hurting someone."

I look at her, trying hard not to break. "I don't know who he was back then. All I know is what he's told me and what he's told the police. I'm sorry."

She stares at me, nodding. She looks around the room and spies my luggage by the staircase. "Are you leaving?"

"I think it's best I go back to the city."

She walks toward me, clasping my hands with hers. "You can't give up on him, Madison. We're family. You have to stand beside him."

"I'm sorry, Josephine. Cooper has to answer for what he's done, and I need to move on with my life."

She turns, as though she's just been slapped. I can't imagine how painful this must be for her, hearing these horrible truths about her son and realizing life will never be the same. But I can't base my decisions on other people's sorrows. I've already been through enough.

She walks to the foyer. I think she's going to leave, instead she opens the front door wide. Roman walks inside.

"What are you doing here?" I ask, taking a step forward.

He doesn't say anything. Both hands are in his pockets, and he leans against the wall.

"I thought you said he took off?" I ask Josephine.

She shuts the door and locks it, then stands beside her son. "I think the three of us need to talk."

CHAPTER 63

June 16, 2006

Roman scrambled to put his shirt on, trying to conceal Celia so she could put on hers. He stood, staring at the flashlight in the distance.

"You know I don't want you bringing girls here," Josephine said. "I'm running a home, not a brothel."

"Mom?" Roman shouted, staring into the dark.

Josephine marched down the dock and froze when she saw the girl's face. "Celia?"

"We can explain," Celia said, her mind scrambling to find a convincing story.

Josephine's mouth was open. She shone her light on Roman, who was looking down at the water in shame. "Are you going to tell your brother about this, or am I?"

"Don't say anything to Cooper," Celia pleaded. "Please. Roman and I... we love each other."

Roman looked at Celia, but not with pleasure. He saw through her charade. The same love she'd just rejected was now being used as a bargaining chip against his own family.

"This behavior is beneath you," Josephine said to Roman. "It's beneath all of us."

Celia was now dressed and came running up the dock at Josephine. "Cooper and I have had trouble for a while now. Roman has been trying to think of a way to tell him—"

"Leave my property." Josephine slung Celia's arms off her. "Now."

"Mama Douglas, I don't want you to look at me differently—"

"Look at you differently?" she cut her off. "This confirms everything I ever thought about you. You're nothing more than Whisper Falls trash. We've entertained you long enough."

"Don't take your anger out on her," Roman said. He walked past Celia and grabbed his mother's arms. "This is my fault."

"I don't want to see that whore on my property again." She turned and made her way down the dock.

"Mama Douglas, wait!" Celia cried. Roman could hear the fear in her voice. He knew she was afraid his mother would ruin her reputation in town. Celia cared about that more than anything.

"Stop calling me that." Josephine turned and shone the flashlight in Celia's face. "I'm not some neighbor by the train tracks."

"Just wait," Celia said, pushing the torch out of her eyes. The light was blinding, making all their heads hurt.

"Get away from me!" Josephine pushed Celia.

Celia stumbled backwards, slipping on a patch of wet grass. She kept falling, arms flailing in the darkness, until her head clunked against the Douglas family rock.

The only thing more alarming than the fall was the silence that followed. Roman moved first, jumping off the dock and climbing down to where Celia had fallen. Josephine walked over slowly. She shone the flashlight on the wounded girl.

Celia's eyes were closed, but her mouth was open. Her limbs were sprawled awkwardly about, and she was still. Roman lifted her head, blood gushing over his fingers.

"Oh my God, Mom," he cried, sounding more like a small child than a young man. "Mom, this looks bad."

Josephine was silent. The hand holding the flashlight started to shake, hindering their only source of light. "Is she dead?"

Roman pressed his hand against her wrist, then her chest. "I don't know. Mom, what do we do?"

Josephine looked scared, but he could tell his mother was thinking. Thinking about the dying girl in the grass and what could happen to them as a result. "Take her out on the water."

"The water?" Roman cradled Celia's hemorrhaging head and kept trying to find a pulse. "Mom, she needs a hospital. She's losing a lot of blood."

"She's already lost too much," Josephine shouted at her son. "If she's not dead yet, she will be soon."

"Mom, we don't know that." Roman was crying in that desperate way people only can when around their parents. He needed counsel and reassurance, but he wasn't getting either.

"Listen to me," Josephine said, kneeling by him. "She's in bad shape. Taking her to the hospital like this will only raise questions. Bad questions, and I wouldn't want you getting in trouble."

"Me? This was an accident—"

"Exactly. There's no point in anyone's future getting destroyed over a simple mistake."

"But she needs help!"

How young Roman seemed when confronted by this situation, and how old his mother turned. While he was falling apart at the seams, she was poised and ready for the next step.

"I'll hose off the blood around the dock. You need to take her to a deep point on the lake. Tie her ankles to a rock and drop her."

Hearing those words shocked him. Hearing them come from his mother's mouth was terrifying. "I can't do that, Mom. I love her—"

"Don't ever say those words again, do you hear me? And I'll never tell Cooper anything I witnessed here tonight," she spat, shining the flashlight on Celia's still face. "You caused this in more ways than one, Roman. Don't forget that."

"Mom? Dad? Is anyone down there?" Cooper's voice called from the house in the distance. Roman and Josephine both turned but didn't see anyone approaching. She switched off the flashlight.

"Be there in a minute," Josephine shouted back, her voice calm and normal.

They heard a door slam, then quiet. She turned back to Roman, clicking the flashlight on.

"Do what I say. Now. Before your brother finds out."

Even if Roman knew what to say, he couldn't speak. He was crying too hard, but he nodded his understanding. Josephine marched up the hill to the house, leaving her son alone in the dark with Celia.

Roman did as he was told. He hoisted Celia onto the boat and rode to one of the deepest points of Whisper Lake. Along the way, he stopped by a cove and found a heavy rock and, using rope from the boat, fastened it to her leg. He found a bottle of his father's liquor in one of the boat's cabinets and drank. The bitter taste soothed him. For several minutes, he sat alone. He listened to the water splash against the hull and gazed at the dazzling stars blinking above. He'd hoped Celia might wake and this could all be avoided. But that didn't happen.

He lifted Celia onto the ledge, staring at the dark water beneath them both. He dropped the rock first, feeling it pull against her body. For a few seconds, he held her still in his arms. As he let go of her waist, he heard a whimper. It was the most frightening sound he'd ever heard.

That sound would haunt him during quiet moments in the years to come.

CHAPTER 64

Madison

The house is silent, except for the crackling of the fire. Roman won't raise his eyes to meet mine. Josephine, however, looks directly at me. Her tears have dried, and there is a deep wrinkle between her brows.

"Roman," I say, my throat raspy. "Why are you here?"

"I told him to come here," Josephine says, placing a hand on her son's shoulder. There's a perceptible wince, but he remains still.

Something about this interaction feels dangerous, but I can't pinpoint why. "If you're trying to help Coop—"

"Cooper is at risk because someone turned him in," Josephine interjects, taking a step closer to me. "Based on your slip a few moments ago, I think that person is you."

I look to Roman, as though he might help me, though clearly that's not what he's here to do. "It doesn't matter who turned him in," I say, flailing for excuses. "He confessed."

"That confession can be thrown out," she says. "As long as there isn't someone to corroborate his story."

I step closer to the fire, feeling the warmth of the flames near my skin. "They won't need anyone to corroborate his story once they find Laura's body."

At the sound of her name, Roman shudders. He tips his head upwards, staring at the ceiling.

"No one has looked for Laura Price in years," Josephine says. "You've been here two months, and they have dive teams swarming the lake?"

"I love Coop, but what he did all those years ago—"

"Don't insult us with your proclamations of love." Josephine sits in the armchair, crossing her legs, without ever breaking eye contact. "Love is unconditional. Mother to son. Brother to brother. Husband to wife. You've betrayed my son, and all of us in the process."

I try not to wilt under her hypnotic stare. "Josephine, I can't imagine how difficult all this must be for you. Learning what Coop did all those years ago."

"Are you that dense? You think I only found out about Laura Price tonight?" She leans forward, ensuring her words sink in. "A mother knows her son."

I blink away tears, trying to remember everything Coop told me. "He said you didn't know—"

"I told her," Roman says at last, stepping away from the wall.

"You knew?"

"Cooper needed help getting rid of the body, so he called me," he says. "I'm the one who drove her back to Whisper and left her in the lake. I had to tell Mom. We were kids. We'd never have managed to cover it up without guidance."

Roman has known about Laura this entire time. It explains why Coop won't tell the police about Laura's remains. He doesn't want Roman to get in trouble. Hell, Coop may not even know where he put the body. I look to Josephine, seeing her for what feels like the first time. "Guidance?" I ask. Even being their mother, I can't believe she'd condone such behavior.

"Cooper was already upset. It was best he never knew about my involvement," Josephine says. She breaks eye contact, looking at the assortment of rings on her hands. "I told Roman what to do with the body. I told him to buy those festival tickets and clean the apartment. The boys made some mistakes, but they did better than last time. At least Laura's body still hasn't been found."

Last time. A cry escapes my lungs, and I take another step back, almost stumbling into the fire. "Celia? Did you have something to do with her, too?"

"You aren't the first woman to try and interfere with my family." She looks at me again, her stare sharp enough to pierce through me.

I'm scared. No one is coming to my rescue. My phone and keys are on the other side of Josephine and Roman, two immovable threats. I focus only on this moment, on this dynamic which is turning unsafe.

"We can figure another way out of this," I say, knowing the suggestion is futile.

"I'm sorry, Madison. Our hands are tied." She looks over her shoulder at Roman. "Get her."

He darts after me, barely giving me time to skirt between the fireplace and sofa. Either way I turn, I'm blocked. This spacious home is closing in. He corners me behind an armchair. I raise my hand to strike him, but he grabs my wrist, twisting it downward. I attempt to kick him, but my strength is no match for his. He grabs my other arm, attaching both wrists with zip ties. He pushes my body onto the sofa.

"Now what?" Roman asks, pacing manically in front of the fireplace.

"We'll take her to one of the rental properties. There's too much activity at the lake," Josephine says.

"My statement is already on record. Even if I disappear, they'll use what I told them against Coop. You don't have to do this." I'm speaking to Josephine, but I hope Roman hears me. Something in his nature makes me think he's not as convinced killing me is the right option.

"The police may have your statement, but you have a habit of telling lies," Josephine says, pulling my attention back to her. "At least that's why you lost your job at the *Chronicle*."

Remembering my career and why I lost it seems foreign now, in this moment of life or death. My breathing slows, as I remember what life was like before I moved here. "What do you know about that?"

"I know everything about it," she says, her lips twisting into a smile. "Cooper had played around in the city long enough. I had to bring him back here, but I knew that wouldn't happen unless you joined him. I'd been in Atlanta three days. Bernard Wright's name was everywhere at that time. I could tell you were a spitfire. You'd chase a story if the right one was presented. All I needed to do was put the pieces in place."

"You planted that story?" All this time I'd assumed Bernard Wright's defense team set a trap and I fell for it. I never dreamed it was Josephine.

"That girl was paid handsomely for the little yarn she told you."

She's enjoying this, revealing just how involved she's been with everything from the start. Celia. Laura. My job in the city. I never realized how crucial a role she played in all these scenarios; I'm not sure Coop knew the measures his mother took to keep things on her terms.

"Can we leave?" Roman asks, scratching the back of his neck. He's antsy, growing tired of hearing us talk. He must have some idea of what gruesome fate I'm about to meet, and he's sick of stalling.

"You don't have to do this, Roman," I tell him, shifting my body to face him. "She can't control you like this."

"She's not controlling me," he bellows, but it's unconvincing. His eyes bounce between us. "I'm sorry, Madison."

"Don't apologize to her," Josephine says. "Besides, we'd never be in this mess if it weren't for you. Haven't you betrayed your brother enough?"

I'm not sure what this comment means, but it's enough to wrestle Roman back into submission. He turns from both of us, waiting for his mother's next order.

CHAPTER 65

Helena

There are cars in the driveway, but in the dark, I don't immediately recognize who they belong to. I park by the main road and walk toward Madison's house. Old habits from spying on her. I can't imagine who she might have enlisted to console her at this hour, but I don't want to interrupt if it's anyone important.

I mount the porch step, peering through the window to see who is inside. Madison is sitting on the couch. Across from her sits Josephine. Pacing between them is Roman, Cooper's brother. A pang of sympathy breaks through for Josephine; some people might expect me to gloat in a moment like this, but I know how painful it is to lose a child. Cooper's gone now, and although punishment is what he deserves, it's no doubt a difficult conclusion for his mother to accept.

It's best not to intrude on this family meeting. I slink down the steps but jerk my head back to the window when I hear a scream. Madison has fallen over the cushions. Roman jerks her to a standing position, keeping one hand on her shoulder. When she turns, I see her wrists are bound together in front of her body. Josephine remains seated, her back to the window. I'm not sure what I'm witnessing, but it can't be good.

I skate back to my vehicle and retrieve my weapon from the glove compartment. I rush back to the porch, looking through the window. Now all three are standing. Josephine is poking at the fireplace, extinguishing the flames. Roman's hands are still on Madison's shoulders. She's crying.

I flatten my body along the house. *Think*, I tell myself. I'm unsure what's happening inside, but clearly Madison is distraught. Footsteps on the other side of the wall pound closer, approaching the front door.

Roman is the first outside. My arms are extended, so that when he steps on the porch, the tip of my gun aligns perfectly with his head. He jumps back.

"What the hell?"

"Back inside," I say, stepping one foot inside the house.

Josephine's pupils dilate when she sees the gun. Whatever they had planned for tonight, they weren't expecting me to intrude with a weapon. I wasn't expecting it either. My arms begin to shake, but my confidence builds when I see the frightened look on Madison's face.

"Get back," I say, using my gun to herd everyone away from the door. I reach behind and pull the knob, locking me inside with my terrified captives.

"Helena," Madison shrieks. "You need to call the police."

Is she frightened for me? Relieved I'm here? It's hard to tell. All I can take in are her terrified eyes and bound wrists.

"What's going on here?" I ask, utterly clueless as to what situation I've found myself in.

"Who are you?" Josephine asks. She meets me with that pious stare I memorized years ago. In the adrenaline-packed chaos, she doesn't remember who I am. After a few moments, recognition sinks in and now Josephine's terror matches that of Madison's.

"They're going to kill me for turning on Coop," Madison says.

"Shut it," Roman says, sinking his fingers into her shoulder blade. Madison writhes in pain. He looks to his mother. "Mom, who is this?"

"It's Helena Price," she answers, never taking her eyes off me. "Laura's mother."

Hearing my daughter's name wilts the poor boy. He lets go of Madison and starts running toward the kitchen.

"Stop," I shout, still unsure of what threat might exist if he leaves. Will he run away? Return with a weapon? Right now, my only advantage is the gun in my hand. I need to keep control of the situation, even if I'm unsure what that situation is. When he won't stop retreating, I close my eyes and shoot.

The pop is loud and jarring, followed only a second later by the sound of Roman's body hitting the floor. Josephine shrieks, pushing past me and Madison to reach her son. Madison falls back on the sofa, her mouth open as she stares ahead. I step forward, trying to assess what damage I've done. My body fills with relief when I hear Roman moaning and see I've only clipped his shoulder. He's hurting, but he's alive.

Josephine, kneeling beside her son, looks at me with tears in her eyes. "What have you done?"

"I told him to stop," I say, lifting the gun again. "Move away from him."

"You're a crazy old woman," Josephine shouts, while obeying my order. She stands, leaving her son on the floor to cup his wound. "Can't you move on with your life and leave us to ours?"

"You're a mother," I say. "You know the answer to that."

"You shot my son!" Josephine shouts.

"Your son killed my daughter!" I scream, and now I'm crying, too. "Don't you have any sympathy for what I've been through? For what your family has done to me all these years?"

For a moment, she sobs, but then she recovers. That arrogant attitude is back and there's nothing but rage reverberating between us. Josephine charges, catching me off guard. Her body pummels into my abdomen, knocking me off my feet and slinging the gun from my hands. I don't have time to retrieve it. I'm too busy fighting off Josephine's blows. We both stop when we hear Roman's voice. He's standing, holding the gun in his hands.

"Shoot her, Roman," Josephine yells. "Shoot both of them."

Madison, her arms still bound in front, moves back. She stares at the gun.

Roman releases a deep breath. Tears snake down his cheek as he looks between his mother and me. "This isn't right."

"It's not about what's right. It must be done," Josephine says. "To protect your brother. To protect me."

"I'm not doing this." He lowers his hand and places the gun on the floor. Using his foot, he kicks the gun, not in the direction of his mother, but to Madison.

Madison lifts the weapon shakily. It's hard for her to grip it with her bound hands, but once she has it, she runs into the kitchen. Josephine tries to chase after her, but I grab her leg, pulling her down.

"What the hell are you doing?" she asks her son, equal parts furious and shocked.

"Changing." He walks to the bar cart by the fireplace and pours a stiff drink. He sits on the sofa. "I'm not going to be an accomplice to this anymore."

Madison returns from the kitchen. She's not holding the gun, probably having hidden it somewhere, and she's unfastened her restraints. She searches the living room, sorting through the mess we've made until she finds her phone. We listen as she provides the 911 operator with an address and the names of all the people inside. Every few seconds, Josephine tries to move again, but I pin her down, until she's finally too tired to move.

"How could you do this?" Josephine whines. "I'm your mother."

"I'm your son," Roman says, swallowing the last of his drink. "How could you do this to me?"

Their exchange references more than what has happened tonight. If what Madison says is true, they'd planned on killing her, eliminating the one person who could send Cooper to jail. Roman reaches into his pocket, pulls out a zip-tie and tosses it to Madison.

Madison comes closer, helping me hold Josephine down long enough to fasten the plastic around her wrists. At least now Josephine no longer has the same range of motion, although I think she's exhausted her will to fight. She turns away from us, her body flat against the floor, and cries.

"Are you okay? Did they hurt you?" I ask Madison. There's still a lot of fear in the room. Every minute that passes feels dangerous and unsure.

"I'm fine," she says, still out of breath. Her eyes dance between Roman and Josephine, making sure they're still docile. She looks back at me with tears in her eyes. "Thank you."

I squeeze her hand, sensing my own tears are about to break free. "Thank you. It couldn't have been easy."

We hug. As she pulls from my embrace, we hear sirens in the distance. The police are coming.

CHAPTER 66

Madison

Three Months Later

I'm watching her. Helena.

She stumbles over the small dunes of sand on the uneven beach. There's a circle of mourners already waiting, each one nodding as she passes. She's carrying a gilded urn. Laura's body was found in Whisper Lake.

Helena holds hands with a man, maybe it's her ex-husband, and they walk to the water. They stand still, the weak waves lapping at their calves. I think they're praying. After several minutes, they walk back to the sand, joining the other gatherers. Each person takes turns speaking, sharing happy stories about Laura and revealing the impact she had on their lives. Former neighbors and teachers and classmates. She was clearly loved.

The wake ends and people walk their separate ways. As Helena exits the beach, she spots me sitting on my bench at the sidewalk. She pauses, then walks closer. She's wearing white, her dress damp from the knees down. I stand, and we hug.

"I'm happy you came," she says, her lips close to my ear. "You could have joined us on the beach."

"I thought it would be best to let you visit with the people who knew her."

She sits beside me. We stare ahead, and for a moment, don't say anything, just listen to the waves crash along the shoreline.

"It's beautiful here, isn't it?" Helena asks.

I nod. I've never been to South Carolina before. The atmosphere is so different from the mountains in Whisper and the streets of Atlanta. I imagine Helena's life is different here, too. Normal.

"Are you back in Atlanta?" she asks.

"Just briefly," I say, looking down. This is the first time I've seen Helena since the night she rescued me. Being this close to her brings back painful memories. "I'm staying with my friend Beth. I accepted a job in another state, so I'll be leaving soon."

"That's wonderful." Helena's voice rises an octave. She's happy I'm making progress. "Change is good."

Helena and I talk on the phone from time to time, mainly when there's a development in the case. Every few weeks there's something, it seems. I think Roman is working on a deal, but Josephine is adamant about going to trial. They made the decision to re-open Celia's case, so more charges could be pending. Then there was news Laura's body had been discovered. Contrary to Cooper's claims that her death was accidental, Laura's skull had multiple fractures. A single fall didn't cause her death; pure rage did. Maybe to him it was an accident. He hadn't meant for her to die. The anger he displayed that night was beyond his own comprehension, ruining so many lives in the process.

I feel the most sympathy for Regina. Her family was taken from her all at once, and yet, I think that's what she needed. Now she can stop worrying about being a Douglas and just be herself. I've only spoken to her once since the arrests, after Laura's body was found. Until then, she was still in denial about Cooper's involvement, but she couldn't explain away a body or multiple skull fractures or Roman's corroboration. I don't think she's completely forgiven me for turning on her brothers, but she's slowly coming to terms with her family's sins. Their faults turned out to be so much worse than she'd wanted to admit. Bailey and I keep in touch; she too is hoping for Regina's forgiveness. It's a long road ahead for all of us.

"How've you been?" I ask. Helena has given me updates over the phone. I know she's started working with a therapist and attending AA meetings, which is a step in the right direction, but it's better to see how a person is actually coping in person.

"I'm doing better. I still miss her, but at least now I have clarity." She smiles. "Today has been really nice, hearing the impact she had on people during her short life. It's important to know she still matters."

The desperation and bitterness Helena once exhibited has lifted. Nothing will bring Laura back, but I'd like to think the old Helena is emerging, piece by piece.

"I'll be in town for a few days," I say. "We should get dinner."

"I'd like that." She stands, smoothing the wrinkles in her dress. "My church is hosting a luncheon following the wake. That's where I'm headed. Would you like to come?"

"I think I'll stay." I smile. I've had my share of feeling like an outsider. "It's been a long time since I've been to the beach."

Helena doesn't push the subject, but she initiates another hug. This time when she pulls me in, my emotions buckle. She feels me shaking and squeezes tighter.

"Thank you, Madison. I'll never forget what you've done for me," she whispers.

I watch her walk away. I think about all the pain she's been through, the pain Cooper caused, and my conflicted emotions in loving him. Bits of those affectionate feelings remain, but I realize now I only loved parts of Cooper Douglas. I didn't have a full understanding of him until the end. Sadly, I don't think he ever understood himself. He was caught between who his family wanted him to be and what the people in his hometown labeled him. The end result was a person who couldn't handle his own emotions, couldn't live in a world beyond his control. At least I was able to bring Helena a small amount of closure, which almost makes my lonely weeks in Whisper Falls, and the heartache that followed, worthwhile.

The breeze picks up, bringing the smell of the sea closer. All around me I hear joyful laughter and gulls calling and the ocean's thundering waves.

I don't know who I am after all this. I don't think I'm a full person anymore—maybe I never was. Instead, I'm all these fragments of a person. A journalist who made a mistake. A woman who fought for others. A lover who made a choice. Most people would say this is where I start over, but I think I'm in the hard middle of my journey.

I just have to keep going.

A LETTER FROM MIRANDA

Dear Reader,

Thank you for taking the time to read *The One Before*. If you liked it and want information about upcoming releases, sign up with the following link. Your email address will never be shared and you can unsubscribe at any time.

www.bookouture.com/miranda-smith

I am thrilled to be sharing this book with all of you, as it's one I've contemplated writing for years. I loved diving into the mindsets of the different characters. Madison, Helena and Celia are all flawed, yet determined in their own ways. *The One Before* explores how the places we encounter and the events we experience shape and change us. I thought Whisper Falls was the perfect setting for all the mayhem that takes place.

I wrote the bulk of this book during the Covid-19 crisis of 2020. It was therapeutic to escape the worries of the world for a few hours by focusing on the problems of my fictional characters. When I wasn't writing, I was reading other great books, many in the thriller and suspense genre. In times of uncertainty, we turn to the arts—fiction, poetry, art, music, dance, theater, film—as a source of comfort and entertainment, and I hope we will continue to recognize the importance of these fields.

If you'd like to discuss any of my books, I'd love to connect! You can find me on Facebook, Twitter and Instagram, or my website. If you enjoyed *The One Before*, I'd appreciate it if you left a review on Amazon. It only takes a few minutes and does wonders in helping readers discover my books for the first time.

Thank you again for your support!

Sincerely,
Miranda Smith

         mirandasmithwriter.com

         MirandaSmithAuthor

         @mirandasmithwriter

ACKNOWLEDGMENTS

There are several people I must thank for helping me through this process yet again.

I'd like to thank the fabulous team at Bookouture. This includes Jenny Geras, Kim Nash, Noelle Holten, Sarah Hardy, Leodora Darlington, Alexandra Holmes, Alex Crow, Jane Eastgate, Natasha Hodgson and everyone else behind the scenes working to make each book a success. This is such an innovative, creative and committed team! Thank you for all you do. I'd also like to thank my fellow Bookouture authors for their support and reassurance.

As always, I must thank my editor, Ruth Tross. You have done so much for my books over the past year, and I'm grateful for the opportunity to work with you. Thank you for your encouragement and insight.

I have a huge support system of friends, family and in-laws. Especially over the past several months, I would not be able to pursue this career without your involvement. Mom and Dad, Carol, Chris, Whitney and Seth, Jennifer, Allison and Tyler: thank you for promoting my books and being there when it all gets a little overwhelming. Although writing is a solitary process, the finished product wouldn't happen without your love and assistance.

Harrison, Lucy, Christopher, Brody and Quinton: I love you. Take care of each other in the years to come.

Lastly, I'd like to thank my readers. There's nothing like the excitement of knowing someone read your book and enjoyed it.

I love reading your reviews, messages and comments. I greatly appreciate the reviewers who continue to spread the word about my books. Without you, none of this would be possible. Thank you.

Made in the USA
Middletown, DE
10 November 2020